# Praise for A Mimi

CH00747406

## Return to Satterthwaite Court

"Wow. Just wow! Those who enjoy raillery and romance get ready to spar & swoon with Kate & Charles!"

—*Austenprose*

## The Work of Art

"Matthews weaves suspense and mystery within an absorbing love story. Readers will be hard put to set this one down before the end."

—*Library Journal* (starred review)

"Strongly recommended."

—*Historical Novel Society*

## Gentleman Jim

"Tartly elegant...A vigorous, sparkling, and entertaining love story with plenty of Austen-ite wit."

—*Kirkus* (starred review)

"Exhilarating...this page-turner shouldn't be missed."

—*Publishers Weekly* (starred review)

"Matthews ups the ante with a wildly suspenseful romance."

—*Library Journal* (starred review)

"Readers who love lots of intrigue and historicals that sound properly historical will savor this one."

—*NPR*

### The Belle of Belgrave Square

"Shiveringly Gothic...Watching Julia blossom away from prying eyes is almost as satisfying as seeing Jasper Blunt pine for her from nearly the first page...For best effect, save this one for a windy night when trees scrape against the windowpanes."

—*New York Times Book Review*

"Mimi Matthews never disappoints."

—Jodi Picoult, #1 *New York* Times bestselling author

"Such tremendous good fun...Julian Fellowes fans will rejoice!"

—Kate Quinn, *New York Times* bestselling author

"This story unfolds like a rose blooming, growing more and more beautiful as each delicate layer is revealed. A tender, luminous romance."

—Caroline Linden, *USA Today* bestselling author

"Mimi Matthews just doesn't miss."

"A grand cross-class romance, a twisty mystery, and emotional internal struggles combine to excellent effect in Matthews's effervescent second Belles of London romance."

"An intoxicating, suspenseful romance. Highly recommended."

## The Siren of Sussex

"A tender and swoonworthy interracial, cross-class romance in Victorian London...Readers will delight in this paean to women's fashion and horseback riding."

"Romance aficionados who love fashion and animals will delight in this tender romance and will be excited to see Evelyn's friends in future installments."

"A tender, empowering love story."

"Matthews brings the Victorian era to vivid life with meticulously researched details and an impossible romance made believable and memorable."

—*Booklist* (starred review)

## Fair as a Star

"Historical romance fans won't want to miss this."

—*Publishers Weekly* (starred review)

"A kindhearted love story that will delight anyone who longs to be loved without limits."

—*Library Journal* (starred review)

## The Matrimonial Advertisement

"For this impressive Victorian romance, Matthews crafts a tale that sparkles with chemistry and impresses with strong character development...an excellent series launch."

—*Publishers Weekly*

"Matthews has a knack for creating slow-building chemistry and an intriguing plot with a social history twist."

—*Library Journal*

## A Holiday By Gaslight

"Matthews pays homage to Elizabeth Gaskell's *North and South* with her admirable portrayal of the Victorian era's historic advancements...Readers will easily fall for Sophie and Ned in their gaslit surroundings."

—*Library Journal* (starred review)

"A graceful love story...and an authentic presentation of the 1860s that reads with the simplicity and visual gusto of a period movie."

—*Readers' Favorite, Gold Medal for Holiday Fiction*

### The Lost Letter

"Lost love letters, lies, and betrayals separate a soldier from the woman he loves in this gripping, emotional Victorian romance."

—*Publishers Weekly* (starred review)

"A fast and emotionally satisfying read, with two characters finding the happily-ever-after they had understandably given up on. A promising debut."

— *Library Journal*

# Books by Mimi Matthews

## FICTION

### Somerset Stories

The Work of Art

Gentleman Jim

Return to Satterthwaite Court

Appointment in Bath

A Lady of Conscience

### Belles of London

The Siren of Sussex

The Belle of Belgrave Square

The Lily of Ludgate Hill

### Parish Orphans of Devon

The Matrimonial Advertisement

A Modest Independence

A Convenient Fiction

The Winter Companion

### Victorian Romances

The Lost Letter

The Viscount and the Vicar's Daughter

***Victorian Christmas Novellas***

A Holiday By Gaslight

***Victorian Romantics***

Fair as a Star

***Gothic Fiction***

John Eyre

———

## NON-FICTION

The Pug Who Bit Napoleon:
*Animal Tales of the 18th and 19th Centuries*

A Victorian Lady's Guide to Fashion and Beauty

# Appointment in Bath

## SOMERSET STORIES
### BOOK FOUR

## MIMI MATTHEWS

*For Jet, the embodiment of pure joy.*

*Chapter One*

*Somersetshire, England*
*November 1843*

"*Are you hurt?*"

Meg Burton-Smythe heard the question long before she spied the gentleman who asked it. She was half-sitting in the mud on the banks of the river by Sefton Bridge, the skirts of her sensible black wool riding habit hoisted above her knees as she examined her injured right ankle. At the sound of the stranger's deep voice, she hastily tugged her skirts back down over her half boots in a fruitless attempt at modesty.

It was too late. The gentleman had already seen her.

He rode up on an enormous white stallion, the late autumn sun at his back, its glimmering rays catching in the threads of his thick golden hair. He was a tall, athletic figure of a gentleman, with a devastatingly handsome face characterized by a strong chiseled jaw, lean cheeks, and firmly molded lips.

A knot formed in Meg's stomach. She was reminded of the fairytales she'd enjoyed as a child. Stories she still read occasionally, about dashing princes on their white chargers, riding to the rescue of damsels in distress.

Unhappy thought.

Given her present predicament, she'd have preferred to be rescued by one of the local farmers. Plain, ordinary, grandfatherly men who wouldn't care how she looked or what an idiot she'd made of herself.

"I've fallen from m-my horse," she said, rather unnecessarily.

Her stammer emerged just as it always did when she was anxious. She suppressed a grimace at the sound of it. What she would have given to sound calm and collected in this moment!

"I can see that." The gentleman leapt from his own mount in one fluid motion. His finely made leather top boots squelched in the mud as he strode, sure-footedly, down the bank.

He was clad in tan Bedford cord breeches that hugged his long legs and a blue, broadcloth riding coat that accentuated the staggering breadth of his shoulders. When coupled with his honey-blond hair and beautifully sculpted features, he didn't just look like Prince Charming, he could have *been* Prince Charming.

Meg's mouth went dry. There was only one family in the county that boasted such golden splendor.

He must be a Beresford.

John Beresford, Earl of Allendale, and his wife, Margaret, owned Beasley Park, the estate that bordered Letchford Hall. Their eldest son, James, Viscount St. Clare was a cold, superior sort of gentleman with ice in his veins and their youngest son, Jack, was an unrepentant rogue with a devilish twinkle in his eyes. Meg knew them both by sight.

But Lord and Lady Allendale had another son. A middle

son, Ivo Beresford, who had spent the last several years away from home, first at university and then abroad, enjoying a lengthy grand tour.

This was surely him, newly returned home to Somersetshire.

Meg privately cursed her terrible luck. It was bad enough that the gentleman coming to her aid should be gorgeous beyond imagination, but that he should be a member of a family as abhorrent to her own family as the Montagues ever were to the Capulets!

"What's her name?" He squinted as he approached Meg's mare. In his boyhood, Ivo Beresford had worn spectacles. He wasn't wearing them now, but judging by the slightly unfocused look in his cool gray eyes, he still required them.

"Rowena," she said.

"Easy, Rowena," he murmured. "I'll not hurt you."

Rowena peered at him through her tangled forelock, glittering malice in her big brown eyes.

"She b-bites," Meg warned.

Mr. Beresford caught Rowena's reins. "She won't bite me." He held the mare's bridle tight as he gave her a pat on the neck. "Will you, old girl?"

Rowena's muzzle twitched. She plainly would have loved to sink her teeth into him.

It was Meg's own fault. She'd handfed Rowena too much when she was a filly. Meg had hoped to form a bond with her—to make her a friend, a partner. Instead, all she'd done was encourage Rowena to nip people's fingers.

Mr. Beresford lashed the mare's reins to a nearby tree before coming to Meg's aid. "Is it your ankle?"

Meg's cheeks warmed, knowing that he'd seen her with her skirts raised. "M-my right one," she said. "I c-can't put any weight on it."

He crouched down beside her on the bank, heedless of the

mud. His hand touched the lacing of her brown leather riding boot. "May I?"

No longer warm, Meg's cheeks were positively scalding. "If you m-must."

He deftly unlaced her boot and slipped it from her foot. His strong fingers moved gently over her stocking-clad ankle and the curve of her instep.

She sucked in a sharp breath.

"Does that hurt?" he asked.

A pained breath trembled out of her as he manipulated her foot. "Yes."

"It's not broken," he said. "Only sprained, I'd guess."

"How c-can you t-tell?"

"If it was broken, you'd be screaming right now. But you're not." He smiled at her, revealing a glimpse of strong, white teeth. "You're only blushing."

Meg could have happily melted into the mud. She knew what she looked like when she blushed. Her entire face and throat turned scarlet. When coupled with her red hair and freckles, it gave her the appearance of a ripe tomato.

"I've n-never fallen from a horse before," she said. "That's why—"

"I don't judge." He slid her boot back on her foot, retying the laces in a loosened bow to better accommodate her injury. "I've been where you are countless times."

She gave him an uncertain look.

"In the mud," he explained. "On my backside." He stood and offered her his hand. "There's no indignity in it. So long as you get back up again."

Meg hesitated for an instant before slipping her gloved hand into his and permitting him to help her to her feet. "*Oh!*" A jolt of pain shot through her ankle the moment she put her weight on her right foot.

"Here. Let me." He slid his hand around her waist. His arm was as strong as a band of iron.

Meg flushed even hotter. At eighteen years of age, she'd only recently left the schoolroom. She wasn't formally out yet. She'd never danced with a gentleman or felt his arm at her waist.

Her heart raced and her tongue tangled over itself. She didn't know what to say, let alone where to look.

How disappointed Miss Adams would be in her! Meg's beloved former governess had taught Meg all she knew of how to conduct herself in company. Meg was meant to be elegant, graceful, and articulate. The very opposite, in short, of how she appeared now.

Miss Adams had departed Letchford Hall in the spring. She was soon to be married in Bath. Meg was happy for her, though not so much for herself. In Miss Adams's absence, Meg had no companion at the Hall to keep her company. No one to leaven the dull days as one drifted inexorably into the other.

The only bright spot had been her solitary rides on Rowena. Unburdened by her governess's insistence that she have a groom accompanying her, Meg had traversed the countryside, galloping over the moors, jumping pasture gates, and exploring the hidden trails that wove along the river. Her daily outings were her sole taste of freedom. A seemingly harmless indulgence, which had now brought her to this.

"It will be less painful once you're in the saddle," Mr. Beresford said, bearing her weight.

Meg doubted it. She nevertheless allowed him to assist her back to her mare. Once there, he grasped her waist in his hands and effortlessly lifted her up into her sidesaddle. It happened so quickly, she had no opportunity to object to the familiarity. Not that she would have done. She'd never have been capable of mounting Rowena without his assistance.

She clumsily hooked her knee over the pommel. "Th-thank you," she stuttered. "Mr.—"

"Ivo Beresford," he said. "And I know who you are. You're Miss Burton-Smythe." He placed her left foot into her stirrup for her. "I'd recognize that red hair and those freckles anywhere."

Meg's already dwindling confidence withered still further.

So much for hoping she'd changed. That the intervening years had turned her from an awkward ugly duckling into a beautiful swan.

"You remember me," she said flatly.

"Of course, I do." Catching hold of his stallion, he vaulted easily back up into his saddle. "You and I are meant to be enemies."

Meg ducked her head, avoiding his gaze as she slowly gathered her reins. She was uncertain how to respond.

He rode up alongside her. "How's your ankle now?"

"Tolerably well."

"Can you manage the ride home?"

"I believe so, thank you."

Mr. Beresford didn't appear convinced. "I'll accompany you back just to be certain."

Her eyes flew back to his. "Oh no, you m-mustn't!" she cried before she could stop herself.

His brows lifted in amused surprise. "Mustn't I?"

Embarrassed, Meg once again bent her head. "I mean... I c-can manage. You needn't t-trouble yourself on m-my account."

There was a long and rather agonizing moment of silence.

"It's no trouble to me," Mr. Beresford said at length. "But I see it would be to you." He circled around her on his stallion, prompting Rowena to flatten her ears. "Very well, we shall part here."

Relief coursed through Meg. She couldn't imagine what

her father would do if he spied her returning to Letchford Hall in company with a Beresford. The very thought of his reaction was too terrifying to contemplate.

"Shall I go first?" Mr. Beresford inquired. "I can gallop away in a trice, if you wish it."

She chanced another look at him through her lashes. "Yes, please. That is…if you would, sir."

Catching her shy glance, the same irrepressible smile pulled at his mouth. "Do you know what I think, Miss Burton-Smythe? I think we should be friends, you and I."

She stared at him, rendered speechless by the scandalous suggestion.

His grin broadened. "Consider it," he said. And then, kicking his stallion into motion, he cantered off over the rise.

Meg was left gaping after him, stunned.

*Friends?* How could a Burton-Smythe ever be friends with a Beresford? It was impossible. Unheard of. The two families hated each other and had done so since well before she was born.

But Mr. Beresford had been kind to her. More than kind. He'd been downright friendly.

And Meg was in desperate need of a friend.

# Chapter Two

Ivo's grin gradually faded as he cantered away. An icy
November wind whipped at his face, obliterating the
last remnants of the warmth he'd felt when assisting the
surprisingly lovely Miss Burton-Smythe back into her
sidesaddle.

Good Lord. What the devil had he been thinking? To
extend a hand of friendship to the daughter of his parents'
oldest enemy, Sir Frederick Burton-Smythe?

He tightened his gloved fingers on the reins, the slight
pressure of his leg guiding his stallion, Snap, along the road
that would take them to Beasley Park. The trees that lined it
were absent their leaves, the countryside cold and wet from the
last of the autumn rains. It stretched before him in a muted
blur—all soft shapes and colors—reminding Ivo exactly what
it was that had got him into this predicament.

It was his own vanity that was to blame.

He hated wearing his spectacles. Oftentimes, it was a
necessity. But not on horseback. When riding, his vision was
just sharp enough to see where he was going. Granted, he
couldn't make out printed signs. And he couldn't recognize

8

faces when at a distance. But the former made no difference when on a familiar path like the one that led to Beasley. As for the latter...

If he'd been wearing his spectacles, he'd have recognized the distinctive red hair and freckles that marked a member of the Burton-Smythe clan from a mile away.

Not that it would have mattered.

Even if he *had* recognized Miss Burton-Smythe in advance, Ivo wouldn't have been so heartless as to have refused to ride to her aid. She'd needed help and he had been only too happy to oblige her. But, as always happened with him, he'd taken things one step too far. It wasn't sufficient that he'd smiled at Miss Burton-Smythe and conversed with her in a civil manner. No. He'd had to go and tell her that they should be friends.

*Friends!*

Ivo huffed a humorless laugh at his own audacity.

His parents wouldn't thank him for cracking open the door between their two warring families. Nor would his brothers and sister. But Ivo couldn't regret his offer to Miss Burton-Smythe. It had been a noble impulse, inspired by his deep conviction in the necessity of progress.

And by all her pretty blushes.

And by her hair—a thickly curling mass of titian red springing loose from its pins.

Strange, that. Not the color of her hair, but the unexpected beauty of it. Of *her.*

It had been ages since Ivo had encountered Miss Burton-Smythe. As a boy, he'd rarely noticed her. And when he had, he'd dismissed her (rather uncharitably) as a scrawny, freckle-faced shadow.

She'd always ducked behind her nurse, swiftly disappearing, whenever their families had crossed paths in the village. A rare enough occurrence. Indeed, for all that Miss

Burton-Smythe had been visible over the years, Sir Frederick might not have had a daughter at all.

Ivo gave Snap another kick as they ascended the final hill toward home. Beasley Park rose ahead—a stately Palladian manor made of honey-colored stone. It had been his mother's childhood home. She'd been Margaret Honeywell then, the only child of a bombastic, horse-mad country squire. Ivo's father had been her childhood love. They'd grown up together at Beasley.

After his father's elevation to the earldom, Ivo's family had removed to Worth House, the family seat in Hertfordshire. But Beasley still held a special place in his parents' hearts. The family returned to it often, spending summers there and occasionally even Christmas, as they were doing this year.

Ivo was nearly a month ahead of them in returning to Somersetshire. He'd planned it so. It had been years since he'd been home. After finishing his final term at Oxford, he'd headed straight to Europe in company with a rambunctious party of university friends. One by one those friends had drifted off on their own adventures while Ivo continued with his rum-soaked guide, Signor Ruggiero, roaming the ancient ruins, museums, and coffee houses of France, Switzerland, and Italy.

He needed time to reacclimate himself to life in England— and to country life in particular.

As he rode up Beasley's expansive gravel drive, a groom jogged out of the stable to meet him. Ivo was nearly upon the fellow before the lad's face came into focus. It was Andrew Cole, a former stableboy. He'd grown into a strapping young man in Ivo's absence.

"Welcome back, Mr. Beresford," he said.

Ivo smiled. "Well met, Andrew. Do I have you to thank for sending Snap ahead to me at the inn?"

"Aye sir. Mr. Partridge said as how you'd be wanting him."

"Quite right, too." Ivo brought Snap to a halt. There were no other stablemen about. "Are you in charge now?"

"Only while Whitson is away with Lord and Lady Allendale. It's he who's head groom."

"Is he just. And he left you to manage in his absence? My congratulations." Ivo dismounted. He tossed Snap's reins to Andrew. "Look after him, would you."

The housekeeper, Mrs. Kirby appeared at the top of the stone steps. A short, round woman of sixty-odd years, she'd been employed at Beasley since Ivo was a boy.

"Master Ivo! Upon my word. How tall you've grown." Tears started in the old housekeeper's eyes. "You are a sight, and no mistake."

Ivo bounded up the steps. "Come, Mrs. K. I'm not so unique from my brothers. If you've seen one Beresford male, you've seen them all." He dropped a kiss on her plump cheek before entering the house. "I trust my valet has arrived?"

Mrs. Kirby followed alongside him through the marble-tiled hall. "He came yesterday with the Italian gentleman."

Ivo stripped off his leather riding gloves. Signor Ruggiero wasn't precisely Italian. Not by birth anyway. But Ivo didn't bother correcting her. There was no point in burdening Mrs. Kirby with the man's tedious history.

"Have you had any word from my parents?" he asked.

"Lord and Lady Allendale are still in Hertfordshire with Lord St. Clare and Master Jack. We expect them back a week before Christmas. Lady Katherine should be returning then as well. She's had her season in London, you know."

"Yes," Ivo said. "Mother wrote me about it in Italy."

His baby sister Kate's debut had been an unsuccessful one by all accounts. A surprising fact—*and* a dispiriting one. At twenty, Kate was a renowned beauty, with a healthy fortune to her name. If she couldn't make a match, there was little hope for the rest of them.

He ascended the grand curving staircase. "Is Partridge about?"

"In your room, sir."

"What about Signor Ruggiero?"

Mrs. Kirby remained at the bottom of the steps. "I've put the Italian gentleman in the rose bedroom." Her lips pursed with evident disapproval. "He's been...ill."

Ivo paused in his ascent, suppressing a grimace. No doubt it was the same illness that had plagued the estimable signore since Ivo and his friends had hired him in Rome. The man loved to drink. He'd rarely spent a day sober since they'd crossed the alps.

"I trust he hasn't been troubling you?"

"He's kept to his room," Mrs. Kirby said. "Mr. Partridge has been looking after him."

God bless Partridge.

The indispensable valet had once served Lord Allendale himself and had traveled with Ivo on the earl's insistence. Ivo suspected his father had originally intended Partridge to be some sort of a watchdog. Lord only knew how well Partridge had fulfilled that office. It was possible he'd written reports to Ivo's father throughout the whole of their time away, detailing every one of Ivo's missteps and misdemeanors.

But Ivo didn't think so.

He trusted the man implicitly.

"I won't be down for luncheon," he said, continuing up the stairs. "I've letters to write. But you may tell Cook to expect me at dinner."

"Yes, Master Ivo. Shall I send a tray to your room?"

"A splendid idea. Send one up for Signor Ruggiero too." If the fellow hadn't eaten yet, Ivo would see that he did. It was the only way to counterbalance the man's perpetual drunkenness.

With luck, Ivo would have him sober enough by the time

his parents, brothers, and sister converged on Beasley Park for Christmas.

As it was, most of the house was shut up. When not in residence, his parents retained only a skeleton staff at Beasley, comprised of Mrs. Kirby, the cook, and a handful of footmen, maids, and grooms. Ivo was glad for the privacy, however temporary.

Entering his bedroom, he found it just as he'd left it on his last visit home from Oxford. The same mahogany four poster stood at its center, draped in its familiar brocaded curtains, and the same blue and gold Aubusson carpets covered the floor. A few remaining leather cases from his travels were stacked on the bench at the end of the bed, the only sign that he'd ever left home.

Ivo shut the door behind him with an audible click. There was a fire awaiting him in the hearth. He came to stand before it, raising his hands to the blaze.

A rustling sound emitted from the bowels of the attached dressing room. Partridge stuck his head out soon after. "Ah. It's you, sir."

"Don't act so surprised," Ivo replied. "We both know you calculated my arrival time down to the minute."

Partridge emerged from the dressing room with a smile. He was a short, brawny man of fifty, with sandy hair liberally peppered with gray. A jagged scar intersected his brow, the remnant of a mysterious encounter he never spoke of.

Whatever had happened, Ivo would wager that Partridge's opponent had come out the worse in the affair. Despite his advancing years, the valet was a man to be reckoned with.

"I confess, you're later than I anticipated." Partridge assisted Ivo off with his coat. "Didn't run into any trouble, did you?"

"Not the kind you mean." Ivo loosened his cravat. "I stopped to render aid to a lady in distress."

"Aye, did you?" Partridge inspected Ivo's coat for wear and tear before draping it over the back of a nearby chair. "Not many ladies in these parts as I recall. Excepting your mother and sister, there's naught but village girls hereabouts."

"You're wrong," Ivo answered before he could stop himself.

Partridge arched his brows. "Sir?"

"Miss Burton-Smythe is a lady."

Partridge went still.

Ivo returned his attention to the crackling flames of the fire, anticipating the valet's censure. "She's the daughter of a baronet, anyway."

"She's the daughter of Sir Frederick Burton-Smythe," Partridge said.

"Through no fault of her own."

"As that may be; the Burton-Smythes are no friends to the Beresfords. Never have been. A dangerous lot, they are."

"For pity's sake, Partridge." Ivo shot the valet a dark look. "You know how I feel about this tendency to cling to the past."

"Yes, sir, but the Burton-Smythes—"

"It's why we're in this muddle. All this emphasis on traditions at the expense of progress. One is supposed to keep doing something just because it's what's always been done before. It's mindlessness. What this country needs is to be moving forward, not forever looking back."

"The country, mayhap. Not your father. You'll find he keeps a keen eye on the past. When he was a boy—"

"Yes, I'm aware," Ivo interrupted brusquely. "The Beresfords take grudge-keeping to the extreme. It doesn't follow that I must leave a lady to perish on the side of the road simply because her father once slighted my own."

"Perish?" Partridge echoed. "Was the lass hurt serious-like?"

Ivo sank into the velvet wingchair by the fire. "No," he admitted. "It was a turned ankle, merely. But you take my meaning."

"Aye, sir." Partridge crouched in front of Ivo to assist him in removing his damp boots. He ably pulled off the first one and set it by the fire. "If you don't mind my saying so…"

Ivo leaned back with a weary groan. In any other servant, it would have been outright impertinence. But Partridge had earned the right to speak his mind. "Oh, go on if you must."

"It weren't a slight, Master Ivo. What Sir Fred did to your father, and to your mother besides…" Partridge removed the second boot. "It were more than that."

A frown compressed Ivo's mouth. "I know."

At least, he thought he did.

As children, Ivo's mother and Sir Frederick had been intended for each other. It had been their parents' fervent desire to see them wed, thereby joining up the neighboring estates of Beasley Park and Letchford Hall into one formidable property. On Squire Honeywell's death, Sir Frederick had even been made Ivo's mother's guardian for a time. He'd attempted to use the position as leverage to force her into marriage.

Naturally, Ivo's mother hadn't succumbed.

She'd roundly rejected Sir Frederick in favor of Ivo's father. Sir Frederick hadn't taken it at all well. Not only had John Beresford been his childhood nemesis, he was also a man long rumored to be illegitimate. For Sir Frederick, who considered his own pedigree something sacred, the insult had been impossible to forgive. There were whispers of a duel. Of devious dealings, brutal bouts of fisticuffs, and false accusations of despicable crimes.

Ivo suspected his parents had never shared the whole of it.

The point was, they hadn't forgotten. Nor had Sir Frederick. It's why he'd christened his only daughter after Ivo's mother. Meg Burton-Smythe was named Margaret for no other reason than pure, unadulterated spite. Sir Frederick had wanted to deliver a final insult to Ivo's father. Even at the expense of his own daughter.

Ivo pitied Miss Burton-Smythe the more for it.

"In any event, it was long before I was born," he said. "I don't plan on shunning the girl. If she and I ever cross paths again, I shall treat her with as much kindliness as I'd treat any other gently bred young lady." He raked a hand through his hair, exhausted by the topic. "Now...what's all this with the signore?"

Partridge flashed Ivo a speaking glance. "Indisposed again, sir."

"When is he not? Have you poured coffee down his throat like we did in Venice?"

"He won't have it. Claims it upsets his digestion."

"Does he, by God. Well, if coffee won't suffice, he can bloody well eat something. Mrs. Kirby is bringing up a tray. See that you're the one to take it into him. I don't want her troubled by any unfortunate remarks."

Ruggiero's compliments toward the ladies became somewhat over-effusive when he'd been drinking. It was another of the man's failings. Ivo couldn't think why he put up with him.

"Very good." Partridge straightened. "Shall I draw you a bath?"

"Deal with the signore first. I have letters to write on business that can't be delayed."

"To your parents, sir?"

"To what constitutes the leadership in this part of the country. I have a proposition to put to them." Ivo stood. "Like I told you, Partridge, I'm looking to the future."

# Chapter Three

Perspiration beaded Meg's brow as her father's aged groom, Timothy, carried her into the cavernous kitchen at Letchford Hall. Her ankle was throbbing. It had been all she could do to make it home on her mare.

The elderly housekeeper, Mrs. Church, and the white-haired cook, Mrs. Stapleton, were seated in front of the kitchen fire, engaged in one of their daily sessions of tea and scandal. They were both in their aprons; both hard-eyed, mean-mouthed, and perpetually disapproving. Between the two of them, they knew all the latest West Country gossip.

On seeing Meg, Mrs. Church rose and hurriedly crossed the kitchen. Small in stature, she made up for her diminutive size with an outsized air of command. "What's happened?" she demanded of Timothy. "Has she fallen from that mare of hers?"

Mrs. Stapleton quickly joined them. She was as plump as Mrs. Church was lean. "Oh, but the master won't like to hear of this. And if she's broken her head, I won't be the one to tell him so. Not me, my good fellow."

"It isn't my head," Meg said. "It's only my ankle. And it's not broken."

The words came easier now that she was in the safety of familiar surroundings. Indeed, among the servants and those who didn't directly threaten her peace of mind, Meg had largely conquered her childhood stammer. Deep breaths and strategic pauses helped.

"Count to ten," Miss Adams had advised Meg as a little girl. "Or twenty, if necessary. It isn't the words that defeat you, but the feelings behind them."

It was true, much to Meg's frustration. Even now, having attained the maturity of her eighteenth year, her stammer was still the most reliable barometer of her unruly emotions.

Mrs. Church's flinty gaze lifted briefly to Meg's face. "I'll be the judge of that, madam." She snapped her fingers at Timothy. "Set her down by the fire."

Meg grimaced as Timothy settled her into the chair where the cook had sat only moments before. He brought a low wooden stool for her foot. "That all right, miss?" he asked.

"Yes, thank you, Timothy. I'm comfortable now." Meg drooped in her seat, exhausted by her ordeal. "Would you see to Rowena, please?"

"Yes'm." Timothy tugged at his brown cloth cap before departing.

Mrs. Stapleton made Meg a cup of tea while Mrs. Church bustled around the kitchen, gathering her supplies. When the housekeeper had cold-soaked bandages sufficient to the purpose, she sank down in front of Meg's foot to remove her boot and stocking.

Meg gritted her teeth through the whole of it.

"Unlucky girl," Mrs. Stapleton murmured. "You'll be abed with your leg up soon, just like your poor father."

"It's already swelling," Mrs. Church remarked.

"Not enough to summon the doctor, surely," Meg said. "I d-don't want to make a fuss."

"Should have thought of that before taking that mare out. And without Timothy to accompany you. I've warned you time and again." Mrs. Church began wrapping the wet bandage around Meg's ankle. "How did the creature unseat you?"

"I was cantering by the river and Rowena stopped short to crop some weeds. I went straight over her head."

"Wretched beast," Mrs. Church said.

Meg instantly rose to Rowena's defense. "She isn't. She's only poorly trained. It's entirely m-my fault. I wasn't as firm as I might have been when I was teaching her."

"You should have let Timothy break her instead of mucking around with the business yourself."

Meg stifled a wince as the housekeeper finished wrapping her foot. "I d-didn't want her broken. It's cruel to crush a horse's spirit."

Or anyone's, she might have added.

Mrs. Church flashed her a perceptive look. "It's a kindness—with horses *and* with young ladies." She tied off the bandage. "Your Miss Adams would say the same."

Mrs. Stapleton brought Meg a steaming cup of tea. "Aye, she would have done and all."

Meg accepted the tea with a quiet murmur of thanks.

She refused to agree with their assertions about Miss Adams. It was true that Meg's former governess had enforced a great many rules and regulations during her tenure at the Hall, but those rules had been meant to shape Meg's personality, not to alter it completely.

"Drink it down," Mrs. Stapleton urged. "The sugar will do you good."

"Excellent for shock," Mrs. Church agreed. She

straightened. "I'll summon a footman to carry you to your room. Then, I'll inform Sir Frederick."

Meg's stomach sank. Her father had been abed for a fortnight, suffering mightily from his gout. He was in no frame of mind to be troubled by anything to do with her. In truth, he seldom was.

Sir Frederick took a dim view of females. Much of that was owing to Lady Allendale. According to what Meg had gleaned from Mrs. Church and Mrs. Stapleton over the years, he'd been in love with the former Margaret Honeywell in his youth. He'd believed they would marry. When she'd jilted him in favor of Lord Allendale, Sir Frederick's disposition toward women had been irrevocably altered. He'd grown bitter and angry over the decades that passed, rather like a turnip—as Mrs. Stapleton had once described him—left to stew in its own juices. What fondness he'd had for his offspring had been reserved for Meg's older brother, Roderick.

But Roddy was gone.

Last Meg had heard, her brother was living somewhere abroad, encamped with a disreputable group of artists and other undesirable persons. She hadn't had a letter from him in ages. Nor had her father as far as she was aware.

"You needn't tell him," she said. "I'll be well enough in a day or two."

———— ❧ ————

IN THE END, IT TOOK MEG NEARLY A WEEK TO recover. At the close of it, she wasted no time in donning her warmest habit, saddling Rowena, and riding away from the stifling prison of Letchford Hall as far and as fast as she could.

Would that it could be farther!

Alas, despite her desire for freedom, Meg was emboldened

to go only as far as the village. There, she stopped at the draper's shop and bought herself a length of pink satin ribbon. It was another modest attempt at rebellion. Her dressmaker was forever insisting that Meg's complexion was ill-suited to pink, even though Meg adored the color.

She was just tucking the parcel into the small leather bag attached to her sidesaddle when a familiar white stallion and his equally familiar rider entered the empty street.

Meg swallowed hard. She hadn't thought to see Mr. Beresford again. Not this soon, certainly.

It was a quiet day in the high street. Approaching storm clouds were keeping most of the villagers at home. Meg sent up a silent prayer of thanks for the foul weather as she used the wooden mounting block in front of the draper's shop to climb back into her sidesaddle.

Mr. Beresford slowed his stallion as he approached. He tipped his black beaver hat to her. "Miss Burton-Smythe. Good morning."

For a split second, she was tempted to ride off without acknowledging him. It's what her father would command her to do. And after all the years of animosity between their two families, surely no one would blame her.

But when it came to the point, Meg couldn't bring herself to offer Mr. Beresford the cut direct. He'd done nothing to deserve it. Not yet, anyway.

"Good m-morning," she replied.

"Your ankle is much improved, I see."

The memory of his hand curving around her stockinged foot, his long fingers both strong and heart-quiveringly gentle, danced through Meg's head. A rush of heat followed, making her blush to the roots of her hair.

That he should mention one of her limbs. And in a public street!

"Yes, th-thank you," she managed. "It's well recovered."

He brought his stallion to halt. A frosty wind rustled the folds of his heavy black broadcloth greatcoat. His top boots were splattered in mud, his drab buckskin breeches hugging his well-muscled thighs like a second skin.

Meg's gaze drifted over him quite against her will, taking in the full magnificence of his figure. The Beresford men were known for their handsomeness, but she'd rarely been privileged to view one of their number from this close a vantage point.

"Have you been Christmas shopping?" he asked.

She shot an anxious glance at the window of the draper's shop as she gathered her reins. Those who spied her exchanging words with a Beresford may not be brave enough to report it to Meg's father, but they'd have no compunction about relaying the news to Mrs. Church or Mrs. Stapleton. Meg would never hear the end of it.

With that in mind, she turned Rowena toward home, giving the mare an encouraging nudge with her heel. "I've finished m-my Christmas shopping already."

It was only a few weeks until the holiday. She'd been accumulating small gifts for the servants and for several of her father's tenants since September. Meg liked to be prepared. Indeed, the single present she'd bought for her father had been wrapped and hidden in her wardrobe for months. She'd struggled with choosing it. Sir Frederick Burton-Smythe was not an easy man to please.

Mr. Beresford kept pace with her on his stallion. "You're more efficient than I have been. As it stands, I only have a few items I picked up during my travels to give my family. A small Swiss clock. A first-rate translation of Dante's Inferno. And some very fine lace I found in Paris. The Dante and the lace will do for my mother and sister. My brothers will have to draw straws for the clock."

Meg couldn't tell if he was jesting. "What about your f-father?"

"Ah. There's a dilemma. What to get the gentleman who has everything?" Mr. Beresford guided his stallion down the high street "What did you buy for your own father?"

"A tobacco box with a spring lid. It's m-made of silver. They have them at Pinnock's Emporium."

"An excellent notion. Regrettably, my father doesn't smoke."

"I saw a silver hand warmer there as well," Meg suggested. "Everyone's hands get c-cold."

"Another splendid idea. I thank you for it." He caught her subtle glance at the street behind them. "You needn't worry," he said. "We weren't observed."

The tension in her shoulders eased a fraction. "How c-can you be certain?"

"I know when I'm being watched. I get the queerest prickle on the back of my neck. It's saved me from peril countless times during my years abroad."

Her curiosity got the better of her. "You were on the continent?"

She knew he'd been on his grand tour, but—despite the gossip Mrs. Church and Mrs. Stapleton regularly brought back to the Hall—Meg didn't know the details of his travels.

"In Italy mostly," he said. "Your brother is abroad, is he not?"

"He is. B-But he rarely writes." Roddy was too busy enjoying his freedom to waste a minute of it in relating his adventures to his younger sister. "It's a p-pity for I should d-dearly love to hear about his travels."

"I don't mind sharing tales of mine, for what they're worth."

To Meg, they were worth a great deal. Village life could be

stifling. There was little excitement to be had except for the variety she gleaned from books. "Did you visit Rome?"

"I did. But it was Florence where I spent the majority of my stay. I took a villa in Tuscany for a time, along with my guide Signor Ruggiero. He claimed he could teach me to speak the language like a native Florentine. Alas, he spent most of our sojourn half-seas at the nearest taverna."

"Oh dear."

"Quite. Fortunately, English public houses don't agree with him half so well."

"He accompanied you home from Italy?"

"He did," Mr. Beresford said grimly. "His history is... complicated. Suffice to say, I'm endeavoring to make him fit for company before my parents return. They're broad minded enough, but I can't imagine they'd appreciate a drunkard roaming the halls, attempting to recite Ovid's *Ars Amatoria* to my little sister."

Meg cast him a glance of alarm. "Is he d-dangerous to ladies?"

"Oh no. Not to my sister anyway. Kate can look after herself."

Meg knew Mr. Beresford's younger sister by sight. Lady Katherine Beresford was a renowned West Country beauty. Only a year or two older than Meg, tales of Lady Katherine's exploits abounded. She and Meg had never been friends. Meg admired her nonetheless. Anyone must do so. Lady Kate, as she was called, was a force of nature.

"It's the signore I worry about," Mr. Beresford went on gravely. "He'd never recover from such a set down as Kate would give him. Better I should sober him up and find him employment elsewhere. A boys' school, preferably."

The two of them rode on past the shops, turning down the country lane that led toward the village church and beyond. Meg leaned forward in her sidesaddle to give Rowena's neck a pat.

"I beg your pardon, Miss Burton-Smythe," Mr. Beresford said at length, "but does your father not employ a groom?"

She bent her head. "He d-does."

"Is this groom, perchance, invisible?"

Her lips twitched with unwilling amusement. "N-No. He's real. But...I d-don't require him today."

"Or last week? You were without your groom then, too."

And paid the price for it, he might have said.

But Meg didn't think he was scolding her. His manner seemed kindly enough. "I prefer t-to be alone when I'm riding."

"I see."

"It's n-not exceptionable. Many young ladies ride alone when they're at home in the country."

"My sister doesn't," he said. "Not that I'm aware."

The horses continued down the lane, side by side. Rowena's gait was steady and sure. She required little guidance. Letchford Hall lay over the hills past the church. The mare could find her way back to the comfort of her home stable from anywhere in the county.

"Is your sister back from London yet?" Meg couldn't resist asking.

It was common knowledge that Lady Kate had gone to town for her first season. Meg had heard Mrs. Church and Mrs. Stapleton speculating on the wealth and rank of Lady Kate's future husband. It was presumed the young beauty would make a spectacular match.

"Not yet," Mr. Beresford said. "She's due back by Christmas. So are the rest of my family. I'm on my own until then."

"I prefer b-being on my own."

A smile tilted his mouth. "Do you? That's singular."

"It's all I've known. Since m-my mother died, it's only b-been me at the Hall. My brother is gone away. And the servants have their duties to occupy them. I had a companion for a time in m-my governess, but she's recently departed as well."

He gave her a puzzled look. "What of Sir Frederick?"

"My father k-keeps to himself. I rarely see him."

"It's not a preference then," he said.

She gazed back at him uncertainly. "I'm sorry?"

"Your being alone. You can't prefer something that's not of your own choosing. Not if you've had no other experiences to weigh against it."

IVO REALIZED ALMOST IMMEDIATELY THAT HE'D once again gone too far. Miss Burton-Smythe's expression attested as much. A spasm of pain crossed her face, as though he'd said something that had hurt her profoundly.

"But you know yourself best," he amended. "To be sure, there are many of my acquaintance who enjoy their solitude. Scholars and—"

"I'm n-not a scholar, sir." Miss Burton-Smythe fidgeted with her reins. "Forgive me. I m-must ride on. I'm...I'm expected back."

Ivo wondered.

She'd said she'd been on her own since her mother died. What she'd failed to mention was that the late Lady Burton-Smythe had died giving birth to her. Everyone knew that. Sir Frederick had been a widower since Ivo was five years old.

It meant that Miss Burton-Smythe had, essentially, been alone all of her life.

She had an older brother, for what the fellow was worth:

the perpetually absent Roderick Burton-Smythe. A strapping, ginger-haired cretin, he hadn't lingered long in Somersetshire. Ivo hadn't seen the man in over a decade. Lord only knew where he was or why he'd been so callous as to abandon his sister to such a fate.

An older brother should do better. He should be interested in his family. He should *care*.

Ivo had naturally gone away from home himself for a time, just as any young gentleman must do, first for his schooling and then to broaden his education with travel. But he hadn't disappeared completely. He'd visited regularly during his years at university. And while in Europe, he'd written Kate and his brothers often. Indeed, Ivo had been a better correspondent than the three of them had been.

"I'm afraid I've offended you," he said.

"No, no," she demurred, ducking her head. "But I m-must go. You're n-not continuing this way...are you?"

A fork in the road loomed ahead. To the right lay the path that led past the church and on to the main road out of town. To the left was the way toward Beasley Park and Letchford Hall.

"No, indeed," he said. "We must part company here."

Miss Burton-Smythe was visibly relieved.

Ivo supposed he should be insulted. He wasn't. Not deeply, anyway. In truth, he was intrigued by her. The quieter she was—the more shy and self-effacing—the greater his desire to engage with her. It was the most damnable urge.

"I have an appointment with Mr. Colfax at the vicarage," he explained. "It's why I was in the village." He patted the pocket of his greatcoat. "I've bought him a packet of cigars. My housekeeper claims they're an indulgence of his."

An unreadable emotion flickered in Miss Burton-Smythe's eyes. It might have been wistfulness. "Are you acquainted with Miss Colfax?"

Ivo hesitated. He couldn't imagine what would bring such a look to Miss Burton-Smythe's face. "I'm not acquainted with any of them," he said. "I was still in Italy when Mr. Colfax arrived to take over for old Mr. Applewhite last year." He slowed Snap, reluctant to part ways with her just yet. "Is Miss Colfax a friend of yours?"

"Not an intimate one. But I d-do know her a little. She c-calls sometimes at the Hall. She's very pretty."

Ivo smiled slightly. "Is she? Lucky me."

Miss Burton-Smythe flinched. "I really m-must get home, sir." Turning away from him, she gave her bay mare a kick in the direction of Letchford Hall. The mare sprang forward.

Ivo was close enough to set a hand on the horse's bridle, preventing the beast from cantering off. "Miss Burton-Smythe—"

"Please let m-me go," she said, refusing to look at him.

An unsettling weight formed in Ivo's chest. Despite his experience of the world, he wasn't accustomed to conversing with ladies who were as sheltered and innocent as she was. It was rather like dealing with a wild woodland creature—a shy doe he was persuading to eat out of his hand. The smallest noise seemed to startle her.

"I will," he promised. "But first...I must tell you..."

Her eyes reluctantly met his.

They were a delicate shade of China blue. Wide, round, and fringed with thick, ink-black lashes. Beautiful eyes, really. Ivo couldn't recall when he'd seen the like of them.

"It's lovely down by Sefton Bridge at this time of year," he heard himself saying. "The place where you fell from your mare? Along the edge of the woods as it runs toward the river? I've been riding that path in the mornings. If you'd like to join me for a gallop tomorrow—"

She drew back. "Oh, but I c-couldn't!"

"Only if you'd like. I ride at eight o'clock sharpish. There's never anyone else about down there at that time of day." He released her horse. "You would be doing me a kindness, really. Unlike you, I'm not made for being alone."

She bit her lip as she stared at him. The torment of indecision clouded her cinnamon-freckled brow. "I-I do like to ride by the river," she admitted at last.

A triumphant smile curved Ivo's mouth. Here was progress at last. Though to what end, he hadn't the faintest idea. He hadn't come home to Somersetshire to foster a friendship with a Burton-Smythe. And he certainly hadn't come to spark up a romance. He was here for one reason only.

He nevertheless felt a certain satisfaction. "Tomorrow, then," he said. "And don't be late."

# Chapter Four

"A railway in Maidenbridge?" Mr. Colfax examined the prospectus that Ivo had given him. Smoke swirled from the cigar dangling from his fingers. He took another thoughtful puff. "That *is* an idea."

"A brilliant one," Ivo said. "Think of the benefit to the local tradesman. A railway would bring all sorts of new people into the village."

"Precisely." Mr. Colfax handed the prospectus back to Ivo.

The two of them were seated in front of a blazing fire in the vicarage's bookroom. It was a smallish parlor at the back of the house, distinguished by an inordinate amount of plaid. Bright red tartan draped the windows and covered the worn sofa and overstuffed chairs. It was a remnant of the last vicar, old Mr. Applewhite, a staid traditionalist who had been firmly tethered to the past.

Mr. Colfax, by contrast, was a younger and more progressive clergyman.

Or so Ivo had been led to believe.

"There are many who would object to it for just that reason," the vicar said. "I admit to reservations myself. Do we really wish to encourage strangers coming into the village?"

"You'd rather Maidenbridge be preserved in aspic?" Ivo set his teacup and saucer down on the table beside his chair. "I must tell you, it's an impossible dream. No place can exist in isolation forever."

"My dear Mr. Beresford, we are hardly isolated here. I dined with twenty families last month."

Ivo suppressed a dismissive retort. What were twenty well-to-do country families in comparison to the hundreds—nay, thousands—of people who might benefit from a railway line?

"It isn't only the people that the railway would bring to Maidenbridge," he said calmly, "it's the benefit our own residents would have of easy access to Taunton and Bath."

"Your business partners mean for this railway line to traverse the whole of Somersetshire?"

"The line would be built in stages. First, the track to Taunton and then beyond. If all goes to plan, we anticipate the project could be completed in seven years."

The vicar raised his cigar back to his lips. "As I understand it," he remarked before taking a puff, "such a scheme would require an authorizing act of parliament."

"You're quite right," Ivo said. "Providing I can obtain the necessary subscriptions for the project, a bill will be presented in the next session."

Lord Pershore, the youngest son of the Marquess of Bruton, was handling that aspect of the business. It was he who had convinced Ivo to join the venture. The two of them were friends from Oxford; both younger sons of the peerage with no set path for themselves in life. Pershore had turned to the railway business as an alternative to his family's tradition of younger sons joining the military or taking up the church as a profession.

Ivo himself had felt no pressure from his family in that

regard, thank God. He had no desire to be a military man. And outside of attending Sunday services, the church held no lure for him. It was the future that had always been his focus. Pershore was keen on the very same. Along with several other of their forward-thinking friends, and two senior advisors who had consulted on the formation of the Great Western Railway nearly a decade before, they'd formed the West Somerset Amalgamated Railway Company.

It wasn't a question of money. On his great-grandfather's death last year, Ivo had inherited enough to ensure his independence. He had no reason to want more. No. This endeavor wasn't about profit. It was about progress.

"Think of what it could mean to our landowners and local businessmen," Ivo said. "Travel would be exponentially faster. It would be easier to ship and receive goods. Not to mention the advantages to the common folk. If a family member is ill and requires a specialist doctor, for example—"

"Yes, yes, these are all persuasive arguments, but do consider, Mr. Beresford. Maidenbridge isn't Liverpool or Manchester. We're a modest community, with no industries of national import."

"Maidenbridge would have a platform halt, not a fully equipped railway station."

The vicar drew on his cigar. "Nevertheless..."

"We have a great many well-to-do families here, as you said yourself. My own family among them. They would all benefit."

"Has Lord Allendale lent his support to the business?" Mr. Colfax asked. "I daresay he must have done."

Ivo hesitated. "As to that..."

The truth was, he hadn't yet spoken to his father on the subject. He was going to do so over Christmas. Until then, Ivo intended to press forward. This was *his* business venture. Not his family's. Something *he* had discovered—and hoped to succeed at—entirely on his own.

"But they're away at present, of course," Mr. Colfax said. "When do they return?"

"I expect them to arrive within a fortnight."

"You must be feeling their absence, on your own at Beasley Park at this time of year, with only the servants to cheer you."

"Not wholly alone. I brought my guide, Signor Ruggiero, back from Italy with me. He's, er, recovering his health. When he's well enough, he'll be taking up employment as a teacher somewhere, or as tutor in a private household. He's fluent in several languages, Latin among them."

"An Italian scholar! Fancy that."

"He's not exactly Italian," Ivo admitted. "Or rather, he is. But not by birth. He's originally from Kent."

"Kent?"

"It's a long story." One that Ivo had no desire to be telling at the moment.

"I'm eager to hear it. I do hope you will bring him to church with you on Sunday."

"Of a certainty," Ivo said. "If he's well enough. As for my father—"

"Yes, yes. His support for your venture would be vital. Though it's her ladyship's support which would be of greater value in these parts. The Honeywell name still carries a good deal of weight here." Mr. Colfax paused, adding deliberately, "As does the name of Burton-Smythe."

Ivo felt the unspoken meaning behind that pause. "I'm aware."

The vicar took another thoughtful puff of his cigar. "I know your two families have been at odds these many years. Mr. Applewhite apprised me of the difficulties when I arrived. I wouldn't presume to advise you, but...I have found that many a parishioner's life has been blighted by nourishing old grievances. Our spiritual well-being is better served by exercising forgiveness and looking to the future."

"I do believe in looking toward the future," Ivo said. "It's my guiding principle."

"Good, good. Then...dare I hope that you have already approached Sir Frederick?"

"Not yet. But I will do, once I've received enough subscriptions from local businessmen. If I have their support, I hope Sir Frederick will be persuaded to lend his as well."

"Happen it might work the other way. Sir Frederick's support could persuade the merchants."

"That may be so," Ivo acknowledged. "I prefer to meet with the townspeople first. I've already written to Mr. Standish and Mr. Horsley. I'm dining with them both this week."

Mr. Colfax stubbed out the remains of his cigar in the small metal ashtray beside him. "You're well on your way, then."

"Not quite. I'm hoping you can point me in the direction of other influential members of Maidenbridge. It's been a long while since I've been home. I'm not as familiar with the townspeople as I was as a boy."

"If you've reached out to Mr. Horsley and Mr. Standish, you've already done your utmost. Outside of your parents and Sir Frederick, they're the wealthiest figures in local society, possessed of the largest properties."

"What of the rest of the town?" Ivo asked. "Wealth doesn't always equate to influence. You yourself have as much impact as Horsley or Standish. People listen to you."

It's why Ivo had called on Mr. Colfax today. The vicar was well-placed to reassure those who might cringe from the prospect of a railway out of fear or ignorance. If Ivo could persuade him to get behind the venture, others would follow.

"Yes, I see." Mr. Colfax's brow wrinkled. "You might

speak with Mr. Pinnock, the owner of the Emporium on Mead Lane. He moved down from London two years ago with his wife and five sons. Mind you, he's not a learned man, but he's full of opinions and possessed of a loud voice. People listen to him."

There was a soft tap at the door of the bookroom. A young lady in a plain wool dress stuck her head in. "Excuse me for interrupting you, father. Mrs. Quint is here to discuss the arrangements for the funeral. You told her to come at eleven, if you recall."

Ivo and the vicar stood. Ivo hadn't met the vicar's daughter yet. She'd been out when he had arrived, much to his disappointment. He owned to a certain curiosity about the girl—an emotion sparked entirely by Miss Burton-Smythe's reaction to the mention of Miss Colfax's name.

"Come in Rose," Mr. Colfax said. "My oldest daughter, Mr. Beresford. Rose, this is Mr. Beresford, Lord Allendale's son, newly returned from Italy."

Miss Colfax curtsied. She was, as Miss Burton-Smythe had attested, a very pretty girl. One of the dark-haired, fair-skinned varieties with liquid brown eyes, plump cheeks, and a swan-like grace to her figure.

"Mr. Beresford," she said. "How do you do?"

He bowed to her. "Miss Colfax. A pleasure."

"I'm sorry I wasn't here to welcome you. I was calling on one of our parishioners. Her baby has been ill."

"You are a credit to me, my dear," Mr. Colfax said. He looked from his daughter to Ivo, with a spark of inspiration. "I say, perhaps you might dine with us on Friday? I'd be happy to invite Mr. Pinnock by way of an introduction."

Ivo exhaled a grateful sigh. He'd been about to suggest something similar. "That would be splendid, sir. Thank you."

"Don't thank me yet. Mr. Pinnock is a self-proclaimed matchmaker. You'll likely regret the acquaintance once he begins meddling in your affairs." Mr. Colfax addressed his daughter. "Tell Mrs. Quint I'll be with her directly. I shall see Mr. Beresford out." He took Ivo's arm as Miss Colfax departed. "A good girl. The gentleman who wins her hand will be a very fortunate fellow."

Ivo's mouth quirked. It seemed that Mr. Pinnock wasn't the only villager with an interest in matchmaking. "Undoubtedly."

The vicar's housekeeper appeared with Ivo's greatcoat, hat, and gloves. "Here you are, sir."

She opened the front door of the vicarage as Ivo put on his things. A faint drizzle of rain had started. The gusting wind blew a few stray droplets into the hall.

"I shall send a note round when I've fixed a date with Mr. Pinnock," the vicar said. "In the meantime, perhaps you might consider making overtures to the Burton-Smythes?"

"Indeed," Ivo said, settling his hat on his head. "I fully intend to."

Meg was sitting alone in the drafty, high-ceilinged dining room at Letchford Hall when a commotion sounded at the doors. The noise wasn't the footman bringing her dinner. Not only the footman, anyway. A crash of plates falling to the floor and a shouted curse at one of the servants announced the unexpected arrival of her father.

"Out of my way, blast you," Sir Frederick bellowed, entering the room.

Meg shot up from her chair. Her napkin tumbled from her lap.

Her father was in his dressing gown, his weight leaning heavily on his thick ebony cane. Sweat glistened on his brow and in his wild, gray-streaked red hair as he limped to his seat at the head of the table. He was obviously in pain.

She moved to go to his side, wishing to offer her assistance, only to falter after the first step. He'd never desired her help in the past and she had no wish to receive a share of the abuse he was presently heaping on the servants.

They scrambled about him, pulling out his chair and setting his place, bowing and scraping as though he were Henry VIII, possessed of the power to send them to the chopping block for the smallest mistake.

"Get me my port," he shouted to one of the footmen. "And tell Stapleton I'll have none of that pap she's been feeding me. Spragg doesn't run this house, I do. I want a steak—rare."

Meg's fingers curled nervously around the back of her carved Jacobean chair.

"And you." Her father's unforgiving gaze fixed upon her. "Stop gawping and sit down."

Stomach quivering, Meg resumed her seat. "Are you f-feeling b-better, father?"

Her father's brows sank. He had no patience with her stuttering. "Do I look like I'm feeling better?"

"N-no, sir."

He scowled. "I thought that governess of yours was to have rid you of that infernal habit? She assured me she had before she up and left us."

"She had," Meg said. "M-mostly."

Except when Meg was with her father.

Or with Mr. Beresford.

Her eyes slid guiltily away from her father's face. To even think of a Beresford in his presence was akin to treason. To be sure, were Sir Frederick truly Henry VIII and not just his uncanny copy, he'd likely have her hauled straight to the scaffold on Tower Green. And if he discovered that she was planning to meet a Beresford male alone...

That would certainly be an excuse for drawing and quartering.

Meg swallowed hard.

She still couldn't quite believe she'd agreed to ride with Mr. Beresford in the morning. How in heaven had he convinced her to do it? To ignore eighteen years of her father's strictures on Lord Allendale's family and thirteen years of Miss Adams's warnings about being alone, unchaperoned, with a young man?

It scarcely mattered now. Given the state of the weather, Meg doubted she'd be able to keep her promise. She couldn't very well ride out to the river when it was raining so awfully.

"Sir Frederick!" Mrs. Church strode in. A harried footman trotted behind her with the silver tray holding Meg's father's wine. "I do wish you'd told me you'd be coming down. I would have had all in readiness."

"Am I now obligated to announce my movements in my own house? Bring me that bottle, Judson."

The footman hastened to fill Sir Frederick's glass.

Meg bit her lip. Her father wasn't supposed to be drinking port or eating red meats. Dr. Spragg had made that abundantly clear during his last visit. Overindulgence could easily trigger another attack. "Father... M-must you have the port this evening?"

Judson hesitated, the bottle frozen in his hand as it tipped over the rim of Sir Frederick's glass.

"Abstaining from it won't cure the suppurating abscess on my leg, will it?" Her father glared at the footman. "Don't dare stop pouring that port, Judson."

"Build up the fire, Hill," Mrs. Church commanded the other footman. "Lucy?" She snapped her fingers at the panicked housemaid. "Fetch a blanket for your master."

"No more fussing, Church," Sir Frederick said. "You make me feel like an old woman." He raised his glass to his lips. "Just see that my steak is made how I like it and leave me be."

Mrs. Church's lips pinched shut. "Very good, sir." She flashed Meg a speaking glance before withdrawing along with the other servants.

Meg was left alone with her father. She cleared her throat. "Father—"

"I said no more fussing."

"Yes, but...Dr. Spragg would n-never forgive me if you—"

Her father silenced her by the simple expedient of bringing his fist down on the table. The place settings jumped.

So did Meg.

"I won't be dictated to by that prosing windbag," he growled. "And I won't stand any lectures from a chit of a girl. If you can't restrain your tongue, you may dine in your room."

Meg was tempted to do so. She'd rather eat alone, with only a book to keep her company, than face her father's ill temper. He was a grumpy man at the best of times, but since his leg ulcer had abscessed, he'd become like a bear with a sore head, shouting at anyone who dared oppose him.

But no. She wouldn't run away. She refused to.

She remained in her seat as the footmen returned one by one, first with the julienne soup, next with mutton cutlets and mashed potatoes, and then with her father's steak and her own small portion of boiled chicken. The two of them ate, mute as two trappist monks, only the clink of cutlery and the continual glug of the port bottle disrupting the silence.

Before Roddy had decamped to the Continent, there had been three of them at dinner. Meg had been all but invisible then. Roddy had commanded most of the attention. But even as the favorite, he'd fallen victim to his share of paternal criticism. He'd left home the instant he came of age, content to leave Meg to bear the brunt of their father's judgment.

Given the alternative, Meg was comfortable with the quiet. However, the more he drank, the more often her father's eyes began to linger on her. She felt the familiar weight of his preoccupied glower. He frequently regarded her thus. In the past, the look had usually precipitated an interrogation. It was no different on this occasion.

"How have you been occupying yourself in Miss Adams's absence?" he asked. "Improving books and silent meditation, I have no doubt."

"I *have* b-been reading a great deal," Meg acknowledged.

Though the books weren't quite of the improving variety. Having exhausted the supply of leatherbound sermons and dry philosophical texts in Letchford Hall's library, she'd returned to reading her favorite novels and romanticized versions of history. Stories about Joan of Arc, the War of the Roses, and King Arthur and his knights. It was likely why her father had taken on the role of the villainous Henry in her mind and why—after but two brief encounters—she'd come to think of Mr. Beresford as something of a Lancelot. Or possibly a Gawain.

"I've b-been riding, too," she said.

"On that mare of yours, yes. Timothy keeps me informed. He says you refuse to allow him to accompany you."

Meg tensed. "I d-don't require a chaperone when I'm on Rowena."

"And if I say that you do?"

She stiffened her spine. On every other subject, she would willingly give way to her father's commands, but not this one. Her solitary rides on Rowena were sacrosanct. "I don't require a chaperone," she repeated more firmly. "I d-don't."

Her father gave her a brooding look. "So, you do have some spirit after all. I've often wondered."

Meg made no reply.

She never knew what it was her father wanted from her.

From her infancy, he'd purported to value meekness and obedience in women, and yet he exhibited contempt for her for having cultivated those very qualities. It made her all the more uneasy when she was around him. She couldn't tell from one moment to the next if she was expected to be quiet and obliging or if she was supposed to try to assert herself. As a result, when in his presence, her emotions—and her speech—were forever in a wretched tangle.

"I suppose I have Miss Adams to thank for that as well," he said, refilling his glass. "God knows you were a mousy enough child before she arrived."

It was halfway to being a compliment.

Meg was heartened by it. Setting down her fork and knife, she inhaled a steadying breath. There was no time like the present. "I've been m-meaning to t-talk to you about Miss Adams," she said carefully. "Now th-that she's left us—"

"You require a new governess? Is that it?" He looked her up and down. "Are you not learned enough, my girl?"

"No," she said. "That is—What I m-mean is... I d-don't need another governess." She folded her hands in her lap. "I'm eighteen."

"I see. You're wanting a season in London." He took another swallow of wine. "What's brought this on?"

Miss Colfax had. That was the unflinching truth of it.

Lady Kate may be the reigning beauty of Maidenbridge, but the vicar's daughter was the angel of the village. Miss Colfax taught at the local school. She called on the sick. She ministered to the poor. She was lovely and accomplished, well-placed to catch a gentleman's eye. *Mr. Beresford's* eye.

The minute he'd said he might be meeting her, Meg had known how it would be. Miss Colfax was perfect. A perfect daughter. A perfect lady; poised to be a perfect wife. While Meg...

Where to begin?

For one thing, Meg wasn't even formally out yet.

What chance had she of catching anyone's interest? She couldn't. Not here in Somersetshire. Not if she had Lady Kate and Miss Colfax to compete against. And certainly not if the only eligible gentlemen in the vicinity were Beresfords.

"If…if I'm to go to London for the season, the m-modiste will n-need t-time to make my c-clothes." Her anxiety at the proposition was so intense, she scarcely managed to get the words out.

But it had to be said.

It had to be done.

She couldn't live at Letchford Hall for the remainder of her life. She wanted romance and adventure. She wanted love.

Her father regarded her for a long moment in skeptical silence. "London is an exacting place. Young ladies on the marriage mart are put under the magnifying glass. Every fault is amplified. The fashionable set would take great pleasure in making sport of your failings."

She held her breath, waiting for him to enumerate them. Her stammer. Her shyness. Her clumsiness. Her abundant freckles. There was no need for her father to recite the laundry list. Meg was well acquainted with each and every one of her flaws.

But he didn't recite them, thank goodness. She supposed even Henry VIII had had his rare moments of compassion.

"Are you prepared for such an experience?" he asked instead.

"No," Meg admitted.

"Well then."

"M-Miss Adams said I m-might have a sort of season in Bath."

"Did she, by God. When might this have been? A final parting shot before she left us? One last attempt at bucking my authority?"

"N-No, sir. She m-mentioned it in her last letter."

"You're in correspondence with the woman?"

"I am." Meg had been writing to Miss Adams faithfully since the governess's departure. Miss Adams was busy with planning her wedding now, but still took time to reply. Her letters arrived with regularity. "Is Bath n-not a suitable alternative?"

Her father cut another chunk from his steak, sawing forcefully through the fat. Pink liquid oozed onto his plate. "Bath," he scoffed. "What other ladies of your quality are presented in Bath?" He tossed her an acid look. "Is this the sort of nonsense that's been occupying your attentions of late? I'm not surprised Letchford Hall is in such a sorry state."

Meg bristled at the reprimand. It was Mrs. Church who managed the day-to-day running of the Hall, by Meg's father's particular designation. If he had a complaint, he should take it up with her.

"I haven't n-noticed anything out of order," she said.

"It's December, is it not?" he retorted. "Where is the greenery? Where are the ribbon bows?"

She began to comprehend. "I'd thought that, since you have b-been so d-dreadfully ill, you would—"

"That I'd prefer my house to look like a mausoleum?" He helped himself to another serving of mashed potatoes. "Do you anticipate my demise, girl?"

"No, sir."

"Then what of the holly and the ivy? What of the jolly Christmas songs on that costly pianoforte of yours?" He raised his glass to his lips. "This is what comes of having no mother to train you," he said uncharitably. "Though she'd have been of no use in this regard. She knew nothing of what it took to be a great lady." He took a long drink. "You have the look of her."

It wasn't a compliment.

Meg knew that to her soul.

After he'd been jilted by Lady Allendale, her father had married Meg's mother, Edith. She'd been a village girl; the daughter of a widowed solicitor. Sir Frederick had wed her for no other reason than to get himself an heir. Edith had willingly done her duty, giving birth first to Meg's brother, Roderick, and then to Meg, before dying in childbed.

Meg had never known her mother. From her infancy she'd been consigned to servants. First a wet nurse, then a nanny, and finally her governess, Miss Adams.

During all those years, Lady Edith Burton-Smythe had lain buried in the family plot in the churchyard. There were no portraits of her in the house. Not even a rough sketch to commemorate her.

Meg had no need of either to dispute her father's claim. She knew exactly who it was she resembled.

A rare spark of temper lent an edge to her voice. "Do I, sir? I understood m-my mother to have fair hair. N-not red."

Sir Frederick's bloodshot eyes narrowed. "Indeed. That hair you get from me. More's the pity." He leaned back in his chair, his glass dangling from his fingers. His gaze drifted around the dining room with growing displeasure. "Drab winter weariness," he muttered. "Have I not earned a measure of the joy of the season? It's I who pay the wages. I who provide food and shelter to my servants and tenants. And to you, my girl. Don't you forget it."

Meg wasn't likely to. "Yes, father."

"I'm not dead yet. This isn't a house of mourning. I want to see Letchford Hall as it was in Christmas's past. The way it looked when my father was alive. Consult with Church, who'll remember."

"What of m-my season?"

"I'll think on it," he said dismissively. "In the meanwhile, focus your attentions closer to home."

It wasn't a suggestion. It was an unmistakable command.

She realized then with a startling clarity that he had no intention of financing a season for her next year. He meant to keep her here, an unhappy prisoner to his whims, rather than risk her shaming him in the ballrooms of London or Bath. He was embarrassed by her, just as he'd been by her mother.

The spark of temper in Meg's veins lit into a full flame. Focus her attentions closer to home? "I shall," she promised him. "Indeed, I shall."

# Chapter Five

S till simmering over the conversation she'd had with her father, Meg woke the next morning, resolved to ride out to meet Mr. Beresford even if it should be raining hailstones. Fortunately for her—and for the temperamental Rowena—the weather proved a good deal more pleasant than that.

The rain had ceased and the dense, wet fog that blanketed the hills was gradually lifting. Frost hollows still lingered in the valleys, the result of icy air collecting overnight, but the sun was making short work of them. With luck, there would be a few hours of brightness before the West Country winter wrapped its chilly fingers back around them.

She arrived at the river to find Mr. Beresford waiting. He wasn't on his horse, however. He was standing on the riverbank admiring the bridge. His white stallion was tethered nearby.

Observing her riding up, Mr. Beresford smiled broadly. "Miss Burton-Smythe. I'd hoped you would find your way to joining me."

A ray of sunlight glinted off something silvery metallic on his face.

*Goodness.* He was wearing his spectacles.

Warmth curled in Meg's belly. She believed she liked him better this way. He was still handsome, but somehow more approachable. "Is anything the m-matter?" she asked.

"Nothing at all," he said. "I was riding along, and seeing as how you weren't here yet, I thought I might as well have a look at the bridge."

"You've seen it b-before."

"Many times. I never cease to marvel. Here." He beckoned. "Come and look."

She bit her lip. Riding with a gentleman alone was one thing, but dismounting and walking with that gentleman was another matter entirely. A young lady was safe on her horse. She couldn't be kissed. She couldn't be ravished.

Though Mr. Beresford wasn't likely to attempt either where Meg was concerned.

Telling herself not to be so silly, she swung her leg over the pommel. Before she could hop from her sidesaddle, Mr. Beresford appeared. He reached up to help her dismount.

"Thank you," she said breathlessly, determined not to blush as his hands closed around her waist and lifted her gently to the ground. Her half boots sank into the mud.

Mr. Beresford took charge of Rowena. He secured the mare to a tree, narrowly avoiding being bitten. "Mind your step," he said to Meg. "The ground is infernally marshy out here. You risking ruining the hem of your pretty habit."

Meg self-consciously smoothed a hand over her skirts. It was her best riding habit, made of chocolate-brown Venetian wool trimmed in a dark mink velvet. The village tailor had cut the jacket daringly closer to her figure to emphasize the curves of her bosom and waist. She'd worn it precisely because she was meeting Mr. Beresford.

Not that anything she owned could compete with the effortless loveliness of the vicar's daughter. It was a dispiriting fact. One worsened by Meg's own overactive imagination. How easy it was to envision Mr. Beresford's reaction to meeting the angelic Miss Colfax!

Returning to her side, he offered his arm. "Allow me."

Meg accepted his assistance gratefully. He led her down the bank, slowly and carefully. The muscles of his bicep were solid beneath her fingers. His greatcoat smelled of sandalwood and leather. Or perhaps it was his own scent—his shaving soap very likely. It was a thrillingly intimate detail. One she'd never have noticed had she not been this close to him.

"It's rumored to have been built during the Bronze age," he said, bringing her up to the edge of the water. The ancient stone clapper bridge spanned the river in front of them, over twenty feet across. "The thirteenth century is a more accurate guess."

Meg reluctantly released his arm. Her boots stuck firm in the mud. She was in no danger of slipping. "I've heard p-people say it was built by the d-devil."

He grinned. "I've heard that, too. Apparently, Satan constructed it for a wager. Locals are only allowed to cross by his leave or risk having their souls stolen away."

"Do you believe that?"

"Not in the slightest. I've crossed this bridge countless times, and my soul is still intact." A smile twinkled in his eyes. "At least, I think it is."

She ventured a timid smile in return. "I don't believe it either. Still...I've only ever crossed it once. I was eight years old, and I took care to walk very quickly."

"A wise course. One can never be too careful where mischievous devils are concerned." He winked at her.

Meg started. No man had ever winked at her in her life!

She didn't know quite how to take it. Was he teasing her? Flirting with her? Or was he merely being impertinent?

But Mr. Beresford didn't seem to mean anything at all by the gesture. No sooner had he made it than he at once returned to the true source of his admiration.

"Do you see those?" He pointed to the piles of rock that rose from the water, forming the bridge's supports. "Slabs of granite, one stacked atop the other, with no mortar to bind them. A crude form of masonry, but an effective one. And those sheets of granite atop—thin but strong."

"They look rather heavy," she managed to say without stammering.

The smoothness of her speech was overshadowed by the triteness of her reply. She stifled a wince. Mr. Beresford was a gentleman of learning. He'd traveled the world. And all she could think to say was that the giant stones looked "rather heavy"?

What had possessed her to make such an insipid remark?

If Mr. Beresford minded, he didn't show it. On the contrary. He greeted her meager contribution as cheerfully as if she'd been a thousand times more eloquent. "Tremendously, so," he said. "The power it must have taken to haul them here! It's no wonder certain of our forefathers believed it the work of the devil."

"It seems a simple enough structure."

"For a cyclops to build, perhaps. Can you imagine the sheer determination? The will to solve a problem, regardless of the effort and inconvenience it might take to execute a solution? That's something missing in our rural citizenry today."

Meg's mouth flattened into an uncertain frown. *She* was a member of the rural citizenry. "You f-find us lacking?"

He smiled at her. "Not you specifically. You're delightful."

Warmth crept into her face.

"No," he said. "It's this propensity to simply accept things as they are."

"What things?"

"The current methods of travel, for one. Given the skill of our ancestors, shouldn't we be farther along by now? The Egyptians built pyramids. The Romans had aqueducts. And here we are, revering the past rather than striving for...for..."

"For what?"

"The moon? The stars? I don't know." He ran an impatient hand through his hair. His blond locks stood half on end. "For myself, I'd be content if Maidenbridge would be willing to entertain the idea of a railway."

Her eyes widened. "There's going to b-be a railway in Maidenbridge?"

"Not as yet. But there will be one day if I have anything to say about it." He turned to her, fixing her with the whole of his attention. "How do you feel about rail travel, Miss Burton-Smythe?"

She took an involuntary step back from him. Looking into his face full force was akin to staring straight into the sun. She couldn't manage it at such close quarters. "I've n-never b-been on a train," she confessed. "I-I've never traveled at all."

"Not even to Bath or Bristol?"

"I've b-been nowhere."

His keen gaze searched her face. "Is that a fact?"

"I d-don't know anyone," she said. "If you d-don't know anyone, you have n-nowhere to go."

"On the contrary. You meet people when you travel. Why, I've been all over the world. You can't imagine the people I've met. Some have remained faithful friends to this day. Others— well. They're just amusing characters. The sort of individuals with which to populate your journal of an evening. You do keep a journal?"

"Indeed, I d-don't."

"Whyever not? Where else is a young lady to confide her secrets?"

"I have n-no secrets."

"Bosh. Everyone has them. But you're wise to keep them to yourself. It lends you an air of mystery. One looks at you and wonders—whatever can the lovely Miss Burton-Smythe be thinking?"

Her gaze briefly fell from his. She retreated another step, shaking her head. "P-please d-don't tease me."

"I'm not teasing. I wonder it myself. You've been excessively quiet on the two occasions we've met. Have you nothing to say to me?"

"I-I..." Her brows knit in frustration. "I *stammer*," she blurted out at last. "In c-case you hadn't n-noticed."

An unreadable emotion softened his gaze. "I *had* noticed, actually."

"Th-then you know why—"

"It's charming," he said at the same time.

She broke off. Butterflies materialized in her stomach, fluttering their wings like mad.

He studied her face. "Is it always this evident? Or does it grow easier on occasion?"

She didn't answer. She was still trying to wrap her mind around the fact that he'd called her stammer charming. That he'd described her as lovely and mysterious. In all her life, Meg had never been complimented even once by a gentleman. And here was Ivo Beresford—a man who should be her enemy—showering her with an abundance of praise.

*Offhand* praise.

Just like his wink, it didn't mean anything. It was all part and parcel of his enviable ease of manner. He had an effortlessness about him. A confidence bred into his bones. It allowed him to say whatever he wished to her and—very likely—to any other young lady he met.

She wondered how he might sound were he actually serious about one of them. Would his voice deepen to a rasp? Would his eyes smolder with feeling? Would he clasp his beloved's hand and gaze soulfully into her eyes?

"I had a friend at Oxford who stammered," he said, graciously overlooking the fact that she'd been rendered mute by his previous question. "Lewis Kitteridge. He was perpetually in fear of his funds being cut off. He used to stutter like a faulty steam engine whenever his father came to visit. Said it was on account of his nerves." His mouth quirked gently. "Do I make you nervous, Miss Burton-Smythe?"

Meg saw no point in denying it. "A little," she said. Surely it must be obvious.

"I see." He seemed to consider her dilemma. "In that case... I suppose we shall have to cure your nerves the same way Kitteridge cured his."

"How?"

"Proximity."

She gave him a bewildered look.

"Kitteridge had to travel to India with his father. They were in each other's company constantly for nearly six months. When Kitteridge returned to Oxford, his stammer was cured. He was no longer afraid of his father, you see. He'd got used to him." Mr. Beresford's smile broadened. "You shall just have to get used to me."

Meg's chin ticked up a notch. A prickle of indignation lent a tartness to her voice. "I c-can't accompany you to India, sir."

His eyes sparkled with appreciative humor at her rare display of sarcasm. "No, indeed. What would the villagers say? Not to mention your father." He closed the growing distance between them. "Given the circumstances, we're left with no other alternative than to simply continue our acquaintance in the manner in which it began."

"Inauspiciously, you m-mean."

"Not at all. You may have been down when I met you, but you got back on your mare, didn't you? You're a competent horsewoman. More than competent, I suspect. We can ride together in the mornings, if you like."

Meg moved slowly toward Rowena. Now they were no longer discussing the bridge, she didn't feel right to linger beside him on the ground. Never mind that her pulse was skipping wildly and her blood fizzing with excitement at the mere suggestion of the two of them meeting again.

"I'd be glad of some company," he said.

"You m-must have lots of p-people to ride with. Your gr-groom or your friends from the village. Miss Colfax is a c-capable horsewoman. She—"

"I'd be glad of *your* company."

Meg's resolve weakened. "I c-couldn't," she repeated faintly, still edging toward her mare. "Forgive me, but...I must get b-back on my horse."

"To ride with me?" he asked. "Or to run away?"

"I *should* run," she said. "I fear I'm n-not brave enough to c-continue our acquaintance."

It was the truth. Despite her show of boldness today, Meg feared her father's wrath. She feared the condemnation of the servants. She even feared the inevitable reaction of Mr. Beresford's family. Indeed, sometimes it seemed as though she'd spent the whole of her life afraid.

But it was a real enough fear this time. If anyone ever found out she was meeting Mr. Beresford—or any gentleman—in secret...

"Nonsense," he said. "You're made of sterner stuff than you realize. Here. I'll prove it to you." He held out a large, black-gloved hand. "Cross the bridge with me."

Ivo didn't expect Miss Burton-Smythe to acquiesce immediately. And she didn't. Indeed, she backed away from him so quickly that her bootheel slid in the mud. She quickly recovered her footing.

"I c-couldn't," she said, continuing her retreat.

Ivo followed her, patiently, unhurriedly, his hand still extended. He felt rather like Apollo pursuing Daphne through the wood. A slow pursuit. Miss Burton-Smythe would have no need to turn herself into a laurel tree to escape him.

"You must want to," he said. "Why else do you ride this way so often?"

She withdrew another step. "Just because I like looking at the bridge d-doesn't mean I want to t-tempt the d-devil."

"We all want to tempt the devil on occasion." He turned his hand palm up in invitation. "Sefton Bridge crosses the Barle, not the Styx. It's only a pile of stones. That's what clapper means in the medieval Latin. It's nothing to be afraid of."

She came to a halt. "I'm n-not afraid."

Ivo's heart ached a little for her. She plainly was. Though why he should trouble himself with bolstering her confidence, he didn't know. It wasn't why he'd come here this morning. He'd wanted to see her again, yes, but his purpose hadn't been to compliment her or to coax her into action. It was her father Ivo needed to coax.

Sir Frederick's support of the railway scheme would be integral to its success. And what better way to engage that support than to befriend the man's daughter? It didn't hurt that Ivo had already scraped an acquaintance with the girl.

Or that he liked her.

And he *did* like her.

"Then come with me," he said. "We'll walk to the other side and then back again. I promise you, you'll return quite another person."

She gave a huff of unwilling amusement. "Because the devil will have stolen my soul away!"

Ivo laughed. She had an unexpected sense of humor. It was hidden just beneath the surface, only emerging when he'd goaded her. It made him want to goad her all the more.

"No," he said. "It's because you'll have faced what you feared. Every time we do so, we emerge stronger from the experience. It's a proven fact."

A disgruntled expression crossed her face, even as she reluctantly slid her hand into his. "Proven b-by whom?"

His fingers engulfed hers. "By me."

She inhaled a deep breath. "I *have* crossed it once b-before in my life."

"Yes, I know. When you were eight." He led her up onto the first granite slab. The river rushed swiftly below. The water was high from the recent rains, rippling and splashing over the frost-tipped ferns, reeds, and outcroppings of rock. "You must have been a daring child. I expect your nanny despaired of you."

Miss Burton-Smythe followed him slowly, holding tight to his hand. Her grip was strong for a lady. Especially one as lithe and elegant as she was. Her snugly cut riding habit skimmed the curves of her figure, its heavy winter wool and thick cording doing nothing to disguise the winsome, long-limbed shape of her.

He'd told her she was lovely. It had been the kind of empty gallantry that fashionable gentlemen dispensed as easily and as thoughtlessly as breathing. It was only after Ivo had said it that he'd realized how thoroughly he meant it.

She *was* lovely. Her mass of curling hair. Her blushing cheeks. Those China blue eyes, both hesitant and eager by turns. And that figure! She was fashioned in the mold of a Renaissance painting. Botticelli's Venus, perhaps. Or the striking red-haired lady—shown both with and without her gown—in Titian's depiction of Sacred and Profane Love.

But Ivo didn't want to think of Miss Burton-Smythe with no clothes on.

He refused to countenance that rogue corner of his brain that was already imagining her with her hair tumbling down around her bare shoulders. That was already wondering whether the liberal gold-dusting of freckles that covered her face and throat covered all the rest of her as well.

Scandalous, unworthy thoughts. He had no intention of acting on them.

"I was exceptionally well behaved," she informed him.

"On the surface, perhaps," he said. "But underneath—"

"No, indeed. I've b-been shy all my life."

"You're not shy. You're inexperienced. It isn't the same thing."

Her fair red brows notched. "How can you tell the difference?"

"You're here, aren't you?" He slowed briefly in the center of the bridge, still holding her hand. Sefton bridge had no railings. The smallest misstep could send one toppling over the edge.

Her eyes went wide as she looked out at the river. An icy mist rose up from the freezing black water, making the moss-covered granite slabs slick under their feet. "Oh m-my," she whispered.

Fog clung to the trees and shrubs on the opposite bank, shrouding the end of the path from view. They might have been walking into nothingness.

"Almost there." Ivo continued on, gently bringing her with him—step by careful step. In no time, his top boots were sinking into the mud on the opposite bank.

Miss Burton-Smythe leapt down from the clapper bridge after him, a huff of laughter in her voice. "My heart is racing."

An echoing laugh gusted out of him. "Mine too. It must be all this tempting the devil."

"I warned you."

"So you did." He kept hold of her hand. Across the river, Snap and Miss Burton-Smythe's mare watched the two of them with mild curiosity. "Shall we go back?"

"Yes," she said.

"After you."

She willingly led the way, a smile on her lips and a confidence in her step as they crossed back over. This time, it was she who jumped down first from the stones. Her cheeks were flushed pink.

"Well?" He made a show of examining her from head to hem. "Has the experience altered you?"

Her bosom rose and fell rapidly under his perusal. "I d-don't know. Do I look any stronger?"

"Let's find out." He retained her hand. "Will you meet me for another ride tomorrow?"

Her smile turned wistful for a moment before fading away entirely. She slipped her hand from his. "I c-can't."

"You can," he assured her.

"It m-may rain again in the morning."

"But if it doesn't..."

She shook her head. Regret was evident in her voice. "I have my duties at the Hall t-to think of. I'm to d-decorate for Christmas. If I'm out of doors at all, I m-must be gathering greenery. The servants will be with m-me. Timothy brings the c-cart and the m-maids and footmen help."

"Then we'll just have to confine our friendship to morning rides."

"The rain—"

"Forget the rain. The snow will come soon. The river path

is at its most beautiful then, all frosted over with ice." He caught her gaze and held it. "I don't mind it, you know. Your stammering."

A flash of furious passion darkened her pale eyes to a vibrant Saxon blue. "I *hate* it," she said. "I'm m-mortified whenever I speak."

Ivo regarded her solemnly. She wasn't a simple country girl at all, was she? A shy little wallflower languishing at Letchford Hall? She was complicated. Fascinating.

"You needn't be," he said. "I believe we do sometimes find words difficult when we feel too much. That you struggle over them isn't a weakness in you. It speaks to your depth of emotion."

She stared at him. "You're n-not teasing me again?"

"No. I mean it. Truly. The important things are often difficult to say."

"Everything is difficult when I'm in your c-company," she replied candidly. "Or when I'm with m-my father. To be sure, it's worse with him."

"Your father makes you nervous, too?" His eyes narrowed with concern behind the lenses of his spectacles. "You're not afraid of him?"

She withdrew back to her mare, avoiding his searching gaze. "Only of his censure. He c-can be a difficult man."

"He has that reputation."

"But he's n-not a bad one," she said. "Not in that way."

Ivo followed after her to assist her in mounting. "I'm gratified to hear it."

"I know your family dislikes him—"

"Our families dislike each other. This feud isn't one sided."

She stopped beside her mare, one hand resting on the bridle. "But it isn't a feud at all. It's...it's a love st-story."

Ivo stiffened at the suggestion. He had no desire to belabor old grudges, but to categorize the history between his mother and Sir Frederick as some variety of romance was passing all bounds. Miss Burton-Smythe was either ill-informed or incredibly naïve. Possibly both.

"How do you figure that?" he asked.

She looked at him with growing uncertainty as she gathered her reins. "Because Lady Allendale refused m-my father and married yours."

"That simple, is it?"

Her brow creased. "Isn't it?"

Ivo helped her back onto her mare. He was careful with her, his hands gentle on her waist as he lifted her up. It wasn't his place to disabuse her of her girlish fancies. Even so, he couldn't refrain from enlightening her. "He was her guardian for a time, your father. Did you know that?"

She darted him a sharp glance. "Her guardian!"

He remained beside her, standing in the mud, while she settled herself in her sidesaddle. "Sir Frederick had the stewardship of Beasley Park after my grandfather died. My mother was left in his charge. He bullied and tormented her. He'd have forced her to marry him if he could. A lesser female would have crumbled under such treatment."

Miss Burton-Smythe's face paled. "Your m-mother told you this?"

"Not directly, no." He'd originally heard it from his mother's former maid, Bessie. Long since retired to a cottage on the estate, old Bessie had been a veritable font of information in Ivo's youth. She hadn't furnished the exact details of Sir Frederick's misconduct toward Ivo's mother, but she'd been clear on the substance of it. "I suppose your father has told you different."

"He's said n-nothing on the subject. What I know, I learned from our c-cook and housekeeper."

Ivo strode down the river bank to untie his stallion. Snap

nudged him hard with his muzzle, threatening to nip as Ivo tightened his girth before mounting. "And what do they say?"

"That my father and your m-mother were promised to each other. And that your m-mother broke that p-promise to wed Lord Allendale."

Ivo vaulted into his saddle. Shortening his reins, he brought Snap up alongside Miss Burton-Smythe's mare. "My mother never promised to marry Sir Frederick. It was only a notion my grandfather, Squire Honeywell, had. He wanted to join the two estates. That was the crux of the idea. It had nothing to do with any affection on our parents' parts."

"But m-my father did love your m-mother," Miss Burton-Smythe insisted. "He m-must have done. Why else..." Her words trailed away. She gave him a look of utter bewilderment. Stark vulnerability shone beneath the surface of it.

"Why else would he have named you Margaret?" Ivo offered a sympathetic smile. "Perhaps you should ask him."

# Chapter Six

Meg returned home with a sour feeling in her stomach. She regretted having said anything about the origins of the feud between their families. It had snuffed out the pleasure she'd felt after traversing the clapper bridge with Mr. Beresford. The hope that had bloomed within her at the symbolism of it. It had seemed, at the time, as if they'd crossed from the past and into the future, leaving the old animosity behind them.

But not any longer.

She'd had to go and ruin it by mentioning her father. By bringing up the fact that he'd loved Mr. Beresford's mother.

Though Meg was no longer certain that it *was* a fact.

"The footmen have carried down the Christmas decorations from the attics," Mrs. Church said when Meg returned. "I've had them put the boxes in the morning room."

"Thank you, Mrs. Church. I'll go through them once I've changed." Meg removed her riding hat and gloves. She passed them to a footman as she crossed the hall. "Is my father awake?"

Mrs. Church's perpetually pinched mouth compressed

into a thin line. "He is. And suffering mightily from coming downstairs last night, as I could have told you he would. I've taken the liberty of summoning Dr. Spragg."

"He was only here three days ago."

"It can't be helped. I must do as I see fit."

Meg hesitated on the stairs. In any other household, it would be she who was giving the orders not Mrs. Church. It was another circumstance Meg could lay at her father's door. He was the one who had invested the wiry little housekeeper with so much authority.

"I'll send Lucy with the hot water," Mrs. Church said before withdrawing.

After washing and changing into a warm, chestnut-colored cashmere day dress, Meg made her way to her father's chamber.

Sir Frederick's room was in a wing of its own, located on the opposite end of the portrait gallery. To reach it, Meg had to pass beneath rows of disapproving Burton-Smythe ancestors, their distinctive red hair immortalized in aged oils and faded watercolors. The gentlemen were all brawny as bulldogs and the ladies equally so. It was how Meg knew she'd inherited her face and her figure from her mother.

Two tall wooden doors marked the entrance to the master's chamber. She tapped softly before entering.

Her father was in his cavernous four poster bed, propped against a stack of pillows. His satin coverlet had been drawn back to reveal his abscessed calf, elevated on a cushion.

"Good m-morning, father," she said.

He glared at her from within the depths of his half-drawn bed curtains. His hair was disheveled, his linen nightshirt opened at the neck. Perspiration dotted his face and throat.

She didn't wait for his reply. Crossing to the windows, she drew open the heavy curtains. "There's sunshine t-today," she said. "It would d-do you good."

"What would do me good is a drink," he growled.

She turned to face him. It was impossible to tell what he meant her to say to that.

Possibly nothing.

"You d-don't want a drink," she said. "It's overindulgence that's c-caused your c-condition."

"I won't be told no."

"Then you m-must t-take it up with Mrs. Church. I won't br-bring you anything b-but plain food and black tea."

He scowled at her. "When did you grow a backbone?"

"I am your d-daughter." Like it or not, she might have added. "The B-Burton-Smythes are a stubborn lot."

"Stubborn as bedamned. I'll not lie down and die to please you and your brother."

Meg couldn't speak for Roddy. The meaning of her brother's absence had been unambiguous. He would remain abroad until he inherited the title. But she was a woman. There was no benefit to her in her father's death.

"I d-don't wish you t-to die," she said. "Only to live d-differently. If you'd refrain from rich foods and drink—"

"You'll keep your sermons to a minimum while you're in my presence. I didn't raise you to be a scold."

You didn't raise me at all, she nearly said. It was the nursery maids, the nannies, and Miss Adams. They had tucked Meg in at night. Taught her to walk and to read. Not her father or her brother, but servants.

"I d-don't recall you overindulging b-before your accident," she said instead.

His brows sank with displeasure to be reminded of the injury he'd suffered two years ago. He'd been hunting and had taken a gate that was too tall for his horse. The resulting fall had bruised his spine. It was the pain of it that had first driven him to double—and then triple—his servings of after-dinner port. He'd claimed it was the only way he could sleep undisturbed.

"If Spragg knew his business, I wouldn't be obliged to," he said. "Has Church summoned the blackguard?"

"Yes."

"Much good he'll do me."

Meg wandered to her father's mahogany dressing table. She absently straightened the brushes, bottles, and shaving implements that scattered its surface. When she'd finished, she did the same to the matched set of porcelain shepherdesses on his mantelshelf. It was an old habit. One she'd picked up in childhood as a way of coping with the nervousness she felt in her father's presence. Bringing order to chaos, Miss Adams had called it. A laudable impulse.

Meg's father took a less favorable view.

"It's the common blood in you," he'd said once. "Your mother's influence."

No doubt it's what he still believed. Why else did his gaze follow her so morosely about the room? She was in every way a disappointment to him.

The thought stayed Meg's hand in the middle of rearranging the two porcelain figures into their proper positions. She may have been raised by servants, but she wasn't one of them. She was a lady. She must learn how to be still.

"When you're finished playing parlor maid," her father snapped, "you can fetch me a wet cloth from the washstand."

She privately flinched at the insult. But it was no more than what she'd already been thinking herself. Moving to the washstand, she filled the basin from the silver pitcher and wet a linen cloth. She wrang it out before bringing it to him. "Are you f-feverish?"

He draped the cloth over his forehead. "I'm suffocating from the heat. Must Church have the fires burning all night and day?"

"The first day of winter is approaching," Meg said. "It's quite c-cold and damp outside. We m-may yet have snow."

"You wouldn't know it," he grumbled. "Douse the fire, girl. It's hot as Hades in here."

Meg obediently retrieved the basin and poured its contents onto the flames. The fire hissed as it sputtered out, emitting a small cloud of smoke. "I wish you wouldn't call me that."

"What's that?"

"'Girl,'" she said. "It's how you address th-the housemaids."

He squinted at her from beneath the cloth on his brow. "You act the part when it suits you."

"But I'm n-not a housemaid. I am your d-daughter." It was the second time she'd felt compelled to remind him of that fact this morning. "I have a n-name. I wish you would use it."

This time he pulled the cloth away completely. He stared at her in the remaining smoke from the fire.

"It's M-Meg," she said, her stammer worsening. "Or M-Margaret if...if you p-prefer."

His expression turned dangerous.

Meg's heartbeat quickened, but she didn't flee. This time, she was resolved to stand her ground. It didn't prevent her anxious hands from moving to straighten her father's coverlet. "If you d-don't like the n-name, why d-did you give it to m-me?"

"To remind me of the perfidy of women," he said.

Her hands stilled on the coverlet. "I thought..."

"You attributed some noble motive?" He gave a derisive snort. "You've been spending too much time with Church and Stapleton. They'll have made a romance of the business. Damn fool old women."

"Wasn't it one?" she asked. "D-Didn't you...Didn't you love Lady Allendale?"

He must have done. It had been the reason he'd never

loved Meg's mother. The reason he couldn't love Meg. And it was surely, without doubt, the reason for Meg's own name. A love story, she'd called it, fully believing it to be true.

Her father's ruddy face darkened like a thundercloud. "*Love* Margaret Honeywell? The devil I did."

"But—"

"She was a pain in my backside. Never listened. Never did as she was told. Always insulting me and treating me as though I were beneath her contempt. But the way she treated *him*." Sir Frederick's eyes blazed. "*He* was the one I was thinking of when I named you."

"Of Lord Allendale?" Meg queried numbly. Her hands fell away from the coverlet. At last, she understood. "You m-mean to say that you…you n-named me out of hatred? As a…a sort of revenge?"

"You're disappointed?"

"I'm humiliated. What must his lordship have thought of m-me?"

"Don't look so cast down. The man's never noticed you, nor has his wife, or that passel of spoiled brats he's sired. They none of them care tuppence what you're called. They don't even know you exist." He leaned back against his pillows with a groan of pain. "Serves me right for indulging in a bit of spite. In the end, your name didn't matter in the slightest."

Meg's chest tightened with suppressed emotion. It burned to the point of pain. "It matters to *m-me*. I th-thought you had named m-me out of love."

It hadn't been for love of her. It had been for love of another. But all these years, Meg had still cherished the belief that it meant something. That by having the same name as her father's beloved, she might—to some small degree—have some of his affection as well.

The look of growing disdain on his face told her how wrong she'd been.

"More romantic claptrap," he muttered harshly. "If this is how you've been focusing your mind in Miss Adams's absence, I shall see to hiring another governess for you without delay. Now make yourself useful. Fetch Church. Find out where that bloody doctor is."

Meg withdrew without another word.

---

"YOU *LOST* HIM?" IVO CAME TO A HORRIFIED HALT AT the entrance to the Beasley Park stables. Snap was obliged to stop short beside him. He bumped Ivo hard with his nose. The stallion's white coat was damp after a hard gallop across the moors. He required a warm blanket and a bucket of hot mash, and was impatient for both.

Partridge hovered outside the stable doors in his heavy coat. He'd been pacing there on Ivo's return from his meeting with Miss Burton-Smythe, waiting to impart the bad news. "There was a letter delivered from the vicarage. An invitation for you and the signore to dine on Friday—"

"Me *and* the signore?" Ivo echoed in disbelief.

"The vicar mentioned that Mr. Pinnock might be interested in hiring a tutor for his younger sons."

"Good God."

"Ruggiero said he was in need of a new suit for the occasion. I thought I'd dissuaded him. But when next I looked—"

"Has he taken a horse?" Ivo handed Snap's reins off to Andrew. The groom's face was peculiarly pale. "You didn't saddle one for him, I trust."

Andrew hung his head. "He being a guest and all...I didn't know I shouldn't—"

"It isn't your fault," Ivo said. "It's mine. I should have

locked the devious scoundrel in his room until I got back." He turned to Partridge. "Pray tell me he wasn't drunk."

Partridge was silent.

*Bloody blasted hell.* Ivo was trying to win over the people of Maidenbridge, not the reverse.

"Saddle another horse for me, Andrew," he said. "Snap is spent. With luck, I can catch up with Ruggiero before he does any lasting damage to my reputation."

Less than five minutes later, mounted on his sister's bay gelding, Ember, Ivo cantered off in the direction of the village. A chill wind bit at his face.

Rain clouds were looming on the horizon, darkening the morning sky. Within an hour, they'd be facing another downpour. Ivo didn't fancy Ruggiero falling victim to it. A drunken signore was bad enough. One crippled by double pneumonia was too tedious to contemplate.

Fortunately, Ivo didn't have to ride all the way back to Maidenbridge in order to find the escaped lunatic. He'd gone no more than a mile when he spied the back end of a chestnut horse ambling slowly down the lane in a zigzag pattern, absent the guidance of a rider.

Ruggiero was slumped in the saddle, his double chin cushioned on the thick wool scarf he wore wound around his neck. He was a portly fellow of indeterminate age. Not more than forty if Ivo was to guess. It was difficult to tell. The signore's heavy black beard and thick side-whiskers obscured his features.

Ivo trotted up alongside him, careful not to spook the man's horse. "You careless blighter," he muttered, catching hold of the horse's reins. "Have you no thought for anyone but yourself?"

Ruggiero snuffled awake. His eyes were bloodshot. "Master Ivo. Buongiorno."

"I'll buongiorno you, you scoundrel. What do you mean

by riding out in this condition? Are you trying to ruin my plans?"

"I require a suit for the dinner party," Ruggiero said in faintly accented English. "To make a good impression on Mr. Pinnock."

"You'll make an impression all right." Ivo turned Ember back toward Beasley Park, leading Ruggiero's mount along with them. "How is anyone to take me seriously with you staggering about the place like Falstaff? Didn't I tell you to remain inside?"

"But Master Ivo, the invitation—"

"A mistake, obviously. The vicar can't expect me to bring you to dinner. His daughter will be there—a gently-bred lady by all accounts."

Ruggiero perked up. "The parson has a daughter?"

"Never you mind his daughter. It's Pinnock I care about. He's an influential voice in the village. I mean to present a serious, sober countenance to the man."

"Sober," Ruggiero repeated mournfully. "Why you English don't like the wine?"

Ivo flashed him a dark glance. "You're English, too, lest you forget it. And enough with that atrocious accent. You're not in Italy any longer, trying to gull hapless travelers into hiring you."

It had worked well enough with Ivo and his companions. For a good six months, they'd all believed Ruggiero to be the native Florentine he'd claimed to be. It had only been later, when the signore was firmly entrenched in their ranks, that Ivo had learned the man's sad story.

"Is a hard habit to break," Ruggiero said.

"It would be easier if you'd cease drinking. Would it kill you to abstain for a week? We might dry you out for a time as we did in Venice."

"Venice." Ruggiero's face screwed up with bitterness at the memory. "A sad time, Master Ivo."

"For you, maybe." Ivo guided Ruggiero's horse through a stand of trees. He didn't trust the signore enough to return the reins to him. "And now this nonsense. Half seas again." He flashed him an accusing look. "You promised that if I brought you back with me, you'd exercise moderation. At least enough that you might find yourself gainful employment."

"It's what I'm trying to do. Find employment."

"Yes. At my expense. Have you no regard for my ambitions? Or, more to the point, for me?"

"I'm grateful for everything you've done for me," Ruggiero said. "Your kindness is more than I deserve."

Ivo dismissed the signore's thanks. He was sorry he'd ever listened to the man's entreaties. Ivo's companions had been wiser. They'd each of them departed, leaving Ivo to handle the settling of accounts with their perpetually inebriated—and increasingly pitiful—guide.

Ruggiero had begged Ivo to take him back to England with him. He'd even wept, saying there was nothing left for him in Italy any longer. He'd claimed he was eager to forge a new life for himself. To finally come home after so many years in exile.

Ivo recalled the conversation with growing resentment. Drat his soft heart! Must he always go about feeling sorry for everyone? The signori of the world. The Miss Burton-Smythes. It wasn't up to him to solve the problems of everyone he met. For once—just for once—could he not focus on his own aims, with no distractions to derail him?

And he *was* distracted, particularly by his burgeoning friendship with Meg Burton-Smythe.

They'd left things awkwardly at the river. It was Ivo's fault, too. He shouldn't have taken umbrage at her innocent assertions. Who was he to disabuse her of her romantic notions about the origins of the feud between their families? He had no right to be telling her that her father had been a bully. And no good reason, either. Especially considering that he needed to smooth the way to speak with the man.

It wasn't the first mistake Ivo had made today. He was determined not to make any others. In future, he would concentrate the whole of his attention on furthering his ambitions with the railway. Damn the rest of it.

"I try to stop drinking," Ruggiero said as they drew closer to Beasley Park. "But the wine—it tempts me."

Ivo scowled at him. "My father won't thank you for drinking his cellar dry. And if my mother catches you in this condition, she'll likely box your ears."

"Lady Allendale is molto formidabile."

"Precisely. That gives you less than a fortnight to get yourself in order."

"Don't require a fortnight," Ruggiero said. "I'll be sober by the dinner."

"You're not accompanying me to dinner at the vicarage," Ivo shot back. "On no account."

"The parson—"

"I shall tell him you've taken ill. You can meet with Pinnock another time, when there isn't so much at stake."

"But—"

"I mean it. This time, I'm going to put my own interests first." Ivo's conscience twinged. "And I'm *not* going to feel guilty about it."

# Chapter Seven

Meg was in her bedroom, nestled in the cushioned window embrasure, working on a new sampler, when Mrs. Church appeared at the door.

"Miss Colfax to see you, miss," the old housekeeper said.

Setting aside her sewing, Meg rose from her seat. She cast a dubious glance out the window. "In this weather?"

Rain streamed down the glass. It had been storming for the last two days. There had been no possibility of taking Rowena out. No possibility of seeing Mr. Beresford again.

Meg was both disappointed and a little relieved. She and Mr. Beresford had parted a trifle stiffly the last time they'd met. Perhaps he wouldn't have wanted to see her again anyway. Not after she'd so stupidly insisted that her father had been in love with his mother.

She knew better now.

"She came in her father's carriage," Mrs. Church said. "Timothy is seeing to the horses." She wiped her hands on her apron. "I've put her in the drawing room. Shall I bring in the tea tray?"

"Yes please." Meg straightened her plain wool gown and

smoothed her hair before descending to the drawing room. It had rarely been in use since her father's illness. The servants nevertheless lit the fires every morning in anticipation of Sir Frederick's arrival. One never knew when he would take it into his head to limp downstairs and bellow his disapproval at the lack of readiness in the common rooms.

Miss Colfax was seated on the old-fashioned damask-upholstered sofa. She stood to greet Meg, the skirts of her modest silk gown swishing softly as she came forward.

The two young ladies curtsied to each other.

"Miss Burton-Smythe." Miss Colfax's milk-and-honey voice was as richly sweet when speaking as it was when she sang in church. "How do you do?"

"Miss C-Colfax." Motioning for the vicar's daughter to sit, Meg took a chair across from her. "What brings you here on such a day as this?"

Miss Colfax resumed her seat. "I come at my father's bequest." She smiled. "And for my own pleasure. For it is indeed always a pleasure to be in your company."

Meg had no reason to doubt Miss Colfax's sincerity. The vicar's daughter wasn't an unkind person. Quite the reverse. It was that very fact that often put Meg out of countenance. How could one ever hope to compare with such perfection?

"You are very good," Meg said. "I'm grateful for the company, of course. Only, the weather is so dreadful."

"Indeed. I have been obliged to cancel our classes today at the village school. The rain has made it impossible. Such a deluge! Mr. Pinnock says Mead Lane is in danger of flooding."

Mrs. Church brought in the tea tray. It held a silver teapot, two porcelain cups, and a small plate of ginger biscuits. "Mrs. Stapleton's baked them fresh this morning," she said, placing the tray on the table in front of Meg. "There's bread and butter as well."

"How divine," Miss Colfax said. "Please thank Mrs. Stapleton for her efforts."

"I shall," Mrs. Church answered. "Will that be all, miss?"

"Yes, thank you, Mrs. Church," Meg said. "I'll ring if we n-need anything else."

Mrs. Church bobbed a curtsy before withdrawing.

Meg poured out a cup of tea for Miss Colfax. "Do you take lemon?"

"Milk, thank you."

Meg added a dash of milk before passing the cup to Miss Colfax. After Miss Colfax had taken it, Meg offered her a biscuit.

Miss Colfax selected one for herself. "You do know Mr. Pinnock? The owner of the Emporium?"

"A little." Meg returned the plate of biscuits to the tray. "I've m-met him once or twice at his store."

"He's coming to dine at the Vicarage tomorrow. Mrs. Pinnock can't accompany him, regrettably. She's visiting her sister in Wales. The poor woman has taken ill with a brain fever. It's that which has prompted me to call today."

Meg gave Miss Colfax a bewildered look as she poured herself a cup of tea. "Mrs. Pinnock's sister?"

"After a fashion, yes. In her absence, Mr. Pinnock means to bring his oldest son, Nigel, to dinner. I fear that will mean only one thing once the port starts flowing. You must know how Mr. Pinnock likes to matchmake."

Meg had heard something to that effect from Mrs. Church and Mrs. Stapleton. "I understand he claims responsibility for two recent b-betrothals in the parish."

"Oh yes. No unmarried person is safe when he's about. And if he brings his son, that will make five gentlemen altogether and only one of me. I don't like to be the sole female, even if my father *is* present. It's never quite comfortable, is it? Retiring to the drawing room alone while the gentlemen remain with their port and cigars? Not to mention the burden on me to perform. I'll be obliged to remain at the pianoforte all evening. You know how these dinners run on."

Meg tensed, anticipating Miss Colfax's request.

"My father suggested I might invite you," Miss Colfax said. "I thought it a splendid idea. That's why I've ventured out in this maelstrom, to ask if you'll join us tomorrow."

Meg took a sip of her tea. "I d-don't often attend dinner parties."

Her father preferred local landowners and men of influence to come to Letchford Hall. Mrs. Church and Mrs. Stapleton had put on many a dinner for them during Meg's youth. Meg had been allowed to attend only a handful of times.

Her experiences with dining in the village had been even less frequent and were mostly confined to dinners with her father at the vicarage during Mr. Applewhite's tenure.

"It will be nothing overly formal," Miss Colfax assured her. "The gentlemen mean to discuss business. It promises to be a lonely evening for me without you there. Do please say you'll come."

"My father is unable to attend."

Miss Colfax nodded in sympathetic understanding. "I presumed as much. His gout is still troubling him, is it not? Dr. Spragg mentioned that he'd had another attack."

"He has," Meg said. It was only to be expected after eating red meat and drinking port. The sugary pudding he'd had last evening hadn't helped matters. By the wee hours, he'd been in agony, shouting at all and sundry. "He's in n-no state to go out at present."

"He wouldn't object to your coming alone, would he?"

Meg lowered her teacup back to its saucer. She didn't *think* her father would object. Not if the dinner was at the vicarage, in company with Miss Colfax and her father. Still...it would be a creditable excuse. Meg was tempted to use it to evade the awkwardness of an outright refusal.

But no.

She hadn't yet been reduced to lying to the daughter of a vicar.

"No," she admitted. "That is...I d-don't think so."

Miss Colfax brightened. "Then you *will* come?"

Meg hesitated. She had no more desire to fall victim to Mr. Pinnock's matchmaking efforts than Miss Colfax did. However...

Were Miss Adams here, she'd have urged Meg to go. To be sure, in her last letter, she'd reminded Meg that attending local dances and dinners was a means of practicing for the inevitable flurry of social events when Meg at last had a season.

*If* she had a season.

Her father seemed in no mind to finance one for her at present.

But perhaps—just perhaps—if he heard that Meg had acquitted herself well at a dinner party in the village, he may be persuaded to reconsider his opinion?

With that in mind, Meg came to a decision. "Yes," she said. "I'll come. If it means so very much to you."

Miss Colfax beamed with gratitude. "Oh, *thank* you. That is a relief. Now, if only Mr. Beresford's sister were in town to accompany him, our numbers might almost be even."

Meg came to abrupt attention. With the thunder rumbling outside and the rain beating against the windowpanes, she couldn't be entirely sure she'd heard correctly. "Mr. Beresford? Is he going to b-be there?"

"Did I not say? It's he who has prompted the entire event."

Meg stared at Miss Colfax, too stunned by the news of Mr.

Beresford's inclusion in the dinner to fully comprehend her meaning. "How do you m-mean?"

"He called at the vicarage earlier this week and wasted no time in securing an invitation to dinner. Indeed, he was rather eager."

Meg's stomach knotted painfully.

Mr. Beresford had met Miss Colfax only once as far as Meg was aware. Only once and he was already eager to dine at the vicarage. He must have been smitten at first sight of the vicar's daughter. He must not have wanted to delay furthering the acquaintance, not for a single moment.

Although...

He'd said nothing about Miss Colfax when he and Meg had met at the river. And when Meg had suggested that he might want to ride with the angelic Miss Colfax instead of Meg herself, he'd swiftly disabused her of that notion.

"I'd be glad of *your* company," he'd said.

"My father has arranged the dinner in order to introduce Mr. Beresford to Mr. Pinnock," Miss Colfax explained. "Mr. Beresford has business to discuss with him, I believe. I'm not clear on the particulars, but I do know it has something to do with Mr. Pinnock's influence in the village."

*The railway.*

All at once, Meg understood. That was why Ivo Beresford was dining at the vicarage. Not because he had designs on Miss Colfax but because he aspired to bring the railway to Maidenbridge.

Some of the tightness in Meg's chest eased. It didn't disappear completely. She sank her voice so the servants wouldn't overhear. "M-My father wouldn't approve of m-me dining in company with Mr. Beresford," she said. "Or with any Beresford."

Miss Colfax regarded her solemnly. "Yes, I've heard about

the difficulties between the Beresfords and the Burton-Smythes. Tell me, do your families have no intercourse at all?"

"Very little in my lifetime."

"But you *have* met them?"

"I have." Some more frequently than others, Meg privately added. "But it isn't my opinion of them that matters. It's m-my father's."

"Will he forbid you attending?"

Yes, he would. There was no question about it. If, that is, he knew about the dinner beforehand. But if he didn't...

The prospect sent an anxious thrill through Meg's veins.

Her dissatisfaction with her father had been growing by leaps and bounds since Miss Adams's departure. Absent her governess, Meg was meant to be treated as a grown-up young lady. One deserving of respect. One worthy of a season. She'd expected as much. Instead, she was fast coming to realize that her father didn't care about her future. Not enough, anyway. Certainly not when it might put his own pride at risk.

In the absence of his attention, Meg resolved to attend to that future herself. It was the only way forward.

"I *will* c-come to your dinner," she replied. "Regardless."

Miss Colfax exhaled in relief. "I'm so pleased to hear it. But...what will you tell Sir Frederick?"

"I shall d-deal with m-my father," Meg said firmly. "Leave him to m-me."

# Chapter Eight

M eg arrived at the vicarage on Friday evening dressed in her newest gown. Made of gold silk, printed with a delicate, contrasting stripe and a subtle floral design, it boasted a snug pleated bodice, long, tight sleeves, and a full pleated skirt that fell into graceful folds around her legs. Meg's corset had been cinched extra tight to accommodate the unforgiving silhouette. She'd felt a little breathless ever since she'd departed Letchford Hall in her father's carriage.

Her corset was only partially to blame.

The true source of her unsteady pulse was seated in the vicarage's parlor, along with the vicar, Miss Colfax, the Pinnocks, and a heavyset black-bearded fellow Meg had never seen before. They were all of them talking companionably, with Mr. Pinnock's voice echoing the loudest. He was a robust man of decisive opinions who didn't shrink from uttering them.

The housekeeper interrupted the gentlemen's conversation to announce Meg's arrival to the vicar. "Miss Burton-Smythe, sir."

Mr. Colfax promptly rose from his chair and came to meet her. The rest of the gentlemen stood as well. They each of them acknowledged Meg with a bow, looking at her with varying degrees of attention. But it was only Mr. Beresford's attention that mattered to Meg. She felt his unfocused gray gaze all the way to her swiftly beating heart.

He was, once again, without his spectacles, but he seemed to see her nonetheless. There was warmth in his eyes and a hint of a smile edging his mouth.

"Miss Burton-Smythe," Mr. Colfax said. "We began to despair of you."

"Am I very late?" Meg asked worriedly.

Miss Colfax crossed the room to join them. She took Meg's hands, pressing them gently in greeting. "Not at all. You're exactly on time."

"Your father was unable to join you, I see," Mr. Colfax said. "Is his health no better?"

"He's still p-poorly, I'm afraid," Meg said. "He...He sends his regrets."

It was partially true.

When Meg had informed her father that she'd been invited to dine at the vicarage, he'd first inquired who else would be there and had then commanded her to convey his regards. He had respect for the Pinnocks, and for the Colfaxes. As for the rest of the dinner guests...

Meg had refrained from mentioning that Ivo Beresford would be in attendance.

It wasn't a secret that could be kept forever. She had no illusions on that score. The vicar's servants would inevitably gossip. So would Mr. Pinnock and his son. Both worked the counters at Pinnock's Emporium and both had a reputation for conversing easily with their patrons.

By this time tomorrow, the whole of Maidenbridge would

know that a Beresford and a Burton-Smythe had dined together on terms of cordiality. Far worse, Meg's father would know. She could only imagine his reaction.

But she wasn't going to think of it. Not this evening.

Tonight, she was resolved to enjoy herself. Tomorrow she'd worry about all the rest of it.

"Come and warm yourself by the fire." Miss Colfax guided Meg to an empty space on the parlor's chintz-covered settee. "You must be frozen through."

"Thank you," Meg said. "It's n-not raining any longer, b-but it is very cold out this evening."

"If the temperature continues to drop at this rate," Mr. Beresford remarked, "we may yet have a white Christmas."

Meg met his eyes as she took a seat. He gave her a faint, reassuring smile. There was a hint of encouragement in it. As if he knew how awkward this evening might be for her and was promising her that all would be well.

She held his gaze for a heartbeat longer than was proper, only belatedly realizing that she was perilously close to staring at him. It was the first time she'd seen him out of his breeches and top-boots. He was dressed in a fine black wool frock coat, a figured silk waistcoat, and an impeccably cut pair of wheat-colored trousers. A dark silk cravat was knotted at his neck, and his honey-blond hair—no longer windswept—was pomaded into meticulous order.

It was too much, really. She'd rather he was disheveled and wearing his spectacles, gazing out at the clapper bridge with an expression of bright-eyed wonder. *That* Ivo Beresford could be met with on terms approaching equality. But this golden God was quite another being entirely.

"English winters," the black-bearded gentleman said in a vaguely accented mutter. "Intolerable."

Meg flashed the man an uncertain look.

"Mr. Ruggiero has lived these past two decades in Italy," the vicar said, introducing him to Meg as the guests resumed their seats. "He was Mr. Beresford's guide on his grand tour of Europe. You know Mr. Beresford, of course. And I believe you're acquainted with Mr. Pinnock and his son, Nigel?"

"How d-do you do," Meg stammered.

"I for one will be glad of the snow." Mr. Pinnock leaned back in his chair. His ample midsection was contained by a checked waistcoat with gold buttons. One of the offerings at his store, no doubt. "We have a new selection of sleds at the Emporium. Don't like to see them languishing in the storeroom unwanted."

Nigel Pinnock nodded along with his father. He was a young man of nineteen, sporting a pair of patchy brown side-whiskers. "There's good sledding in Shropshire. The winter here is nothing to the winters we had there."

"You're not thinking of returning, I hope," Miss Colfax said from her place beside Meg on the settee. "We've all come to rely so much on the Emporium."

"We won't be departing just yet, miss, never you fear," Mr. Pinnock replied. "If we do, the store will remain. It's a dream of mine to have a Pinnock's Emporium in villages across England." He looked to Mr. Beresford. "Daresay it seems a small enough dream to the son of an earl."

"Not at all," Mr. Beresford answered. "Prosperous shopkeepers are the result of a prosperous village. To my mind, your ambitions are all to the good."

"You're ambitious yourself, I understand." Mr. Pinnock cast a significant glance at Meg. "In every respect, it seems."

Meg willed herself not to blush under Mr. Pinnock's scrutiny. She supposed it had been too much to hope that he would confine his remarks to next-day gossip. It seemed the convergence of a Burton-Smythe and a Beresford was too scandalous a subject to ignore, even for courtesy's sake.

But Mr. Beresford *did* ignore it. Both his gaze and his attention remained firmly on Mr. Pinnock. "I see nothing wrong with keeping one's sights set on the future," he said. "Nothing has ever been achieved by looking backward."

"As Lot's wife would attest," Mr. Colfax interjected dryly.

The vicar's attempt at levity was effective. The gentlemen chuckled and Miss Colfax smiled with relief at an awkward moment averted.

"Quite so," Mr. Pinnock said, returning his focus to Mr. Beresford. "The vicar mentioned that you're touting a rail station in Maidenbridge."

"A platform halt," Mr. Beresford clarified. "It's not as obtrusive as a railway station, but it's equally as convenient to the villagers."

"Dangerous, more like," Nigel said.

Mr. Beresford turned to him with interest. "How so?"

"Don't want to live too close to a railway. Causes all manner of ailments, I've heard."

"Does it, indeed?" Miss Colfax murmured. "How fascinating."

"Aye," Mr. Pinnock concurred. "It's the motion of the train that does it. I've read accounts of folk being driven mad by the vibrations. It shakes something loose in their heads, I reckon. Might have the same result for people living near a station, or one of them platform halts, as you describe."

Mr. Beresford's mouth hitched in an amused half smile. "Those are old wives' tales. That, and elaborate fabrications conjured up to sell newspapers."

Mr. Pinnock's brow wrinkled with doubt. "You dispute the truth of them?"

"Wholeheartedly. There's nothing dangerous about living near a railway. Not unless you stand on the tracks in the path of an oncoming train."

Miss Colfax gave an elegant shudder. "How wretched. Does that happen often?"

"Rail accidents occur but rarely," Mr. Beresford said. "When they do, they're usually an engineering matter. Nothing so exciting as you might read in a penny horrible."

"Still," Mr. Pinnock said, "one doesn't like to take the risk."

"And why not?" Mr. Beresford inquired. "The greatest achievements in our history have been brought about by risk takers and dreamers. We shouldn't be afraid of their ideas. We should embrace them. Indeed, we should follow their example and take a few risks ourselves."

Meg listened to him avidly, captivated by the energy in his speech. In repose, Mr. Beresford was as coldly beautiful as his father and brothers, but when he was speaking about the railway—or about something as seemingly simple as a medieval clapper bridge—his face lit with glorious animation. He became at once both more dazzling and all the more approachable.

"Some risktakers end up in the parish graveyard," Mr. Pinnock said sagely. "Isn't that so, parson?"

The vicar reluctantly agreed. "There's danger in being too ambitious."

Mr. Beresford leaned forward in his chair, his excitement over the project backed by a seriousness that denoted the substance of his ambition. "The railway is coming regardless. It's already poised to expand across England. The only question is, how soon will it come to Maidenbridge."

"Master Ivo likes his trains," Mr. Ruggiero remarked to Meg in an overloud whisper.

Mr. Beresford flicked his former guide a quelling look before resuming his conversation with the Pinnocks. "If we construct a platform halt in Maidenbridge, think how many new shoppers it will bring into the village. Residents of other villages in other counties who will soon be clamoring for a Pinnock's Emporium of their own."

Mr. Pinnock's face grew thoughtful. He plainly hadn't considered this aspect of the business. "You feel it would aid in my expansion?"

"I'm confident it would," Mr. Beresford said.

The housekeeper came to the door of the parlor. "Dinner is served, Vicar."

"Excellent." Mr. Colfax stood. "Shall we continue this discussion in the dining room?"

---

IVO WASN'T PUT NEXT TO MISS BURTON-SMYTHE AT dinner, much to his disappointment. He had Miss Colfax on his right and Mr. Pinnock on his left. Miss Burton-Smythe was seated across the table from them between Ruggiero and the vicar. Ruggiero was talking to her about something, gesturing wildly with his hands as he often did when he was passionate about a topic.

A frown notched Ivo's brows.

He couldn't think what the man could be saying, but judging by Miss Burton-Smythe's closed expression, it was nothing she found very entertaining.

Not for the first time, Ivo regretted having brought Ruggiero with him. He'd fully intended to leave him at Beasley Park, but once again—as so often happened—the man's entreaties had weakened Ivo's resolve. Ruggiero was, after all, trying to reestablish himself in England. What could it really hurt to allow him a brief meal at the vicarage and an even briefer conversation with Mr. Pinnock?

But Ivo hadn't reckoned for the presence of Meg Burton-Smythe.

He hadn't seen her since their disagreement by the river. Despite his invitation, she'd failed to appear to ride with him. Never mind that he'd waited for her at Sefton Bridge each morning. That he'd lingered in the rain, only giving up when the elements grew too fierce to withstand.

Returning to Beasley today as the storm set in and the driving rain soaked his greatcoat, Ivo had been convinced he'd never see her again.

He'd only discovered she'd be in attendance after he'd arrived at the vicarage. The news had knocked him back a step. Her appearance moments later, wearing a dinner dress of form-fitting gilded silk, had knocked him back again.

She was uncommonly pretty in her riding habit. Out of it, she was heart-stoppingly gorgeous. Her gown shaped to her figure with aching detail, as alluring in its simplicity as Aphrodite's girdle. The sensuous effect of it was only aided by her loosely knotted coiffure. No longer twisted into compliance, her vibrant red locks were gently caught up in a pair of opal-studded combs, with curling tendrils left free to frame her gold-dust freckled face.

He found his gaze drifting to her throughout the meal, even as he conversed with Mr. Pinnock about the railway and Miss Colfax about, among other things, his two brothers.

"Lord St. Clare is expected home for Christmas, too, I hope." A glimmer of feminine expectation shone in Miss Colfax's usually placid face. "It's been too long since I've seen him in church."

Ivo cut into his roast potato. He wasn't surprised she should be asking about his older brother. James Beresford, Viscount St. Clare was the heir to the earldom. He was also, objectively, the best looking of all the Beresford brothers. Ladies were perpetually swooning over him wherever he went, undeterred by James's starchy demeanor. Ivo felt rather cruel to encourage any of them, especially someone as decent as Miss Colfax.

James would never, after all, lower himself to marry a mere vicar's daughter. He had his sights set on someone grander. A duke's daughter, very probably. Someone from a morally upright, well-established, and well-monied family. It wasn't a mercenary ambition on James's part. It was a redemptive one. Practically from birth, his sole concern in life had been to rehabilitate the Beresford family's scandalous reputation.

And it *was* rather scandalous, truth be told.

Their grandfather had turned highwayman for a time. And niggling rumors still persisted that their own father, Lord Allendale, had been born on the wrong side of the blanket. James had taken the old gossip to heart. He considered it his duty to right the wrongs of the past and firmly establish the Beresfords as a respectable family.

Ivo supposed it was because James was the heir. The majority of the burden had always been on him. Whereas Ivo and Jack had been free to live and to love as they liked—within reason, of course.

"St. Clare is still in Hertfordshire with my parents," he said. "He'll return on the eighteenth. My sister's expected shortly thereafter."

"I shall be glad to see her again," Miss Colfax replied.

He gave her a vaguely curious glance. His sister had never mentioned the vicar's daughter in any of her letters. "Are you acquainted with Kate?"

"We've taken tea together several times since I arrived in Maidenbridge last year. She's very..." Miss Colfax's forehead puckered, at a loss for what she could say to describe the rebellious Lady Kate.

Ivo didn't wonder. The two young ladies were as different as chalk and cheese. "Yes, she is *very*," he agreed with a chuckle.

"She certainly was when last I saw her. I'm pleased her character has resisted reformation."

"I didn't mean to imply anything about her character," Miss Colfax said. "I found her exceptionally amiable. She's a great sportswoman, is she not?"

"A persistent one. She doesn't concede defeat easily."

"I expect she'll be returning from London having made a conquest of all who met her."

Ivo wasn't so certain. Not every gentleman appreciated Kate's spirit. To be sure, there had been some fellows over the years who had found her conduct downright alarming. But she was beautiful and had a generous fortune to her name. That carried more weight with the male sex than Ivo cared to admit.

He cast another discreet glance at Miss Burton-Smythe.

Doubtless she was possessed of a generous fortune, too. Her father wouldn't have settled it all on that wastrel, Roddy. Not if he cared for his only daughter, that is.

When the next course was served, Ivo made an effort to refocus his attentions on Mr. Pinnock. The tradesman was loud and opinionated. It wouldn't do for him to go around the village spouting nonsense about railway vibrations driving people mad.

"Have you ridden on a train?" Ivo asked him.

"I've not had that pleasure, no sir." Mr. Pinnock's spoonful of boiled custard paused briefly on the way to his mouth. "If it is a pleasure."

"It's an exhilarating experience, not an unpleasant one. The convenience alone is enough to fire the senses. A man can run up to London in no time at all, without the trouble of coaching inns or the danger of injuring his cattle."

Mr. Pinnock swallowed his mouthful of dessert with a cynical smile. "I suppose you require investments."

"As any business venture would. Though the costs of

subscriptions are vastly outweighed by the benefit to those who endorse the scheme."

"You've met with Mr. Horsley and Mr. Standish?"

"I have." Ivo had dined with them earlier in the week.

"What do they have to say about a railway in Maidenbridge?"

"They're keen on the idea."

It was partially true. Both men had pledged their support, contingent on Ivo obtaining the backing of his parents and Sir Frederick. Ivo had promised them that the Beresford and Burton-Smythe endorsements were forthcoming, knowing full well that the latter was still very much in question.

Ivo had no regrets. He was confident that, when he finally met with Sir Frederick, the man could be persuaded to see reason. Sir Frederick may be an ogre in his personal dealings, but he'd never been accused of falling short in matters that affected Letchford Hall. A railway would benefit him as well as it would the tradesman and villagers. Coal, crops, and anything else produced on his estate could be transported with ease.

Mr. Pinnock seemed to read his mind. "And Sir Frederick? What of his opinion? He's in favor of your venture, I presume, if his daughter's presence here is any indication."

"She has nothing to do with the business," Ivo said.

"More to do with pleasure, has she?" Mr. Pinnock smiled smugly. "No need to deny it. I've a gift for spotting these things. The butcher's recent engagement is down to me. So is the chemist's. But a Beresford and a Burton-Smythe! Now that would be a feather in my cap."

The vicar had warned Ivo about Mr. Pinnock's propensity for making matches. Ivo nevertheless felt a distinct flare of annoyance with the man. "My interest is solely in the railway," he said. "As I told you before, a platform halt in Maidenbridge has the power to revitalize the village."

Mr. Pinnock was temporarily diverted. "With more business for the Emporium?"

"And easier shipments of goods."

Mr. Pinnock nodded slowly. "Mayhap it's time I bought a rail ticket to see what all the fuss is about. Can't promise to endorse the scheme until I do."

A surge of accomplishment lifted Ivo's spirits. "Naturally. One must be sensible about these things."

He was prepared to say more when he heard Miss Burton-Smythe's voice from across the table, haltingly interjecting during a pause in Ruggiero's endless soliloquy.

"I b-beg your pardon," she said. "I seem to have spilled wine on m-my gown."

The entire table looked at her as one.

She held her half-filled glass in her hand. Her countenance was pale beneath her freckles.

"That's easily remedied," Miss Colfax said, setting aside her napkin. "Our housekeeper has all sorts of salves in the kitchen. She can remove any stain that hasn't set in yet." She began to get up. "I'll walk you down."

Ivo and the other gentleman moved to stand.

Miss Burton-Smythe rose from her chair in a flurry of gold silk skirts. "Pray d-don't trouble yourself. I c-can find the way." With that, she swiftly fled the dining room.

Ivo stared after her in the flickering candlelight. A frown curved his mouth as he returned to his seat. There had been no wine stain on her dress. None that he could see. He cast an accusing look at Ruggiero.

The signore responded with a bewildered shrug.

"Poor dear." Miss Colfax spread her napkin back over her lap. "She *is* easily flustered, isn't she? I shall give her five minutes to compose herself and then go after her."

"No," Ivo said. "Leave her be. It's time she wants, not company."

Miss Colfax's gentle smile turned quizzical. "You speak as though you knew her."

"I do," he said. He was beginning to, anyway.

If Miss Burton-Smythe wasn't back in five minutes, he'd go after her himself.

# Chapter Nine

Meg had not, in fact, spilled her wine. Despite her anxiety at being in company, she wasn't so fumble fingered as that. It was Mr. Ruggiero who had driven her to flee. Him and his endless stories about Ivo Beresford's compassionate heart.

Initially, Meg had listened with avid attention, eager to hear anything about Mr. Beresford. She was, to her embarrassment, developing a bit of a fascination with the man. But as Mr. Ruggiero droned on, it became clear that every account of his employer's life in Italy contained a similar theme. No matter how wretched a person's situation—no matter how the world had shunned them—Mr. Beresford could always be counted on for a kind smile and a sympathetic word. He was, as Mr. Ruggiero insisted, a gentleman who took pity on the misfits of society.

It wasn't very long into the man's soliloquy that it had begun to occur to Meg that she was very likely one of them.

And that hadn't been the worst of it.

She passed into the narrow downstairs kitchen, with its flagstone floor and sprawling, rectangular softwood table scattered with the leavings of cut vegetables, flour dust, and the remnants of the meal that had been served upstairs.

The cook was having a cup of tea with the scullery maid in front of the fire—a short respite after having finished preparing the final course for the vicar's guests. She scrambled up from her wooden chair at the sight of Meg. The maid followed suit, nearly spilling her tea.

"Can I help you, miss?" the cook asked.

"I th-thought I spilled something on m-my gown," Meg said, "but I was m-mistaken." She felt like the veriest liar. To be telling fibs at the vicarage of all places! "I shall just...g-get some air."

"You'll catch your death," the cook warned as Meg reached to open the back door.

Meg didn't heed her. She ducked out of kitchen, into the frosty, starlit darkness of the yard that led to the privy. A small oil lantern hung from a post next to the water pump, protected by the jut of the roof. She stopped beside it, folding her arms around herself against the chill.

The cold night air was just what she required to compose herself. A minute or two and she'd be calm enough to return to the dining room.

Though what she really wanted to do was go to the stable and command Timothy to hitch the horses and drive her home. Indeed, as she stood, shivering beneath the eaves, she seriously considered it.

But it was impossible.

For one thing, she didn't have her cloak. For another, she may be timid as a mouse at times, but she was no coward. She'd come here, hadn't she?

Gooseflesh rose on her arms beneath the silk of her sleeves. If she lingered any longer, her teeth would begin to chatter. She was just straightening her spine to return to the house when the back door opened and Mr. Beresford entered the yard.

Meg's breath stopped in her chest. "What are you d-doing out here?"

He closed the door behind him and came to join her. "The same as you are, I expect," he said. "Enjoying the fine weather."

The last thing Meg wanted was his pity. "I'd rather b-be alone."

"I gathered that. What I don't know is why." He examined her in the dim light cast from the lantern. "Did Ruggiero say something to upset you?"

"Is that likely?"

"It is," Mr. Beresford said frankly. "He hasn't yet learned to set a guard on his tongue. It's bad enough when he's drinking. When he's sober, it's worse." He paused, studying her face. "It wasn't the *Ars Amatoria*, I take it."

"N-No."

"Then what was it he was talking about with so much enthusiasm?"

Meg saw no reason to dissemble. "You."

"I see." His brows notched. "Or rather... I don't. I've nothing in my past to make a lady race out of room on hearing of it."

"N-No, indeed. You're perfect."

He snorted. "Hardly. If that's what he's been telling you—"

"He t-told me only that you rescued him. He said he was languishing in Rome, with n-no funds t-to support him, and m-might surely have died if you hadn't come to his aid."

"Rubbish. It wasn't that near of a thing. It's true, he was without funds. And he'd taken to begging outside the Coliseum. But he wasn't at death's door."

"Why d-did you help him?"

"Because we needed a guide. He can speak the language fluently and he'd been up and down the country countless times. Not to mention the fact that he was one of us."

She gave him an uncertain look. Her lips were going numb from the cold. She was beginning to sorely regret having stepped outside without her cloak.

"He's an Englishman, born and bred. He went to Italy on his grand tour twenty-odd years ago." Mr. Beresford paused, frowning. All at once, he shrugged out of his frock coat and, in one fluid motion, draped it around her shoulders without so much as a by your leave.

Meg started. She was poised to object to the intimacy when a delicious warmth settled over her, too wonderful to refuse. Goodness, if this is how toasty an article of Mr. Beresford's clothing was, his body must be hot as a furnace! She listed toward him a fraction quite against her will, her shivering frame instinctively desiring more of his heat.

He remained close to her, continuing his speech as though he hadn't just spiked the temperature of her blood by several degrees. "After his father died, Ruggiero ended up stranded in Rome, without a penny to his name. He decided to remain. Said it was better to be a pauper in sunny Italy than left cold and humiliated back in Kent. Problem was, the longer he stayed, the worse his circumstances."

"What had that t-to do with you?" she asked.

"Nothing at all. But he has no one else to help him—no friends or family remaining in England. And he wanted to come home. It was past time he did."

"So you t-took it upon yourself t-to rescue him."

"I dispute that it was a rescue. But yes, I did help him, first by hiring him and then by bringing him back with me. Why not? He practically threw himself in my path."

"As I did." Her breath was a visible puff in the chill night air.

"I beg your pardon?" The glow of the lantern illuminated the gleaming white of his linen shirt and shimmered in the silk of his shawl-collared waistcoat.

Absent his coat, his tall, lean frame was even more imposing. He was obviously strong. Not at all a dandy or a soft, country squire prone to indulging himself. His midsection was lean, his muscles hard, and every inch of him as magnificent as any Arthurian hero.

But heroism wasn't always romantic. Sometimes it was unwanted. Unwelcome. Especially if it was motivated for reasons abhorrent to a lady.

"I threw m-myself in your path," she said. "That day by Sefton Bridge. It wasn't on p-purpose, but... Of course you m-must help me. You always d-do help sad figures such as m-myself."

His brows shot up. "You're implying that I felt *sorry* for you?"

"Didn't you?"

"No," he said. "I—"

"And th-that isn't the worst of it," Meg said.

Her heart trembled against her ribs, like a bird battering at the bars of its cage. She knew what would happen if she spoke the next bit aloud. Their budding friendship would be over before it had fully begun. Ivo Beresford would depart from her life. But if what Mr. Ruggiero had told her was true, her friendship with Mr. Beresford was no friendship at all.

"What can be worse?" he asked.

She steeled herself. "Is it true that you m-must have my father's approval in order to b-build your railway extension?"

Mr. Beresford stilled. He was silent for a full three seconds. And then: "Yes. It's true."

Meg's heart dropped. No longer fluttering, it went cold in her breast. "Is th-that why you suggested we should be friends?"

His gray eyes darkened like twin storm clouds. "Is *that* what you think?"

"Is it?" she pressed.

"No it isn't, by God," he said fiercely. "For heaven's sake, Meg. Do you hold yourself in such low regard?"

She wouldn't be diverted. No matter that he'd never used her given name before. No matter that his question stung her to the soul. "It isn't about m-me," she shot back. "I d-didn't suggest we m-meet to go riding under...under f-false pretenses."

"I didn't—"

"You said you were on your own and th-that you'd be glad of the company. You d-didn't say anything about m-my father."

He scowled down at her. "Because your father was the last thing on my mind, drat it all!"

"But he *was* on your m-mind?"

Mr. Beresford opened his mouth to deny it only to close it again. It was answer enough.

The clatter of pots echoed from the kitchen, a reminder that they weren't alone. There was nothing that happened here that wouldn't be remarked on the instant they returned.

She stiffened with indignation at the position he'd put her in. To have to confront him here of all places. "You shouldn't have c-come after me. You'll only subject m-me to gossip."

"The dinner is over," Mr. Beresford said. "The gentlemen have retired to their cigars. Pinnock wishes to hire Ruggiero to teach his younger sons. They're engrossed in a discussion about methods of instruction, and the vicar and Pinnock Jr. are halfway to planning the latter's grand tour. I excused myself to check on my cattle. None of them know I've come after you."

"What about Miss C-Colfax?"

"She's withdrawn to the parlor. She'll be awaiting you there."

"Then I shall join her." Meg slipped off his coat. Thrusting it into his hand, she moved to brush past him.

He caught her arm, arresting her step. "We're not done with this conversation."

"There's n-nothing more to say."

"Not here, no. But tomorrow. Meet me at Sefton Bridge at sunup. We'll talk then." His fingers curved around her silk-clad flesh in an insistent grasp. "And don't shirk as you did the last two days."

Meg's eyes jolted to his, startled and uncertain.

"I waited for you," he said gruffly.

Her heart gave a hopeful thump. She did her level best to ignore it. "It was raining. I-I c-couldn't—"

"You could," he said. "You will." He loomed over her, refusing to release her until she'd agreed to see him again. "Tomorrow. Promise me you'll come."

"I-I—"

"Say, I promise you, Ivo."

Meg could no longer disregard the pounding of her pulse. He'd never looked at her quite that way before. Great goodness, it was very near a smolder. She drew in a breath to refuse him, but a refusal didn't emerge. "I p-promise you, Ivo," she heard herself whisper instead. "Now let m-me go."

Mr. Beresford's hand fell from her arm. Meg didn't wait for him to reply. She didn't even look at him. Clutching her skirts, she fled back into the house.

# Chapter Ten

The next morning, the minute the cold light of dawn had burned away the low-lying fog, Ivo was up and in the saddle, riding to meet Meg. He arrived at the river early. All the better to cool his blood. A good night's sleep hadn't done it. He'd been as aggravated when he woke up as he'd been when he retired. Aggravated with himself—*and* with her.

Not only had she thought the worst of him (understandably so), she'd provoked him into near incivility. She'd made him feel...

But lord only knew *what* he'd been feeling last night.

It hadn't been friendly, that was for certain. Indeed, he'd thought for a moment, looming over her in the moonlight, holding her arm in his grasp, that he might bend his head and kiss her. The impulse had nearly overpowered him.

Dashed inconvenient.

The last thing he wanted was an entanglement. He was only three and twenty for God's sake. And Meg was a Burton-Smythe!

It wouldn't do. It simply wouldn't. And yet...

He couldn't let her go.

Ivo was pacing by the clapper bridge, slashing his riding crop among the frost-tipped undergrowth, pondering that very dilemma, when she arrived on her mare. She rode up to the same tree where he'd tied Rowena on the last occasion they'd met and dismounted without waiting for his assistance.

Relief coursed through him, obliterating what remained of his irritation. He'd suspected she wouldn't come. He could scarcely have blamed her. She had every right to doubt his motives. And he meant to tell her so.

He strode up to meet her, coming to an awkward halt. "You came," he said, rather stupidly.

Her face was pale beneath her freckles. "I promised I would."

"And you keep your promises, of course," he said. "I would expect nothing less."

She didn't reply, only looked at him. There were no shy blushes. No flustered stammerings. Just taut, unrelieved silence.

The distance between them grew by the second.

If he left things too long, all would be lost. She was already retreating from him. Not physically—not yet—but in every other way that mattered. He'd realized last night how little he wanted to lose her.

"What did you wish to speak to m-me about?" she asked at last.

Ivo didn't waste time with prevarication. "It did occur to me that I might use you to advance my interests with your father," he admitted. "But not when first we met. That day under the bridge, when I suggested we be friends—that was genuine."

She folded her arms. The velvet-trimmed brown wool of her winter riding habit pulled tight across her shoulders.

"How c-could it have been? Our families d-despise each other."

"I'm my own man, Meg. My family commands my loyalty, but not blindly. What happened between our parents went on a quarter of a century ago. It had nothing to do with either of us."

"That m-may be so. It still d-doesn't explain why you'd ever wish to be my friend. Indeed, I d-don't believe you did. Not in earnest."

A gust of ice-cold December air whipped through the trees, rustling Ivo's hair. Down the bank, Snap stamped his hooves and shook his head. When the wind was up, he'd rather be galloping, not tied to a tree while his master made a bumbling apology to a young lady.

Ivo forged on, ignoring the weather. He was determined to make things right, even if he must swallow pride. "Because you don't see yourself as I do. You're too caught up in worrying over your stammer and your other imagined shortcomings. It's distracted you from noticing what anyone else can perceive quite plainly."

She stared at him with equal parts hurt and indignation. "And what is th-that, pray?"

"You're stunning," he said bluntly.

She blinked. It was the only indication that his assessment had surprised her. That, and the shadow of vulnerability that crept into her gaze.

"*And* you're kind," he added. "The way you handle that fractious mare with so much gentleness and devotion? The way you smiled when we crossed the bridge together? The way you held my hand? Any gentleman would be honored to have five minutes of your time. That's all I wanted."

Doubt etched Meg's brow. But she didn't stop him.

He was emboldened to continue. "Perhaps I was curious, as well. I've wondered about you over the years. About what it was like to live up at the Hall, with only your father and the servants for company. As a boy, I daresay I made you into a bit of a fairytale."

She bent her head, brow still drawn. Her voice fell quiet, confessing, "We're b-both guilty in that regard."

He smiled slightly. "Don't say you've been idealizing me?"

She glanced up at him through her lashes with a flicker of ruefulness. "I read too m-many stories about King Arthur."

Ivo made an exaggerated wince. "Good God. You haven't imagined me that philanderer?"

Color rose in her cheeks. "No. N-Not him." She didn't volunteer who it had been.

Ivo supposed it must be one of the treacly, romantic characters. Lancelot or Galahad, very likely. But he didn't tease her on the subject. This was no time for levity. They hadn't yet settled things between them.

"That just proves it," he said. "We've been aware of each for a long while. The day we met, it was only natural I should be interested in you."

"As a c-curiosity."

"No," he said. "As a young lady."

This time when she glanced up at him, their gazes locked and held.

He looked at her steadily. "I did want to be your friend, Meg. I still do."

Her bosom swelled on a deeply indrawn breath. "I'd like t-to believe you, Mr. Beresford—"

"Ivo."

"Ivo." Her blush deepened. "But you admit you wanted m-my father's help, too."

"The two needn't be contradictory."

"I suppose n-not, but—"

"Besides, I wouldn't say I require his help. Merely his endorsement. So long as the other residents of Maidenbridge know he doesn't oppose a railway, they'll be willing to support the scheme." A rogue doubt struck Ivo. He frowned. "I say, he wouldn't oppose it, would he?"

Meg bit her lip.

Her very pink and very kissable lip.

Ivo's attention fell to her mouth. He forced it back to her eyes, ignoring the startling clench of longing in his belly. "Would he?" he repeated when she didn't answer.

"I d-don't think so," she said. "He's quite progressive with his m-methods on the estate."

"Yes. That was my thinking. The rancor he feels toward my family has never driven him to do anything that would hurt the land." Ivo uttered a wry huff. "Though it's certainly compelled him to do other things."

A nameless emotion crossed Meg's face. She moistened her lips.

This time he couldn't keep himself from staring. From thinking about what those lips would feel like. Taste like. Her mouth was appallingly sinful for a girl of eighteen, just out of the schoolroom.

"I asked him about what you said," she told him.

His gaze returned to hers as though he was waking from a fleeting dream. How long had he been staring at her lips and envisioning kissing her? He seemed to have lost the thread of the conversation.

"You were right," she said. "He didn't name m-me out of love."

Ivo suddenly understood. His attention sharpened to a knife's edge. Good lord. She truly had asked her father why he'd named her Margaret. Ivo could only imagine how *that* conversation had gone.

"Indeed," she went on, "his m-motives were quite the opposite. I suspect I d-did it out of...out of..."

"Spite," Ivo supplied grimly.

"Yes."

"I thought as much."

Her mouth trembled. "Did you?"

"It's what my brothers and I have always believed. It's no reflection on you."

"Yes, it is. Had he loved me, he wouldn't have used m-me so. But he doesn't. He'd rather have no d-daughter at all than be c-cursed with the likes of a disappointing c-creature like me."

Ivo's temper erupted with a scorching fury. "He *said* this to you?"

"He d-didn't have to say it."

He took an instinctive step toward her, only stopping when the skirts of her riding habit brushed his legs. "Any man would be proud to have you as a daughter," he said fiercely. "You're...You're..."

She waited, lips parted on a suspended breath. "What am I?"

"Sweet. Gentle. Kind. Everything I've said you are and more." He flung a hand toward the bridge, reminding her of how they'd first met. "You didn't give me the cut direct for starters."

She appeared offended by the suggestion. "I could never have c-cut you. Not after you c-came to my rescue so splendidly."

"Well. I made the mistake of taking you for a damsel in distress. More fool me." He turned back to her. "You're stronger than you appear, aren't you? I look forward to the day you realize it for yourself."

MEG HAD NEVER BEEN ACCUSED OF BEING STRONG before. She found she rather liked it. Particularly because Ivo hadn't referenced her strength with contempt. He'd sounded as though he respected her. As though he was eager to see her come into her own.

She stood a little taller on the river bank, arms loosening from across her chest. She'd been holding them so tightly a cramp had started in her elbows. "I hope I *am* strong. I shall need be when m-my father finds out we've dined together."

Ivo's brows lifted. "He doesn't know yet?"

She shook her head. "He was abed when I returned last n-night, and he sleeps late in the m-morning now he's suffering from his gout. He t-takes laudanum, you see."

"He must wake up eventually."

"Inevitably. I expect the servants will have t-told him by the time I return from m-my ride. He'll be as cross as a wild b-boar."

Ivo's countenance was at once grave with concern. "He won't hurt you?"

Meg's eyes widened. "Oh no, n-never. You wouldn't suggest such a thing if you knew him."

"I know *of* him. I know he doesn't take kindly to young ladies who oppose him."

"I d don't oppose him."

"You're here now, aren't you?"

"Yes, b-but...that's our own secret. Even if m-my father learns of the dinner, he'll never know of our meetings here."

"Our *continued* meetings." Ivo's tone brooked no argument.

Meg had no wish to argue. "Yes, exactly."

He hesitated, his eyes betraying a momentary flare of doubt before he once again surged ahead. "I realize the risk is unequal. Your father isn't likely to be as forgiving of our friendship as my parents will be. But we're not doing anything wrong. No more than any other couple who walk or ride together. As country pursuits go, we're well within the bounds of propriety."

What he said was true to an extent. Unmarried couples often walked and rode together. They even drove together, providing it was in an open carriage. That didn't mean it didn't cause remark. On the contrary, too much time spent in a particular gentleman's company—even if that time was expended in a wholly respectable fashion—could lead people to draw only one conclusion. It must be a romance. A love affair. A relationship that would lead either to marriage or straight down the road to ruination.

Meg recognized the fact even as she dismissed it. Society's opinions mattered little when weighed against the demands of her heart.

"It's all right," she said. "My father c-can't stop us being friends."

Uncertainties on that score still lingered at the back of her mind. But her conversation with Ivo had largely laid them to rest. She believed he meant the things he'd said to her. That she was kind. That she was strong. That she was stunning.

Stunning!

Meg held the compliments close to her heart. She would never forget them, not so long as she lived. Not even if Ivo Beresford disappeared from her life tomorrow.

Though she fervently hoped he wouldn't.

A shadow of a smile touched his lips. "Shall we walk by the water?" he asked, offering her his hand.

She took it without hesitation. "Yes, please. So long as it's n-not raining."

His fingers instantly engulfed hers. He was strong and sure beside her, not leading her, but walking with her, matching her step for step as they descended to the river. She knew beyond doubt that he wouldn't let her fall. That she could depend on him to hold the course.

"It isn't going to rain anymore," he said. "Snow is coming. Can't you taste it in the air?"

"You can taste snow?"

"Taste it, smell it, feel it. I have a sense about the weather. The snow especially. When I was a lad, I used to love mucking about in it with my brothers. We had sled races and snowball fights, and we built the most appalling snowmen. We're a rambunctious lot, my family. The opposite of yours, I expect."

As they walked together, holding hands, the disparate pieces of Meg's soul seemed to shift and organize into a new configuration. One that didn't provoke anxiousness or the fidgety desire to bring order to chaos, but instead offered the promise of safety and assurance.

Perhaps this was how Britannia might feel, were she a living entity. To stride through life with a golden lion as one's companion. There was a delicious security in having someone formidable at your side.

"I love the snow," she said. "But we n-never did those things at the hall."

Ivo flashed her a dark glance. "Your father didn't allow them?"

"It wasn't th-that." Meg made an effort to disabuse him of his poor impression. Just because her father had named her out of spite, and just because he was grumpy and churlish, didn't mean he was an out-and-out monster. "He isn't a terrible person, you know."

"No?"

"He m-may not love me, but he doesn't strike me. He doesn't lock me away in the tower."

"A low bar."

She bristled at the scorn underlying his words. Stopping on the riverbank, she turned to face him. "He hired the b-best governess to instruct me. He affords m-me the finest clothes I can find in Maidenbridge. He d-doesn't refuse me the things I need."

Ivo's expression softened with something like compassion. "Is love not something you need?"

Meg's burst of indignation fizzled as swiftly as it had arisen. Had she not been holding Ivo's hand, she might have felt a little lost. She refused to show it. "I shall have it eventually," she vowed, sounding more certain than she felt. "I m-mean to marry for love."

His gaze sharpened. "Marry whom?"

"I d-don't know. I shall have to wait and see who pursues me in Bath."

Her heart gave a hopeful thump as she looked up at him. Was there any chance he'd follow her there? Any chance he might court her? Marry her?

Oh, but she wished it would be so!

In all her life, Meg had never met a gentleman she liked half as well as Ivo Beresford.

Admittedly, she hadn't met many. Only spotty local lads or toplofty members of the local gentry. The former were sometimes impertinent, but the latter paid her no mind at all, not even when they dined with her father. Bran-faced, she'd overheard one of the young men call her once. A girl whose only appeal was her fortune, and that scarcely a temptation with a father as menacing as Sir Frederick.

Could Ivo stand up to her father? Would he even want to?

"Bath!" he exclaimed. "Is that where you mean to have your season?"

"Yes."

"What on earth for?"

"I d-don't want to go to London. I'm n-not as bold as your sister."

"No one is as bold as my sister. Not even me."

Meg's mouth tilted up at the corners.

He smiled back at her, gray eyes gleaming behind his spectacles. "She'll be a bad influence on you," he warned. "I mean to introduce you to her just the same."

"Do you?"

"Why shouldn't I? Why shouldn't we all of us be friends? I see nothing very wrong with the idea."

She gazed at him in increasing bemusement.

His smile broadened. "What?"

"Nothing. Only that you're so..."

Congenial. Handsome. Kind. Any one of those could have been used to describe him—and no doubt *had* been countless times. But they weren't any of the words that sprang to her lips.

"You're so very... odd," she blurted out.

Ivo burst out laughing.

A tide of blistering heat suffused Meg's face. "Oh, I b-beg your pardon! I d-didn't mean to—"

"It's all right. I daresay I do seem odd to someone like you—*and* to everyone else in Maidenbridge. I've never seen the point in wasting time on the past. We've too much to accomplish to be distracted with trivialities." Raising her hand to his lips, he pressed a swift kiss to her gloved knuckles. "Speaking of which..."

"Yes?" she asked breathlessly.

"When do you suppose it would be best for me to call on your father?"

Her pulse surged. "You wish to visit Letchford Hall?"

"I must do," he said. "My business can't proceed until I speak with Sir Frederick about the platform halt."

The railway. Of course.

For a moment, Meg had thought...

But no. Naturally he wouldn't be calling at the Hall out of

personal inclinations. She'd known him only a few weeks. And he'd promised her friendship, nothing more.

Yet, he'd kissed her hand just now.

That wasn't friendly, was it? That was something else.

"I daresay tomorrow is out of the question," he said. "No one wants to discuss business on Sunday. And he may still be peevish about our having dined together at the vicarage."

Peevish was one way of putting it.

"Very probably," Meg acknowledged. A pit formed in her stomach at the reminder of what awaited her at the Hall when she returned from her ride.

"What about Monday?" he asked. "I could come after luncheon, if you think he'd be fit for company."

"You're n-not afraid of him?"

"Afraid of Sir Frederick?" A flicker of amusement crossed Ivo's face. "I'm not afraid of anyone, Meg."

She blinked. How was that possible? Surely everyone was afraid of someone. "But he m-might say things. He m-might lose his t-temper."

"So what if he does. His words can't harm me." Ivo gave a reassuring press to her fingers. "Anyway, I'm not applying to him for a bank loan. All I want are his opinions on the railway. Once I have them, I'll know best how to proceed."

Her hand was warm in his grasp. She felt the energy of him—the confidence and ambition—all the way through the fine kid leather of her glove. If it was possible to derive courage from another person, Meg derived it from him in that moment.

"Shall I ask him?" she inquired.

Ivo's brows elevated. "On my behalf? I should think not."

"Not on your b-behalf, no," she said. "I wouldn't presume. But I c-could find out his thoughts. It m-might help you decide how b-best to approach him."

The idea seemed to grow on him by degrees. "Yes. That would be helpful, indeed. But you needn't feel obliged—"

"I don't."

"And you needn't put yourself at risk—"

"What risk?"

He searched her face. "I thought *you* might be afraid of him."

Meg took a deep breath. "I'm n-not," she said at last. "N-Not anymore."

# Chapter Eleven

When Meg returned to Letchford Hall, she went straight up to her bedroom where she washed and changed into a plain wool dress. She was just finishing repairing her hair when Mrs. Church poked her head in the door.

The old housekeeper's perpetually sour countenance was unusually blank. "Your father wishes to see you, miss."

Meg's stomach tensed. She cast one final look in the mirror of her dressing table. Her thick hair was twisted back in a simple chignon, her twilled silk gown neat and pressed. Miss Adams had once said that a lady's toilette provided a degree of armor in difficult situations. As Meg rose from her seat, she hoped it was true.

Exiting her room, she turned in the direction that led to her father's wing.

Mrs. Church stopped her. "He's in his study."

Meg's already pounding heart gave a decided lurch. If her father had managed to dress and come downstairs, all the way to his study—a room he hadn't occupied since his fall from his horse—it meant his anger had reached frightening proportions.

She smoothed her skirts. She'd told Ivo she wasn't afraid of her father. And she wasn't.

She refused to be.

"Thank you, Mrs. Church," she said.

The housekeeper lingered a moment. She looked as though she very much wanted to say something. To scold Meg, no doubt, for having broken bread with a Beresford.

Meg gave the woman a level stare. If she wasn't going to be afraid of her father, she certainly wouldn't be frightened of one of her own servants. "Is there anything else?"

Mrs. Church pursed her lips. Something in Meg's face persuaded her to hold her tongue on the subject. "No, miss."

*That's what I thought*, Meg uttered silently.

Like her father, Mrs. Church and Mrs. Stapleton claimed to value meek obedience in a young lady. But they none of them really did. What they respected was strength. Meg was no longer going to hide hers to please them. It served no purpose at all except to diminish her in their eyes—*and* in her own.

From now on, she was going to assert her wishes, come what may, even if her father *did* bellow and threaten like Henry VIII. He couldn't, in reality, send her to the tower. This wasn't the Middle Ages.

Shoulders set, she made her way down the hall to the main staircase. She descended the marble steps, her skirts clutched in her hands. Her father's study was at the back of the house, near to the library. She found him there, seated behind his massive Jacobean desk, engaged in writing a letter.

He was in his paisley silk dressing gown, worn over a pair of loose-fitting wool trousers. Perspiration beaded his brow. He was obviously still in pain.

She hesitated on the threshold. "You wanted m-me, sir?"

No amount of resolve could completely quell her stammer in his presence.

Sir Frederick didn't look up from his letter. His quill pen continued scratching over the page with unusual force. "Come in and close the door behind you."

Meg worried her lip with her teeth as she shut the door. The curtains were drawn over the windows, leaving the study to look as out of use as it had been in the previous months. Only the small fire crackling in the grate and the single candle flickering on her father's desk leavened the darkness. They cast shadows across the heavy furnishings, streaking over the floor like long fingers reaching out to her.

Knees trembling, Meg walked to her father's desk. She sat down in one of the two leather-upholstered armchairs arrayed across from it.

Her father dashed the nib of his quill into the inkpot, splashing a drop of black ink onto the blotter. "I didn't invite you to sit."

On any other occasion, Meg would have leapt straight back to her feet. But not this time. She remained in her chair, reminding herself that she'd done nothing wrong.

Nothing that he knew of, at least.

He didn't have any inkling that she'd been meeting Ivo by the river, only that she'd dined with him in company. It was a minor sin in comparison. Indeed, it was no sin at all.

The thought restored Meg's courage. "You'd rather I stood in f-front of you like a servant b-being dressed d-down for breaking a vase?"

It was quite the most impertinent thing she'd ever said to him.

Impertinent enough that he finally stopped what he was doing to glare at her. "*What* did you say to me, girl?"

"I asked you if I—"

"You dare take that tone with me?" He cast aside his quill,

leaving his letter unfinished. "You who have gone behind my back to do what I've expressly forbidden any member of my household from doing?"

"What is th-that?" If he wanted to accuse her of something, he'd have to do so outright. She wasn't going to do his work for him.

Stark fury glittered in his face. "Was there or was there not a Beresford at the vicarage last evening?"

"Th-There was."

"You *dined* with him." He made the accusation sound as if she'd committed a mortal sin. Doubtless it was one, as far as he was concerned.

"I d-dined with Mr. Colfax and his d-daughter," she said. "They had other guests as well."

"A Beresford."

"Yes."

"You didn't think fit to inform me of it when you begged my permission to attend this farce of a dinner?"

"What objection c-could you have had to Mr. B-Beresford?" Meg asked. "He isn't, after all, his f-father."

Sir Frederick leaned across his desk. "Don't test me, girl. You know my feelings on that family."

Meg clasped her hands in her lap, praying her courage wouldn't desert her. "What of m-my feelings?"

He heaved himself to his feet to tower over her. His eyes burned with outrage, even as he grimaced from the pain in his ulcered calf. "You presume to have feelings for one of those preening jackanapes!"

Meg shrank back in her chair. A blush crept into her cheeks. Yes, she did presume. She presumed very much. Ivo had been fixed firmly in her daydreams—and in a few of her sleeping dreams, too—ever since the first day they'd met.

But that was none of her father's affair. He had no right to examine the contents of her dreams—or of her heart.

"I'm not t-talking about *him*," she said. "I'm t-talking about attending d-dinners and dances. Learning to c-conduct myself in company. I'm eighteen."

"So you keep saying." He grudgingly sank back into his seat, more to accommodate his leg than to retreat from the field of battle. His burst of white-hot anger, though temporarily assuaged, was in no way vanquished. "You will not dine at the vicarage, or any place that hosts any member of that family. Do you understand me? Disobey me again and the consequences will be severe. I've already written Colfax on the matter. The man should know better than to have allowed you to set foot into his house when a Beresford was present."

"Mr. Colfax is a vicar. He b-believes in forgiveness."

"He may believe in what he likes, damn him, but he'll not defy my wishes. Nor will you, my girl. From now on, you're forbidden my carriage."

Meg's mouth fell open. "*What?*"

"You heard me."

"But it's winter!"

"You have your mare for brief errands around the estate. For anything else, you can send one of the servants." He picked up his quill "That will be all."

Meg stayed in her seat. She wouldn't be so easily dismissed.

He was forbidding her the carriage in December? It wasn't fair! What of long shopping trips in the village? Or late afternoon or evening calls when the snow set in? She couldn't very well ride Rowena in such weather. And the dainty pack on Meg's sidesaddle wasn't big enough to accommodate any purchases larger than a small parcel.

Her father was punishing her disobedience by stealing her independence away. It wasn't being locked in the tower precisely, but it may as well have been.

She felt a tide of building fury in response to it. "If you

want me to c-consort with gentlemen who aren't B-Beresfords, then why have you forbidden m-me a season?"

"I've done no such thing."

"You all but have. I've t-told you I'd like a season in Bath. It's where I'll m-meet someone whom I c-could marry. Miss Adams has said so. She approves of the p-plan."

"Miss Adams is not my master." He dipped his quill back in the ink pot and, shaking the excess away, resumed his letter. "It's I who will decide when you're ready to enter the world, not a servant. And not you, my girl."

"Very well." Meg played her next card with no little anxiety. "If I m-must remain in Maidenbridge, then I must c-consort with Beresfords. Lord Allendale's sons are the only eligible g-gentlemen about."

That regained his attention.

His fingers clenched so hard around his pen, the quill threatened to snap.

"Lord Allendale," he spat, glaring up at her. "*Lord Allendale.* Do you have any inkling who that man truly is? He's a baseborn nobody! A bastard. Everyone knows it."

Meg recoiled from his anger. But she wasn't wholly surprised by his accusation. She'd heard some of the old rumors from Mrs. Church and Mrs. Stapleton. The earl had been the product of his father's brief union with a lowly kitchen maid. Some still whispered that it had been an illegitimate union, but the old earl—the present earl's grandfather—had had his son's marriage lines. He'd long ago proven that his grandson was no bastard.

"Why would you say th-that?" she asked.

"I knew him of old. We were raised together, Me, Margaret, and *him*. He was no heir to an earldom then, that much I can tell you. He had more in common with the stables than he did with fortune and breeding. A feral wolf in sheep's clothing, as likely to steal your jewels as a common highway robber."

"I don't b-believe it."

"You don't, do you? You think him too elegant and charming to resort to such tactics? To rob someone? To wound them? And why do you suppose my right shoulder pains me whenever the weather turns? *That* is a remnant of your great Lord Allendale's civility."

Meg was almost afraid to ask. "How do you m-mean?"

"He shot me, point blank, the blackguard. Cold-blooded as they come. *And* it's the arm with which I hold my whip. Never could ride as well after that. Indeed, you might say my present injury is down to him. Had my shoulder been in better order, I might have—"

"You surely can't blame Lord Allendale for your horse f-faltering at that fence!"

"I do blame him!" her father retorted. "For that and more. He's a conniving opportunist. Traits he's passed on to those sons of his, you can believe it."

She shook her head. "I d-don't. You've never even m-met Mr. Beresford."

"Ivo Beresford," he said scornfully. "Is that what he's called? I suppose you thought him the handsomest devil in five counties."

"He is handsome."

"Aye, I'll bet he is, the lustful dog. I know the look of him. Just like his father." His words dripped with contempt. "Stupid girl. To have your head turned by such a pathetic specimen of a gentleman."

Meg's **fingers** curled into fists in front of her. "You accuse him of n-not being a gentleman, and yet, you would address your own d-daughter in that fashion?"

"I'll address my own daughter as I see fit."

"You are unworthy, sir."

His gaze shot to hers. A vein pulsed in his forehead. "Tell me, then," he said in a tone of dangerous calm. "What was this golden prince like? What compliments did he ply you with to win your devotion? For you must be far gone indeed to have found your voice at last."

Heat burned in her face. "He isn't like th-that."

"You've met him but once and are already an authority?"

"No," she said. "I only listened to him." It wasn't a lie. She'd listened to Ivo on all the occasions they'd met. He was that energetic and engaging. Whenever he spoke, he held Meg in thrall.

Sir Frederick snorted. "He has something to say, does he? About me, I don't doubt."

"No indeed," she protested. "He n-never speaks of the past. N-Not hardly at all. It's the future he talks about."

"What is *that* supposed to mean? The future? What future?" Her father's eyes drooped under the weight of his sinking russet brows. "If you mean to tell me he's spun you some fool's story about his intentions toward you—"

"Why a f-fool's story?" she interjected before she could stop herself. "What's f-foolish in the idea that Mr. Beresford m-might have intentions toward me?"

"Many a rake has employed similar tactics in order to dishonor a girl. I won't have my daughter taken advantage of by any man, least of all a Beresford." He gripped his desk. "What lies has he told you? What promises has he made?"

Meg exhaled an exasperated breath. "You've g-got it all wrong. It's the railway he thinks of, not young ladies. That's the future he talked about at dinner. He spent most of the evening in discussion with Mr. Pinnock."

"Pinnock!"

"Mr. Beresford has already m-met with Mr. Standish and Mr. Horsley. They all agree with his p-plan to bring the railway to Maidenbridge. It only remains for you and Lord and Lady Allendale to lend your support."

Her father leaned back in his chair. "So, this is why he's paying you attention. He's using you to get to me."

Meg bristled with indignation. "It's n-not always about you! There are other concerns in the world. If you would b-but stop thinking of yourself for f-five minutes—"

"You mind your impertinent tongue, girl," he growled.

"It isn't impertinent to t-tell you to stop indulging your own vanity."

"By God, if this is a Beresford's influence—"

"It's a Burton-Smythe's influence!" Meg's temper exploded in a startling conflagration, burning away what remained of her timidity, and taking her stammer along with it. Before she knew it, she was on her feet. "*Your* blood is what runs in my veins, not Beresford blood. My temper is entirely owing to you. You passed it to me by birth and it's you who's provoking it!"

His brows elevated to his hairline.

She belatedly realized she was shouting. A dizzying sense of her own feminine power struck her. She felt a trifle giddy.

No one ever shouted at her father. Not even Roddy during his worst fits of temper. Indeed, Roddy had preferred to leave England entirely rather than stand up to Sir Frederick. That Meg should be the one to do so now, despite her years of timidity, was shocking to them both.

"I don't mean to be disobedient," she said, "but I won't let you bully me any longer. I am your daughter."

He stared at her as though seeing her for the first time. "So it would seem."

"And I am n-no fool," she added for good measure. "Though I *am* only just out of the schoolroom. And though I haven't seen anything of the world."

His mouth curled in a perturbed frown. He glanced down

at the letter he'd been writing. "This is to an employment agency in London. I write to inquire after another governess for you."

Meg's temper sputtered out like a vanquished candleflame. "Another governess?" She formed the hated words, but no sound came out to voice them.

"After learning of your dinner with that Beresford boy, it seemed to me you were in desperate need of one. Miss Adams has been gone but half a year, and look at you." He regarded her, his frown deepening. "Just look at you."

She unclenched her fists, using her damp palms to smooth her skirt. "Nothing is wrong with me. I am as God—and m-my family—has made me."

"So you are," he muttered. Abruptly, he crumpled up the letter.

Meg held her breath. She didn't dare ask his motives. And he made no effort to explain them.

"My leg is aching," he grumbled. "Have Church send for Spragg. The bottle of tonic he's given me has only a single drop remaining."

"Yes, f-father."

"As for that Beresford boy..." He tossed the crumpled letter into the hearth. It burst into flame, swiftly shriveling away to ash. "You may tell Colfax to send him to me after Christmas. I'll speak with him then. But not in a secretive roundabout fashion, with that damned vicar providing neutral ground. If young Ivo Beresford desires words with me, he can apply at the front door of Letchford Hall."

# Chapter Twelve

The next morning, the first flakes of snow fell on the frozen West Country landscape, as delicate as white gossamer feathers fluttering down to earth.

Ivo met Meg at the river. They didn't dismount this time. It was too cold for walking, much to Ivo's regret. He'd have liked to hold her hand again. To smell the faint fragrance of her rose perfume. Instead, he settled for a gallop across the moor, the two of them neck-and-neck, both laughing as the wind whipped at their faces.

It was only after they'd slowed to a walk to rest their horses that she told him about her interview with her father.

At least, she told him what she deemed fit to tell him. Ivo had the distinct suspicion the interview hadn't been as pleasant as she conveyed.

"So, he'll see me?" he asked.

"He will."

"All he requires is that I stop by the Hall?" It was hardly a concession. Indeed, it was what Ivo had intended to do in the first place.

"Yes. That's all. But it must be after Christmas. He enjoys

the holiday too much to allow commercial matters to intrude. He doesn't ever entertain business until after Twelfth Night."

"Who knew," Ivo murmured. "Sir Frederick is a jolly fellow after all."

Meg gave another short laugh. It was a soft, husky sound. A private laugh, just for the two of them. It sent a throb through Ivo's vitals to hear it.

"Not jolly, no," she said. "But he enjoys the pageantry of the holiday. And he likes when I play carols on the pianoforte."

"Do you play well?"

Meg guided her mare down the path that led back to the river. "Creditably well. Miss Adams taught me."

Ivo rode alongside her. He kept a strong contact on his reins, taking care to keep Snap from playfully nipping Rowena's neck. The mare didn't appreciate the stallion's overtures. She repeatedly warned him off with bared teeth and flattened ears.

"Your Miss Adams figures frequently in your stories," Ivo said.

"She was a good lady and a very dear friend," Meg replied. "Though she *was* only with me as a form of employment."

"When did your father hire her?"

"She came to Letchford Hall when I was but five years old. The day she left for Bath, I wept for hours in my room."

Ivo shot her a concerned glance. He didn't like to think of her weeping about anything. "I'm sorry to hear it."

Meg's face was still flushed from their gallop. A lock of red hair had worked free from her chignon to curl about her freckled cheek. Ivo's gaze was drawn to it relentlessly. His fingers itched to smooth it away.

A dangerous impulse.

It was a lover's liberty, not that of a friend. Only a

gentleman who had a lady's heart would make so free with her person.

Unaware of his attention, Meg absently brushed the stray lock from her face herself as they continued into the woods that bordered the river. Frost glittered on the branches of the trees and sparkled in the low-lying grasses.

"She gave me such good advice," she said. "I always knew where I was at when she was around."

"Could your father not have enticed her to remain in some other capacity? A lady's companion, perhaps?"

"My father had nothing to do with her leaving. Miss Adams had a distant family connection. A Mr. Philips. He was widowed two years ago and had a mind to remarry. They're to be wed in the spring. She traveled ahead to begin making arrangements with the gentleman's mother. Miss Adams is staying with the lady at her townhouse. I still write to her practically every day. I daresay she must be tired of my letters."

"Who could ever tire of hearing from you?"

"You're kind to say that—"

"There's no kindness in it." He paused, mouth tugging into a smile. "Did you realize, we've just had a whole conversation and nary a stammer to be found?"

Meg stilled on her mare. She plainly hadn't realized.

"You were right. It must only happen when you're nervous. Which means..." His smile broadened. "You're no longer nervous with me."

She bent her head. The rosy flush in her cheeks deepened. "I suppose n-not."

"But I'm making you nervous to mention it, aren't I? Never mind. I won't reference the subject again. We can pretend this exchange never happened."

Her pale blue eyes flickered with unwilling amusement. "Ivo..."

"Yes, I know. I'm odd. I won't apologize." He grinned.

"Tell me more about this Miss Adams of yours. Will you ever see her again?"

"I hope I will, when I go to B-Bath for my season."

Ivo's grin faded, his cheerful mood dwindling. He didn't want to contemplate Meg enjoying a season in Bath. Didn't want to envision the legion of suitors who would no doubt pay court to her there. For many, her fortune alone would be enough of an inducement to make their proposals. But she was beautiful, too, and modest and intelligent and—

"Do you ever visit Bath?" she asked offhandedly.

He shook his head. "Not since I returned from the Continent."

"It's—It's a lovely city, I've heard."

"Beautiful. Quite diverting, as well. There's a marvelous confectionary shop there, as I recall. Makes delicious marzipan." He glanced at her. "Do you like marzipan?"

"Very m-much. Our cook, Mrs. Stapleton, m-makes it every Christmas. She just finished a batch yesterday."

Ivo marked the return of her stammer. He wondered what he'd said to provoke it this time. They were only riding together quietly, not discussing anything distressing save for her season. And that was only distressing to him, truth be told.

He'd met many ladies during his travels. But the peculiar thumping of his heart and strange ache in his stomach had only emerged during his recent visits with Meg. By God, but he liked her. He wished they might be together like this always.

It was a foolish inclination. A boyish one, too. Nothing lasted forever.

He cleared his throat. "How are the, ah, decorations coming?"

"I'm n-nearly finished. Timothy and the footmen have helped bring in the pine boughs and other greenery. I've tied the holly and ivy with ribbon b-bows and frosted the leaves with a solution of alum and boiled water. And this afternoon, Mrs. Church is assisting me in gilding the fruit and nuts."

Ivo couldn't imagine decorating for Christmas with only the servants to help. It seemed a depressing way to usher in the holiday. "We've done nothing at Beasley yet," he said. "My family will see to it when they return."

"Could you not have the servants make things ready?"

"My parents would be offended if the servants attempted to decorate for them. We Beresfords prefer doing the job ourselves."

A troubled look came over her. She slowed her mare. "When will they be back?"

"Kate is expected on Friday. My parents the day after."

"Does that mean... Will we still b-be able to ride together?"

"Is that what's troubling you?"

"I m-merely thought—"

"Of course our rides can continue. Though not with the same frequency, I fear. My family keeps me woefully busy during the holidays. One of my siblings is always attaching themselves to my outings. It's difficult to escape Beasley without someone marking my whereabouts. But it's not impossible. Anyway, they're not to know you and I are meeting each other. Even if they did manage to discover it..." He trailed off with a frown.

The closer it came to his parents returning, the more Ivo was plagued by misgivings. Not about Meg. He had nothing to doubt about his friendship with her. It was explaining that friendship to his family that was the problem.

His mother might understand, but his father wouldn't. And James certainly wouldn't. Ivo didn't look forward to a season of tedious sermons from his straitlaced older brother.

"What?" Meg asked. "What would they d-do?"

Ivo gave her an eloquent grimace, more for humorous

effect than to alarm her. "Lecture me endlessly, that's all. It's nothing I can't withstand."

Meg didn't appear mollified. The same cloud of worry hung over her, darkening her face. "The quarrel b-between our families is decades' old. B-Both sides are f-firmly entrenched."

"Don't dwell on it," Ivo said. "I don't intend to. It's a habit, merely. And like all bad habits, must be broken eventually."

"My father claims your father shot him," she said.

Ivo started. "He *what?*"

"He says that Lord Allendale shot him in the shoulder."

Ivo instantly recollected the long-rumored duel between his father and Sir Frederick. "When did this supposedly happen? Was it before my parents married?"

"He didn't volunteer the circumstances. But they remain keen in his mind. His shoulder still pains him, you see. It has ever since I was a girl. I never knew the cause of it."

"My father has never mentioned any such thing."

"Would he?"

"Possibly not," Ivo allowed. "My parents are..." He hesitated over how best to describe his parents' still passionate love affair with each other. "They're, ah, very much consumed with their own interests. They rarely mention your father."

"He hasn't forgotten. He injured himself in a fall from his horse two years ago. He b-blames the weakness in his shoulder. Which m-means, he blames your father."

"Does he, just," Ivo mused.

"It's n-nonsensical, I know."

He looked at her as their horses walked on. "I begin to wonder if he hates us more than my family hates him."

"*Does* your family hate him?"

"I don't know. They must still feel something for him to have forbidden our association with your family for so long. It's dratted awkward, I must say."

"It is," she agreed. "I-I wouldn't like them to judge m-me on my f-father's past behavior."

He felt a surge of tenderness for her. "They wouldn't. They're reasonable people when it comes to it. And they love me. It must be enough that I l—" Ivo broke off abruptly, astonished by what he'd almost admitted. "I *like* you," he amended. "That's all that need be said on the matter."

A soft smile curved Meg's mouth. "I like you, too, Ivo."

He stretched out his hand to her across their horses. She took it without hesitation. He pressed her fingers warmly. "Then we're in accord."

"Perfect accord."

# Chapter Thirteen

Over the next week, as the weather grew colder and intermittent flurries of snow continued to fall, Meg met Ivo every morning by the icy river. They walked and rode, talked and laughed, and shared more than she could ever have imagined sharing with any gentleman, a Beresford least of all.

He always took her hand at least once during their meetings. Sometimes he winked at her and twice he'd kissed her gloved fingers. Nothing scandalous. And likely nothing very meaningful, except to her.

Meg treasured every touch and every glance. She memorized the deep rumble of his laugh. The way his gray eyes twinkled behind his spectacles. The way he listened to her with his whole attention, turning thoughtful when she was serious, and smiling broadly when she edged ahead of him during their impromptu races across the moors.

He let her win, of course, though he never said so. But Meg recognized it well enough. Rowena could never outpace Snap. She was a lazy creature at the best of times, with a gallop that had more in common with a canter. A safe mount, Meg's father had called her. Only fifteen and a half hands at the withers and eminently suitable for a lady.

"You can try Snap if you wish," Ivo said later that week, when the two of them had returned to the woods by Sefton Bridge after a rousing ride.

It was time to go home. They both of them knew it. They'd been out for over an hour and they didn't have the luxury of time. Not today. Dr. Spragg and one of his specialist associates was due at Letchford Hall and Lady Kate was arriving later this afternoon at Beasley Park. There was too much to be done.

But Meg wasn't ready to say goodbye just yet. Nor was Ivo, if his suggestion was any indication.

She brought Rowena to a halt beneath an old oak tree. "Ride Snap? You're not serious."

"Deadly serious." Ivo dismounted. He secured Snap to a tree. "Don't you want to know what it's like to go as fast as the wind?"

She smiled. "You and your obsession with speed. First trains and now—"

"You'll love it." He came to assist her down. His tone turned teasing as his hands closed around her corseted waist. "Come my girl, don't be shy."

She gripped his shoulders as he helped her to the ground. She was provoked into a laugh. "It's not shyness. It's common sense."

"Are you afraid Snap will be too much for you?"

Rowena stood untethered behind Meg. The mare's head hung and her eyes drooped. She was too tired from her exercise to roam.

"He *is* too much for me," Meg said. "He's nearly seventeen hands."

"Nonsense. A horse's height has nothing to do with his degree of difficulty under saddle. Anyway, you're as good a rider as I am. A firm leg and a soft contact and Snap will be butter in your hands." Ivo's own hands lingered at the swell of her hips.

Meg's heart skipped a beat as she gazed up at him, still smiling. Proximity hadn't cured her of the butterflies that materialized in her stomach whenever he touched her or looked at her that way. She doubted if it ever would.

He gazed back at her steadily, his own smile dimming the longer his hands remained. He'd never before held her for this long after helping her to dismount. Usually, he let her go the instant her feet were steady on the ground.

But today he was in a peculiar mood. He was looking at her so strangely. His spectacles glinted in the rays of cold winter sun that filtered through the oak's branches.

"Ivo," she said.

His throat bobbed on a swallow. "Yes?"

"Why don't you wear your spectacles all of the time?"

Her questions seemed to surprise him. What had he thought she was going to ask him?

"My spectacles?" He uttered a short laugh. "Vanity, I suppose."

"I d-don't believe it."

"It's true. It isn't easy being the least attractive member of a handsome family. I must compensate as best I can. If it means my vision must occasionally be blurry, then so be it."

She searched his face. "Who's said you're the least attractive?"

"My brothers, for a start. Plenty of young ladies, too. There's not a one of them who hasn't used their opportunity of meeting me to ask after my brother James. I'm practically invisible compared to all his splendor."

"I've n-never asked about Lord St. Clare."

His expression softened. "I know you haven't. Bless you for that."

She raised her hands to his forearms, squeezing them tightly. "You are handsome, Ivo. Indeed, I like you b-better with your spectacles."

"Do you?" His fingers curled at her hips. "Not as well as I like you, I'd wager."

"Now you're just being silly." She moved to step away from him, but he turned to follow, still holding her fast. Something behind Rowena seemed to catch his attention.

His mouth curled, his smile returning in a rush. "Look up, Meg."

"What is it?" She followed his gaze to the oak branch above. Her heart lurched.

A disconcerting note of huskiness infiltrated Ivo's deep voice. "It's mistletoe."

Meg was grateful for the support of his hands. She felt, rather suddenly, as though she might swoon. "I d-didn't know it grew here."

"Nor did I. You're not to think I persuaded you to dismount merely to have my wicked way with you."

She blushed fiercely.

"But," he added gravely, "the customs of the season must be respected."

Meg stared at him. She couldn't think. She couldn't breathe. One moment he was staring back at her, gray eyes glimmering with amusement. The next, that familiar gaze had grown uncommonly warm and serious, and then...

Oh, and then.

He was bending his head to kiss her.

---

Ivo's lips pressed gently against Meg's beneath the frost-covered sprig of wild mistletoe. A brief, chaste kiss.

The sort one would give a friend. That's what Ivo had intended.

But he wasn't prepared for the feel of her. The way her lush mouth softened beneath his, their breath mingling so sweetly. It was as intimate as an embrace, making his heart thunder and his blood surge with heat.

She smelled of rose water. Of snowflakes, starched petticoats, and the faint fragrance of the orange she'd eaten for breakfast. He tasted it on her lips. Both sweet and citrus tart.

His hands slid up to her waist. The bones of her riding stays creaked beneath the press of his fingers as he kissed her again, drawing another trembling sigh from her lips.

The soft curve of her bosom rose and fell against his chest. She gripped tight to his forearms. But she didn't recoil from him. She received his kiss with every sign of willingness. Of *pleasure.*

Two kisses might have led to three or more if Ivo hadn't regained mastery of himself. Drawing back, he pressed his cheek to hers as he caught his breath. The silkiness of her skin sent another rush of heat through his veins.

"Have I presumed too much?" He huffed an unsteady laugh. "Don't answer that. I know I have."

"I d-don't mind."

"I mind. This isn't why—" He stopped himself. "I'm sorry. I didn't mean to get so—"

*Bloody hell.*

He cursed his own inarticulateness. Had she any idea how that kiss had affected him? He suspected not. She was far too innocent.

"It's all right." Her hand fluttered to his jaw in a brief, conciliatory gesture. Her touch was infinitely gentle.

Ivo wished suddenly that he could feel the naked press of her fingers against his cheek. He was tempted—frighteningly tempted—to take hold of her hand and strip away her leather glove.

But he'd already dared enough.

Anything more and he may as well take himself straight off to Letchford Hall to apply to Sir Frederick for permission to wed his daughter. Indeed, only a rogue would trifle with a girl this way if he didn't intend to marry her.

"I'm sorry," he said again. This time, by some miracle, he managed to release her. Retreating several steps, he raked a hand through his hair. "I must blame the mistletoe. Potent stuff, that."

Meg didn't reply.

He rambled on, filling up the void between them, not entirely sure what he was saying. "Apparently even more potent in the wild. I haven't been this affected by the kind that's been cut, tied, and hung up in a doorway, that's for certain. It should be made illegal."

She bent her head.

His conscience was seized with guilt. "Meg—"

"I-I should get back," she said.

Guilt rapidly gave way to a sense of desperation. He masked it with a cheerful smile. No doubt it looked more like a grimace of pain. "Don't say I've scared you off?"

"N-No," she said. "Of course n-not."

He obviously had. He could have kicked himself for it.

After all the progress they'd made together. The friendship they'd developed during their rides and walks and endless conversations. Meg had come to trust him and he'd damaged that fragile trust by taking advantage of her like any scoundrel.

The mistletoe had been but a convenient excuse. The truth was, Ivo had been longing to kiss her for days.

Meg may not know it for a fact, but surely she recognized it on some level. Why else would she be so eager to leave?

She caught hold of Rowena's bridle. "It's only m-my

father," she stammered. "I c-can't miss his appointment with the d-doctor."

Ivo followed her back to her mare. "What about your ride on Snap?"

She drew up her reins. "Perhaps another d-day."

He was afraid to touch her again, but there was nothing for it except to help her mount. She couldn't manage it without his assistance. Taking hold of her waist, he tossed her back up into her sidesaddle as quickly as possible, trying to ignore the tantalizing feel of her.

"When?" he asked.

She glanced down at him as she arranged her habit skirts. "I b-beg your pardon?"

"When can we meet again?" He remained by Rowena's side, gazing up at Meg with unusual solemnity. "It can't be Saturday or Sunday. Not with my parents arriving. But next week, the moment I can get away, we can continue riding together as always."

"Everything just the same," she said quietly. It was both a statement and a question.

Ivo hastened to reassure her. "Exactly the same. This doesn't change anything, I promise you."

A flare of some unnamable emotion flickered in Meg's eyes. It was gone in an instant, replaced by an equally unreadable look. "No," she said. "I know it doesn't."

# Chapter Fourteen

"Is that everything?" Ivo wandered around Ruggiero's empty bedchamber, eyes alert for stray books or any lingering scrap of clothing.

"It is, sir." Ruggiero fastened his battered trunk. "Mr. Partridge saw to it while you were out riding."

"Did he?" Ivo murmured. If Partridge had been responsible for gathering the signore's effects, one could be sure that, once the man departed Beasley Park, no traces of him would remain. "God bless Partridge."

"Aye, sir," Ruggiero agreed. "A most efficient man."

A most efficient man who had presently absented himself.

Ivo had returned from his tumultuous meeting with Meg to find the signore preparing to leave, with no trace of Partridge in sight.

Ruggiero's departure wasn't entirely a surprise. Pinnock had made him an offer of employment several days ago. The signore had accepted, of course. Ivo had heartily encouraged him to do so. But now...

He leaned back against the window embrasure. Folding his arms, he regarded his former guide with decidedly mixed feelings. As irritating as Ruggiero could be, and as aggravating his vices, Ivo felt a distinct responsibility for the man. "You're certain this position will suit?"

"Is good place with Mr. Pinnock." Ruggiero paused. A sheepish smile brushed his lips. "It *is* a good place," he amended. "Steady work."

"Respectable work. He won't tolerate any nonsense."

"This I know."

"If the wine tempts you again..."

"It won't." Ruggiero retrieved his leather portmanteau from the bench at the end of the bed and carried it to join his trunk by the chamber door. "I drink when I'm missing the way it was. You know. In the before times."

Ivo nodded in grim understanding. Ruggiero had suffered mightily being left impoverished and stranded in a country far from home. A more resourceful—and perhaps less emotional—man might have made a success of it. But the signore had felt the sadness of his alteration in circumstances too keenly to bear without the assistance of drink. After so many years in exile, it was a miracle he'd survived his own weaknesses.

"What's to prevent you missing the way it was when you're teaching Mr. Pinnock's children?" Ivo asked.

"I have a place now," Ruggiero said. "No need to be melancholy. Mr. Pinnock...he has many sons. All ages."

"Quite so. Play your cards right, and you're guaranteed a decade of employment at least. And a glowing reference afterward, I endeavor to hope."

"I'll make a success of it."

"I know you will," Ivo said. "You're more than your circumstances."

Ruggiero's eyes glistened with repressed emotion. "That's what you told me in Rome."

"I meant it. Humans have an infinite capacity for change. We've no need to fear it. To change is to survive."

"As you say. We must look to the future." Smoothing his brown cloth frock coat, Ruggiero drew himself up with dignity. "I'll pay you back the cost of my passage with my first wages."

Ivo straightened from the window. "Don't be stupid. In any event, I consider it an investment. In ten years' time, I'll likely have children of my own. They'll need to learn their Latin and Italian. Keep yourself in good order and who knows? You might find yourself returning to my employment."

Ruggiero's smile broadened into a grin. "I give you my blessing for strong sons."

"It's the girls who are strong in my family. I fear the men are merely much put upon. Which reminds me." Ivo drew out his pocket watch and checked the time. "Providing the weather holds, my sister's coach should arrive by five."

"Pity I'll miss her."

"Yes," Ivo said dryly. "A great pity."

---

*THIS DOESN'T CHANGE ANYTHING, I PROMISE YOU.*

Meg spent the afternoon seated beside Mrs. Church and two of the housemaids in the Letchford Hall kitchen, Ivo's parting assurance playing over and over in her head.

He'd kissed her.

He'd kissed her.

Yet, he'd said it didn't change anything. And perhaps it hadn't, for him. But for Meg, it had changed *everything*.

She'd realized as his lips had first brushed over hers, that she was falling in love with him.

Or perhaps she'd already fallen.

It had happened so gradually she didn't know where it had begun. One moment she was stammering and blushing at him, dazzled by his beauty, and the next they were laughing and confiding in each other. Clasping gloved hands and exchanging confidences.

He was her friend. Of that she was certain. But somewhere along the way, he'd become something more. Not just a romantic daydream come to life, but a bespectacled, flesh-and-blood gentleman who held her trembling heart in his palm.

She felt all at once the full, stark vulnerability of her position. To unabashedly adore someone who didn't adore her in return. It made her want to weep. To rage. To pour out her painful insecurities to a friend who might offer their advice and consolation.

Oh, but she wished Miss Adams was here!

"Have a care, miss," one of the maids said. "You'll gild your fingers."

Meg started. She'd been so lost in her own melancholy ruminations that she'd let the goldleaf she was using to wrap acorns flake off all over her hands. "Oh dear. Thank you, Lucy. How c-clumsy of me."

Mrs. Church shot Meg a narrow look as she gilded a walnut. "You're in a world of your own today," she remarked. "Have been ever since you returned from your ride."

Meg willed herself not to blush under the old housekeeper's scrutiny. "I have m-many things on my mind. My father's illness chief among them."

It was partially true. The specialist physician that Dr. Spragg had brought with him earlier had only served to reiterate Dr. Spragg's recommendations. Worse, he'd advised an even stricter diet for Sir Frederick, with no alcohol, sweets, or red meats at all.

Meg's father hadn't been best pleased. He'd quarreled with

both gentlemen, questioning their education, their breeding, and their basic good sense. Neither man had been able to stand up to him. Instead, they'd reserved their stern words and dire warnings for Meg. As if she could exert any influence!

"Huh," Mrs. Church gave a doubtful grunt. She added another perfectly gilded nut to the row she'd already completed. "He'll not get any better till he permits Cook to alter his menu."

Mrs. Stapleton nodded from her place by the stove where she stood, stirring a pot of leek soup. "A haunch of venison, that's what he's requested for dinner. Venison, I tell you! I had four chickens ready, and then he says—"

"There is to be no venison," Meg said. "No red meat whatsoever. The doctor commanded it."

"I don't answer to the doctor, miss," the old cook replied.

"You will answer to me," Meg replied in a voice of surprising calm.

The housekeeper and cook exchanged an astonished glance.

Mrs. Church turned to Meg. Her mouth compressed in a line. "We answer to Sir Frederick, as we always have. He's master here."

Setting aside her work, Meg rose from the table. "And I am mistress," she said. "No venison, Mrs. Stapleton. We will adhere to Dr. Spragg's menu."

Mrs. Stapleton sputtered. "But Sir Frederick—"

"I will inform my father." Meg felt the weight of the servants' stares as she departed the kitchen. Let them gawp! She didn't have to answer to anyone save her father. And she wouldn't defer to him either, not if he persisted in being unreasonable.

She'd promised herself she'd cease fearing his temper—*and* his judgment of her. It was a difficult habit to break, but one she'd been endeavoring daily to overcome. The grudging respect he'd shown her since their last quarrel had only served to encourage her.

Her father would never admit it, but he admired strength, even if it *was* possessed by a lowly female. Knowing that emboldened her to seek him out, despite knowing it would only lead to another confrontation.

Sir Frederick was in his bedchamber, still sulking after the doctors' visit. Clad in his dressing gown, he sat in a chair by the window, his leg elevated on a tufted velvet ottoman. An edition of the *Times* lay spread across his lap unread as he dozed.

She rapped once at the half-open door. "Father?"

He snuffled awake. "What's that?"

"It's only m-me."

His brows sank as Meg entered and crossed the room to join him. "What do you want? Come to repeat Spragg's lectures, have you?"

"No indeed." She stopped by the window. The chill weather had iced over the glass at the corners, making the panes appear as though they were set in frosty-white frames. "I've only c-come to tell you that I've given orders to the kitchen."

He went rigid with ready anger. "You? Giving orders in *my* kitchen?"

"My kitchen as well," Meg said. She repeated what she'd told the servants, "I am m-mistress here."

He glared at her in blank amazement, too taken aback by the declaration to formulate a quick reply.

She took full advantage. "It's m-my duty to see to the running of the household, n-not Mrs. Church's. The housekeeper and c-cook must properly consult with me."

Her father's face mottled with outrage. "Who says so? Miss Adams again? Drat her interference!"

"Miss Adams didn't invent the rules. She m-merely taught

them to me. And she's n-not wrong, is she? As your daughter—"

"*As my daughter*, you will obey me." He refolded his newspaper, snapping the pages with uncommon force. "I see what you're about. All this rigmarole is a way of circumventing my orders in the kitchen. You mean to starve me as Spragg and his brainless compatriot would have you do. But starvation is no cure, my girl, regardless of what these supposed medical men say."

"You shan't starve, father," Meg said. "And you shan't die."

A sudden spasm of emotion flashed across her father's face. His voice took on a gruff undertone. "I'll wager you're eager to see me suffer, though, aren't you? After I forbade you my carriage—"

"Don't talk n-nonsense." She sank down on the ottoman next to his leg, careful not to touch his bandaged calf. Her skirts pooled around her slippered feet. "It was unfair of you to forbid me the carriage, but that isn't why you m-must let me take charge. It's because I am the only lady in the household. And I am a Burton-Smythe. You diminish us both by investing Mrs. Church with so m-much power."

"Diminish myself? Rubbish."

"It isn't rubbish. Mrs. Church begins to believe she has m-more rights to Letchford Hall than I do. The other servants follow her lead. What would Roddy think were he to return home and find a housekeeper acting as m-mistress here?"

Her father scowled. But this time he didn't argue. On the contrary, he seemed unsettled by her argument. It was plainly one he hadn't thought of before. "Have you heard from your brother?"

"No. Not in ages." She paused. "Have you?"

"He applies to me for funds, the bounder. Racking up debts all over Europe, with his degenerate friends. The only time he writes is to inquire about advances on his quarterly allowance. That's all the respect he shows me—the same esteem he'd hold for a banker."

Meg felt a twinge of sorrow. She and Roddy had never been close, but he was still her brother. She'd rather he returned to Somerset than traipse the Continent for years on end without a thought for his duty. "I'm sorry for it. I don't know why he won't come home."

"Oh, he'll return soon enough. The moment I die, he'll be on the next steamer from France."

Meg couldn't dispute it. Roddy had always been keen to take over as head of the family. Unfortunately, he had no head for business, only a reckless enjoyment of money. Once in his grasp, she didn't doubt but that he'd run the estate straight into the ground. "You shan't die, father," she said again. "But you m-must change."

Her father scoffed.

"You must," she insisted. "Beginning with your diet."

He rubbed his sullen brow as though staving off a headache. "You'd have me celebrate the holidays with no roast beef? No plum pudding?"

"Christmas isn't about pudding," she said. "It's about family. We must find joy in each other."

He gave a hoarse bark of derisive laughter.

She gazed at him in mute entreaty.

His laugh dwindled. A look of dawning comprehension came over him. "By God. You're serious."

"I am," she said. "M-Mother is dead. Roddy is gone. We've only each other."

He examined her face. "What in blazes has brought on this sentimentalism? You're not ill, I trust?"

"It's n-not an illness. It's Christmas. I don't want to spend it alone."

# Chapter Fifteen

"Where are you off to so early?" Jack Beresford entered the stone stables as Ivo was saddling Snap.

The youngest of Ivo's brothers, he was tall, blond, and possessed of the Beresford family's famous good looks. He was also possessed of the Beresfords' notoriously competitive spirit.

"I thought we might have a race," he said.

"Not today." Ivo tightened the girth on his saddle. "I've an appointment to keep."

"An appointment with whom?"

"A friend."

"Ah. A friend." Jack grinned. "Say no more."

"It's not like that." Ivo went to fetch Snap's bridle.

"If you say so." Jack followed him. "It certainly explains why you've been in such a foul mood since our return home."

Ivo didn't like to admit how right his brother was.

It had been six days since he'd last seen Meg. Six days since their kiss. A damnable way to leave things. He'd wanted to ride out to meet her the very next morning. But Kate's arrival had prevented it. His parents' and brothers' arrival the following day had further delayed Ivo's plans.

Not a moment seemed to pass when he wasn't importuned by one of his siblings.

"I'm not used to so much excitement anymore." Ivo returned to bridle Snap. He eased the bit into the stallion's mouth, sliding the headpiece over his ears. "You, James, and Kate have been at me since you came home. I've not had a moment's peace."

"You've been gone two years. We're merely making up for lost time."

"By deviling me to death?"

"Naturally." Jack scratched Snap's neck. "Who is this friend? Is she pretty?"

"*She's* none of your business." Ivo lowered the stirrups on his saddle. The leathers snapped sharply. "And I don't admit that it *is* a she."

Jack was unconvinced. "Have a care, big brother. Not all the young ladies hereabouts are pure as the driven snow. You'd best consult me before pledging your affections, lest you end up in the clutches of some conniving wench who's already had a go at me and James."

"How flattering."

"Not saying you're third best, but—"

"Quite."

"You're still my brother. Don't like to see you getting mixed up with anyone inappropriate."

Ivo glared at him across Snap's withers. "Like who for example?"

Jack shrugged. "I'm not so ungentlemanly as to name names, but..." His mouth quirked. "There are a few tradesmen's daughters who are no better than they ought to be."

"I'm not looking to marry anyone," Ivo said.

"That's a relief. It's Kate who's expected to make the first match. Then James, of course. Pity she's unmarriable and he's so blasted picky. By the time the pair of them come to the point with anyone, you and I will be past it."

Ivo vaulted into his saddle. "Are you quite finished?"

"Are you sure you don't want to race?"

"Another day, Jack. Now let me go." Ivo didn't wait for permission. He trotted out of the stable, exiting the yard through the low gate that led to the pasture. He prayed Jack wouldn't follow him.

Tradesmen's daughters? Good lord. During Ivo's two years away, it appeared that his younger brother had become the village lothario. And here Ivo was worried about harming the family name by an association with a Burton-Smythe! God help Jack if he got a local girl in trouble.

A perilous wind nipped at Ivo's face as he cantered toward Sefton Bridge. Though the snow hadn't fully set in yet, the weather had grown colder with each passing day, frosting the brown hills with ice and freezing over the river. Soon winter would come in earnest, blanketing the whole of Somerset in white. But not yet. Not until after Christmas, Ivo suspected.

Arriving at the river, he rode along the path through the trees for nearly half an hour, both his breath and Snap's gusting clouds of steam in the cold air, before Meg finally appeared.

She was riding toward the bridge, bundled up in her brown wool habit with the velvet collar. Absent her riding hat, her plaited red hair was left on full view to gleam in the winter sun.

His heart stopped to see her.

But she didn't see him. Arriving at the water, she hopped off her mare and tied her loosely to a tree. Then, giving her skirts a shake, she made for the clapper bridge with single-minded intention.

*What the devil?*

Ivo was off Snap in a flash. "Meg!"

She jolted to a halt, one booted foot on the stones. Her eyes widened. "*Ivo.*"

He advanced on her. "You don't mean to cross the bridge, do you?"

Her shoulders were set. "As you see."

"What in God's name for?"

"Because I can." She climbed up onto the first granite plank.

"Wait!" He strode to join her. "If you must do it, let me help you."

"I don't require your help. I can do it on my own." She kept walking. The frozen river glittered menacingly beneath her.

Ivo's pulse skittered with alarm. He didn't want to scare her, but if she slipped and fell—and she very well might given the slickness of the icy stones—she could come to genuine harm. "Meg—"

"Please stop talking," she said. "You're only distracting me."

Ivo's hands clenched into fists at his sides. She was being reckless. Careless. Anyone could have told her not to cross the bridge in this weather. One wrong move and she'd fall straight through the ice and end up trapped underneath it.

Good God! She'd been intending to cross the bridge before she'd known he was there! Had an accident happened, she'd have been all alone, left to the mercy of mother nature—who had no mercy at all in Ivo's experience.

Her boot slid dangerously on the plank an instant before she reached the other side. Recovering her balance, she hopped down onto the opposite bank.

Ivo exhaled the breath he'd been holding. "You madwoman!"

She flashed him a roguish smile. Her cheeks had a beautiful cold-weather flush. "I'm halfway safe!" she called back. "And so is my soul!"

He laughed in spite of himself. "Can you make it back without assistance?"

"I can." She quickly put action to word. In minutes, she'd once again successfully traversed the frozen river, returning safely to the bank.

Ivo took her hand without asking permission. He helped her down from the stones, though she clearly didn't need him to. "Why would you do that?"

"This isn't the first time," Meg said. "I've been doing it every day since last we met."

He was appalled. "What on earth for?"

"It's a challenge I've set myself. You were right, you know. Every time I do it, I feel stronger."

"That's laudable, but..." He retained her hand. "The bridge is dangerous when the weather turns colder. I'd really rather you didn't attempt to cross it again unless I'm here."

She slipped her hand from his. "What have you t-to d-do with it?"

It was an airy, unconcerned question. Or so she must have intended.

Her stammer gave her away.

The guilt Ivo had been experiencing since he'd kissed her returned in a violent rush. He felt like the veriest cad. "I care about you," he said. "Obviously."

"Because we're friends."

"Exactly."

"Do you wrap all your friends in c-cotton wool?"

"No, but—"

"I'm p-perfectly capable of looking after m-myself." She climbed back up the bank. "As I've just proved."

He trailed after her, belatedly registering something she'd said. "You've come back here every day since last we met?"

Her frame betrayed a faint stiffness. She stopped to stand by Rowena.

Ivo hadn't thought he could feel any worse. "You weren't waiting for me, were you?"

"N-No. I knew you couldn't come."

"Then why—"

"I was riding here long b-before our acquaintance. I shan't stop n-now you're gone."

"I'm not gone," he said. "I wanted to come sooner. I thought I'd be able to earlier, but my brothers and sister are as persistent as deranged gnats. It's taken me days to break free of them. Even this morning, Jack pursued me to the stables. He wanted to ride with me. I told him no."

"Is th-that all you told him?"

"I said I was meeting a friend."

Meg absently stroked Rowena's neck. "You had b-better catch Snap before he runs away."

The stallion had wandered up the bank. He was standing along the edge of the trees, his nose to the wind.

Ivo cursed vividly. He stalked off to catch his horse. When he returned with him, Meg was already back up on her mare. She must have used a fallen log to mount.

Worse and worse.

Clearly, she still hadn't forgiven him for taking liberties.

A knot formed in Ivo's stomach. He didn't know if it would be better to address the subject or to ignore it. The latter seemed the wiser course. After all, he'd already apologized and promised her their friendship would remain unchanged. What more could he say to reassure her?

Placing his booted foot into the stirrup, he swung into his saddle. He brought Snap up alongside Rowena. "Shall we ride together on the moors?"

"I'm riding back toward the Hall." She kicked her mare into a walk.

Ivo wasn't so easily put off. "Then I'll ride with you," he said, following her. "Perhaps by the time we reach Letchford Hall your temper will have cooled."

She cast him a sidelong glance. "I'm n-not angry with you."

"No?"

"I don't get angry."

His brows lifted.

"Even though I *am* a B-Burton-Smythe," she added. "My f-father's temper is abhorrent to me."

"Nothing wrong with a bit of temper. Anger doesn't frighten me." Ivo paused. "Losing your friendship does."

She looked at him again. This time their gazes held.

"Please don't be cross with me, Meg," he begged.

Her face softened. "Ivo—"

"I did try to come."

She sighed. "It's n-not that. I knew you wouldn't be free once your family returned."

"Then what?" he asked. "You're not still upset about that stupid kiss under the mistletoe?"

She ducked her head. "N-Not upset, no."

"Thank heaven for that." He gave a rueful grimace. "I've been raking myself over the coals since we parted. I'd rather anything than upset you. Indeed, I nearly wrote to you on Saturday to offer my apologies again, but... I daresay that would have done more harm than good."

Meg smiled slightly. "Very p-probably. Miss Adams says a gentleman shouldn't write an unmarried young lady. N-Not even one who is a f-friend and only a friend."

"Miss Adams is right. Still, one can't live the whole of one's life by the rules in an etiquette manual. My sister doesn't, nor do my brothers. Nor do my parents, come to that. How boring it would be if we all did."

"Is your f-family well?" she asked as they ascended the rise.

"Tolerably so. My sister has returned from London in good order, and my brothers are much as I remember them."

To be sure, both James and Jack looked the same as when Ivo had left home, though certainly taller and possessed of more muscles. As for Kate, her time in London hadn't resulted in an engagement, but it did appear to have had an appreciable effect on her ladylike decorum. She'd been crocheting something when Ivo had left the house, much to his dismay.

"Kate will be returning to town in the new year," Ivo said. "She has a particular ball to attend in February, after which she'll stay on for another season. I'm making the most of her company while I can."

"What of your p-parents?" Meg asked.

"In good health," Ivo said. "They're still settling in. I've yet to find a moment to talk to my father about the railway."

It was a source of some frustration. That, and—admittedly—no little relief. Ivo had a suspicion that it would be better to speak with Sir Frederick first. And that couldn't be done until after Twelfth Night. Until then, Ivo's business plans were in limbo.

"I expect he'll hear about it eventually," Meg said. "From the vicar. Or from Mr. P-Pinnock, Mr. Standish, or Mr. Horsley."

Ivo had considered that possibility. "I doubt it. He's too busy to tolerate company at present. And anyway, Pinnock, Standish, and Horsley would never call on him. My father isn't overly fond of the villagers in Maidenbridge. It's *your* father the tradesmen look to." He squinted into the sun. "How is he, by the way? Still plagued by his gout?"

"Endlessly. Though I d-do have him on a n-new regime. He won't admit to it, but he seems to be a little b-better."

"I'm pleased to hear it." He glanced at her. "Will he be well enough to make merry with you at Christmas?"

"That may prove difficult," Meg said.

"Now *that* I'm not pleased to hear," Ivo said. "I don't want you to be on your own. Not at this time of year. It's inhuman."

"It's what I'm used to. One c-can get used to practically anything, I find."

"How extraordinarily depressing."

"I d-don't think so."

"Poor little thing," he teased. "You don't know any better."

Her lips quivered with unwilling humor. "I'm n-neither poor, nor little."

"Littler than me, my girl. I have a mind to spirit you away somewhere more cheerful. Bath perhaps." He flashed her a roguish smile. "What do you say to that? We could visit the confectioner and dine on marzipan and iced ginger cakes."

She smiled in return, beguiled by the fantasy. "I could visit Miss Adams."

"Quite right. If we're going to dream, why hold ourselves back?"

Her smile dimmed a little. "It is a lovely dream. But only a d-dream, isn't it? We're not likely to see Bath together."

Ivo didn't answer. Not directly. He didn't want to make her any promises. He was certainly in no position to do so. "When the railway comes, a journey to Bath will be no more trouble than a carriage drive to Taunton. Everyone will see it then."

She briefly turned away from him. "I pray the railway will c-come soon."

"So do I. Until then, we must think of another way to keep you from being alone at Christmas."

"Oh b-but I won't be." Her smile returned, a tad cautious, as though in contemplation of an event of decidedly mixed happiness. "My father isn't in a m-merry mood, to be sure, but he has promised to spend m-more time with me."

Ivo pulled a face. "I don't know if that's better or worse than a solitary holiday."

"Better, I hope. Though...n-not wholly comfortable, I expect."

They both laughed.

Letchford Hall loomed in the distance—a sprawling baroque monstrosity made of red brick. It was the closest Ivo had ridden to the place in an age. It was just as imposing and isolated as he remembered from his boyhood. An ogre's castle. That's how he'd thought of it. A place one avoided at all costs.

"I should go the rest of the way alone," Meg said.

Ivo reined in Snap. "Of course."

"Thank you for accompanying me this far."

"It was my pleasure. Will you...that is... I don't expect I can get away again until after Christmas. Shall we promise to meet for a ride in January?"

Her brows notched. "You're c-calling on my father then, are you not?"

"I plan to."

"Then we may f-forego the ride." She turned her mare toward home, kicking her into a trot. "It will be too c-cold anyway. I can't keep taking Rowena out in this weather."

"What do you suggest?" he asked as she rode off. And then, in vague desperation: "I must see you again!"

Meg glanced back at him over her shoulder, her beautiful face aglow. "You will. When you come to the Hall, I shall give you tea and cake!"

His face spread into a grin as she cantered away.

When she'd disappeared, Ivo turned Snap back toward the main road, still smiling like a besotted fool. Now he was alone, there was no reason to skulk in the woods or creep along desolate moorland paths. There was no danger of anyone observing him with the daughter of his parents' enemy. He trotted in plain view, back toward Beasley Park.

He'd gone no more than a short distance, approaching the crossroads to the village, when a grand, black lacquered carriage rolled through the intersection. It stopped in the middle of the path, blocking Ivo's way. The Earl of Allendale's golden crest glimmered on the door.

Ivo hauled Snap to an abrupt halt. The stallion stamped his hooves in protest.

The carriage window lowered and James Beresford, Viscount St. Clare looked out with a glacial stare. "Ivo."

Ivo's stomach fell to his boots. "James."

A young groom hopped down from the backboard to take hold of Snap's bridle. It was Andrew Cole. He cast Ivo an apologetic glance as he gripped the reins, preventing Ivo from riding off.

"Dismount," James said to Ivo. "And get in. Andrew can take your stallion back to Beasley."

"Like hell," Ivo retorted. "I'm in no mood to talk with you."

"*I'm* going to talk," James said. "You're going to listen."

# Chapter Sixteen

Ivo sank down across from his brother onto the velvet-upholstered seat of their parents' carriage. James had always been high-handed and officious, but this was something else. Indeed, his face was as coldly implacable as their father's sometimes was when he was obliged to deal harshly with someone.

Ivo didn't like it one bit. James may be older, but he wasn't *that* much older. He was only five and twenty, for God's sake. Ivo glared at him. "Were you following me?"

"Don't insult me," James said. He was dressed in a dark suit and an immaculately tied black cravat. It stood in stark contrast to Ivo's own ensemble of rumpled greatcoat, horse-hair-covered breeches, and muddy top-boots.

During all the years Ivo had known his brother, he'd rarely seen him out of countenance. James wore his clothes—and his familial dignity—like a suit of armor. On returning from his grand tour, Ivo had hoped to find his brother had changed. And James *had* changed. For the worse, it seemed. He was, if possible, even more frozen in ice than he'd been when Ivo had left England two years ago.

James rapped once at the ceiling, signaling the coachman to drive on. "I had no need to follow you," he said. "I already knew where you were headed."

A bolt of surprise rattled Ivo's composure. He quickly recovered himself. "Ballocks."

"You and Miss Burton-Smythe have been meeting each other all month, I take it."

This time, Ivo could think of nothing to say. He stared at his brother in blank astonishment.

"Partridge informed me," James said.

Had Ivo received a blow, it couldn't have hurt as deeply. His own valet had betrayed him? Bloody hell. "He would never. He's too loyal."

"He *is* loyal," James said. "To father."

"Then why didn't he go to father?"

"Because he's not heartless."

"I'd rather he'd told father than you," Ivo said sourly.

"No," James said. "Mother and father aren't going to hear of this. We're going to sort it right now."

The statement sounded very much like a threat.

Ivo might once have been intimidated by it. In boyhood, his brother had been a dominant force in his life. But Ivo wasn't the same lad who had left home two years ago. He'd seen something of the world. He had thoughts and opinions of his own. Who he consorted with—who he cared about— was none of James's affair.

"There's nothing to be sorted," he said.

"Have you made her any promises?" James asked.

"I don't know what you're talking about."

"Because if you have...I must tell you that you risk being sued for breach of promise."

"*What—?*"

"Under no circumstances will you be permitted to form an alliance with that family. Not if I have anything to say about it."

Ivo's temper rose swiftly. "You may say what you like. No one's stopping you."

"Only a scoundrel would inflict a connection with the Burton-Smythes on mother. If you knew the extent of the bad blood between our families—"

"Yes, I know. We hate each other. They abhor us and we despise them, and so it's always been and so it must continue. I comprehend that much. But however justified the cause of the quarrel, it's in the past."

"Our parents haven't forgotten. Nor has Sir Frederick, you may depend on it."

"I don't give a toss for Sir Frederick. As for mother and father..." Removing his tall beaver hat, Ivo raked his fingers through his hair. "Anyway, I don't admit to having made any promises. I'm not a fool, James."

"No, indeed. You've only been meeting the girl in secret for weeks. Laughing with her. Smiling."

Ivo scowled at him. Dash it all, how much had his brother observed today? "Is laughing with a girl a crime now?"

"Not if it's done in the proper sphere. With the blacksmith's daughter or one of the other village tarts."

"Tarts, are they?"

"Girls who know how to play the game, not young ladies who consider a solitary pleasantry tantamount to a declaration of intent. Unless, of course, you consider Miss Burton-Smythe to be a member of the former class?"

"Don't you *dare* compare Meg to a West Country lightskirt," Ivo growled.

Something dangerous flickered in James's glacial gaze. "By God, Ivo. Don't tell me your heart is engaged."

A muscle ticked in Ivo's cheek. He hadn't realized how hard he'd been clenching his jaw. "And what if it was?"

"I wouldn't believe it. For if you've done this thing, then you must have no heart at all."

The carriage rolled on at a steady pace, the interior of it crackling with palpable animosity. They weren't traveling toward Beasley Park. They were taking a circuitous path around the estate. A journey that, no doubt, wouldn't end until James was convinced that Ivo would give up his association with Meg.

All that remained was for Ivo to convince him. It was no easy task. Ivo had never been as adept at disguising his feelings as his older brother.

Relaxing his jaw, he leaned back in his seat with a hollow laugh. As an effort at subterfuge, it fell utterly flat. "This is too Shakespearean," he said. "Next you'll be droning on about ancient grudges leading to new mutinies."

"It's no joke."

"Then what is it?" Ivo asked. "I know mother refused Sir Frederick in order to marry father. And I know they fought over her. It was a duel, I suppose."

James gave him an alert look. "Who told you that?"

"There have long been whispers of a duel. I didn't fully credit them until now. Apparently, our father shot Sir Frederick in the shoulder."

"*Who* told you that?"

"Miss Burton-Smythe," Ivo admitted.

James's gray eyes smoldered. "This is exactly why you shouldn't be speaking to her."

"Yes. I see. Better I be kept in complete ignorance."

"You're not ignorant. You know the substance of the feud. It should be enough."

"It isn't. Not when it begins to impact the future of an innocent young lady. It's one thing to shun Sir Frederick because of his past actions, but to include his daughter in the grudge, as though her father's sins somehow accrue to her—"

"You can't separate the two of them. An association with the one must naturally lead to an association with the other. Sir Frederick won't accept it any more than we will."

"*We*?" Ivo repeated. "You don't speak for everyone in the family, James."

"Do you imagine this won't hurt the family?" James asked. "That Sir Frederick won't start spewing his lies again? Telling anyone who'll listen that father has no right to hold the title? All you're doing is hitting a hornet's nest. It's *that* which should concern you."

"It does. But not as much as it concerns you, apparently." Ivo's eyes narrowed. "Which makes me wonder, why do you seem to know so much more about the past than Jack and Kate and me? Merely because you're the oldest and an absolute pain in everybody's arse?"

"I'm the heir," James said simply.

"Ah yes. Of course. That old justification. Well let me take leave to inform you, my Lord St. Clare, that I am *not* the heir. I am my own man, with my own means, forging my own path in this life. If I choose to go riding with a girl then I'll damned well go riding with her. I don't care if she's a goddess, a goblin, or a blasted Grecian fury."

"A goddess," James murmured. "I see."

A prickle of heat crept up Ivo's neck. He was silent for a time. And then: "You would like her."

James looked at him steadily. "It doesn't matter."

"She's a good person. A sweet, gentle person."

"It. Doesn't. Matter."

Anguish twisted in Ivo's gut. "Oh, doesn't it, just?"

"You're not to see her anymore. That's an end to it."

"By your command?"

"Yes."

"But you don't command me, James."

"Try me, Ivo," James said. "You won't like how this ends."

Ivo's jaw clenched harder. In that moment, he could have happily throttled his brother. Someone needed to.

Though it was doubtful there was a gentleman alive who could best the insufferable heir apparent. James may be a sentient block of ice, but he was fit and capable, as likely to level an opponent with a punishing blow as with the Beresfords' legendary skill with a pistol.

No. If ever anyone was to knock him down, it likely wouldn't be a man.

"Do you have something else you wish to say to me?" James asked mildly, appearing to comprehend the violent trend of his younger brother's thoughts.

"Only this," Ivo replied. "I hope to God that one day— and I pray it will be soon—you meet a lady who knocks you for six. An entirely inappropriate, unsuitable female who turns your world upside down and wipes that blasted overconfident look from your face once and for all."

James was unmoved. "I look forward to making her acquaintance." He rapped hard on the ceiling of the carriage again. "Take us back to Beasley!"

# Chapter Seventeen

M eg celebrated Christmas with her father in the pine-bough and holly-and-ivy festooned drawing room of Letchford Hall at half past ten the following Monday. There, she gave him the silver tobacco box she'd purchased for him and received his single gift in return.

She looked up at him after opening it. "Figured silk?"

Her father was seated across from her in a wingchair Mrs. Church had arranged for him by the blazing fire. His thick, carved ebony cane leaned beside him.

He'd made an effort this morning, combing his graying red hair into order and abandoning his dressing gown in favor of a deep green frock coat and dark trousers. It had taken a toll. There was a paleness to his ruddy features and a glimmer of sweat on his brow. Though his health was improving, he had a long way to go yet. Descending the stairs from his rooms was still a trial, even with the assistance of his cane and two of the footmen.

"French silk," he said. "I'm assured it's the latest thing for young ladies."

Meg withdrew the folded fabric from the box. Pale apricot

in color, with a finely wrought floral pattern of darker apricot sprigs, it was easily more than ten yards altogether. "Assured by whom?"

"One of my correspondents in town. Claims this weave is being used by the best modistes in London and Paris at the moment to outfit ladies of fashion."

She ran her fingers over the silk, marveling at the feel of it and the way it shimmered softly under her hand. "What a beautiful color it has. There's almost a golden hue in the light." She looked up at him, offering a tentative smile. "Thank you, father."

He inclined his head. His own gift sat on the inlaid table beside his wingchair. He'd been measurably appreciative of it, though his gratitude hadn't prevented him from pointing out that Dr. Spragg had forbidden him using tobacco. Which made Meg's gift all but useless to him now.

She returned her attention to the bolt of fabric. "It's almost too beautiful," she remarked absently. "It seems a shame to waste it on a dress that I'll only wear in Somersetshire."

"A waste, is it?" Her father puffed up with indignation. "Rubbish. You've a position to uphold in the county. *My* position. The minute you're caught in out-of-season rags, the villagers will assume I'm in financial difficulties. I won't have people thinking I can't afford to keep you turned out in the latest fashions."

Meg carefully refolded the silk, returned it to its tissue-lined box. Despite spending more time with her father, and receiving a kernel more of his respect, he still didn't recognize her as an individual. She only existed as an extension of him. A poor, feminine shadow who could never live up to the splendor he imagined was due the Burton-Smythe name.

His disappointment in her didn't precisely hurt. Not any longer. But it never ceased to sting.

"I shall have my dressmaker m-make a ball gown," she said quietly.

"Now that *would* be a waste," he replied. "I'll be hosting no balls in the foreseeable future. Have the woman run up a dinner dress. You can wear it when we dine of an evening."

"Surely my f-future holds more than lonely d-dinners here at Letchford Hall?"

His brows lowered. He despised the sound of her stammer. And he hated the suggestion of her having a season even more. "What else would it hold, pray?"

Meg didn't wish to argue on Christmas. Still... "You've yet to render an opinion on m-my having a season in Bath."

"I haven't come to a decision as yet."

"Then you *are* c-considering it?"

"I consider a great many things. Were you aware that Smithson is complaining about the roofs on the tenant cottages again? Or that Leonards is talking of selling the freehold to his sheep farm? The very land we've leased the past decade and more? Your pleasure jaunt to a local watering hole weighs poorly in comparison to the concerns of the estate, my girl."

"It's not a p-pleasure jaunt. It would be my c-come out. You m-must see that I—"

"I see no such thing."

She opened her mouth to argue.

He waved her into silence with an abrupt sweep of his hand. "Yes, I'm aware you're eighteen. Still a young enough chit, by my reckoning. You have another year yet before we must needs be troubled by thoughts of your taking part in the season. And when we do trouble ourselves," he added ominously, "that season will be in London, as is proper for a girl of your pedigree."

"Mother had n-no pedigree," Meg replied under her breath. "As you so often remind m-me."

Her father glared at her for a long moment. "Your mother's low birth is nothing to the Burton-Smythe name. If a baseborn scoundrel masquerading as an earl can parade his jumped-up offspring through the drawing rooms of polite society, then I bloody well can send my daughter to London to make her curtsy to the queen."

"Must you bring Lord Allendale into things?"

"Lord Allendale—the very name is laughable! And now his son thinks to court my good opinion on the railway? I have a mind to crush the impertinent pup under my bootheel."

Meg would like to see him try. Ivo mayn't be a bully—he mayn't be unreasonable—but he was no weakling. "I trust, when he c-calls on you, you'll think of the benefit the railway would bring to Maidenbridge before you succumb to your worse instincts."

"*If* he calls," he said. "I take leave to doubt he'll come. None of their number have darkened Letchford Hall's door in twenty years and more. They haven't the courage."

"They have the reputation for b-being courageous. Even Lady Katherine. She's just returned from a season."

"A failed season, Church says."

"You shouldn't encourage Mrs. Church to gossip. What's to stop her from spreading tales about m-my own season—or lack of one?"

"You shall have a season," he said. "Once I'm persuaded you're up to snuff."

Meg set aside her gift. She doubted he would ever be persuaded. She couldn't fully conquer her stammer, after all. Not to his satisfaction. And she had red hair and freckles, too—though he must take the blame for that.

Under other circumstances, she would have been inclined to accept his endless delays. What else could she do? But she had a particular reason for wishing herself away from Somersetshire. If only she could get to Bath—if only she could meet someone else—she might stand a chance of forgetting these wretched feelings she had for Ivo Beresford.

Meg no longer suspected she was falling in love with him. She *was* in love with him.

All those days they'd been apart after their kiss had confirmed it. She'd returned to the river on every one of them, hoping against hope that he'd be there to meet her. That the intimacy they'd shared would be enough to draw him back to her side, never mind that he'd told her he wouldn't be able to see her again until the following week. Reason hadn't mattered. Only unreasoning emotion.

That first day, when he hadn't come, she'd succumbed to tears. But after that...

She'd made herself cross the bridge alone.

It wouldn't do to spend the rest of her life frightened and pining. She wouldn't be that person. She was resolved to face her fears. And if Ivo couldn't love her...

Well.

Surely someone else existed who could. Meg only had to find him.

# Chapter Eighteen

I vo's Christmas with his family was as all of their holidays together—boisterous, chaotic, and loud. It was made even more so by the discovery that Kate had invited a potential suitor to join them for an impromptu house party in the new year. Between the teasing, the questions, and the expressions of parental concern (mingled with guarded optimism), the focus had been well and truly off of Ivo and his doings.

It didn't mean he'd been at liberty to get away. His family had put him to constant use, hauling in a yule log, chopping down a Christmas tree with his brothers, and climbing ladders to hang mistletoe, boughs of holly, and endless garlands of pine for Kate and his mother.

And then there had been Partridge to contend with.

Or Brutus, as Ivo had taken to addressing him.

"What was I to do, Master Ivo?" the unrepentant valet had inquired when Ivo had taxed him with his betrayal. "The honor of the family was at stake."

"I would you'd have been less concerned with the family honor and more concerned with my happiness," Ivo had

166

snapped in reply. "All you've done is ensure I'm made miserable."

"You may dismiss me, if you like, sir."

"And have an even worse spy put in your place? I think not. But I'll know better than to confide in you in future." Ivo had leveled him with a menacing glare. "And if I find you poised to stab me in the back again, I've a mind to box your ears."

His warnings hadn't deterred Partridge from keeping a keen eye on Ivo's movements as the season progressed, no doubt with a mind toward reporting those movements to Ivo's older brother.

Even when the holiday was over and Ivo at last had a moment to ride out toward the river undetected, his sister managed to intercept him at the entrance to the stable, demanding his assistance in finding one of her miscreant cats who had disappeared in the attic.

Thwarted from his aims, Ivo grudgingly trudged beside her through the snow, back toward the house and another day without Meg.

His sister walked beside him, hands thrust into the warmth of a fashionable velvet muff. She was a copy of their mother—a petite, vibrant young beauty, with mink-brown hair and sapphire blue eyes. Her older brothers were largely hers to command and she knew it. But there were limits.

"Could you not have asked one of the servants for help?" Ivo asked crossly.

"They'd be useless in luring Tabby out," she said. "He doesn't trust them the way he trusts the family."

"If that's the case, you might better have asked Jack."

"Jack's gone into the village. I couldn't wait on his return. If I leave Tabby to his own devices much longer, he may get stuck in one of the attic walls."

Ivo made no reply, though he knew she was very likely right.

His sister flashed him a look. "Why so grumpy?"

"Because," he said, "I require time alone on occasion. I've grown accustomed to my own company these two years."

"Nonsense. You're the last person one could accuse of enjoying a solitary state."

"Perhaps I've changed?"

"I doubt it. You traveled Europe with Pershore, Quimby, and the rest of your university friends. *And* you returned with your guide in tow. How is the elusive man doing in his new post, by the way?"

"Settled in with the Pinnocks, by all accounts. Sober, miserable, and entirely out of trouble. Mr. Pinnock is probably exerting himself to find a suitable match for him. He'll have the signore leg shackled before the year is out, mark my words."

"I should have liked to meet him."

"I'm confident you shall eventually. Ruggiero was quite curious about you. He appreciates a pretty girl, the bounder."

"I wish all gentlemen were so inclined."

Ivo cast his sister a sidelong glance. "Speaking of gentlemen... Who is this Charles Heywood, really?"

"I told you," Kate said. "A former naval lieutenant of excellent family. He has a sister, as well. A charming girl with eyes that are two different colors—one blue and one brown. Jack and I met them last week when we called at Heywood House."

Ivo had heard tell of her impulsive journey to pay an unannounced visit on the mysterious ex-lieutenant. Kate must be very well gone indeed if she had stooped to chasing a gentleman down at his family's country home. "Yes, but who is he to *you*?"

"No one." Kate's gem-like eyes gave a mischievous twinkle. "Not yet. But he will be by the time I've finished."

"That sounds ominous."

"It's nothing of the sort. I only mean to court him. We'll walk and ride, and talk and dine. He can play games with us the first evening, which will show my skills at cards and charades to excellent effect. And then, the second evening, we shall waltz together."

"Where? There are no local assemblies at present, and it's too late to plan a ball."

"We have no need of either. We'll simply clear the drawing room. You, Jack, and James can take turns dancing with the lieutenant's sister while the lieutenant and I—"

"You and your elaborate plans."

"Don't disparage them. One must plan if one wants to succeed." Kate's expression turned thoughtful as they tramped up the snow-covered drive. "Granted, we'll be woefully short of ladies, but that can't be helped. There's no one hereabouts worth inviting save the vicar's daughter and she caught cold while visiting her father's parishioners. Which is all to the good. I shouldn't like the lieutenant to meet Miss Colfax. She's too perfect for words. My own personality might suffer by comparison."

Ivo sighed. As an older brother, it was his duty to discourage her calculating romantic schemes. To counsel caution—and reason. But he didn't feel much like warning Kate against her heart when his own heart was in such a sorry state. "What if mother and father don't approve of him?" he asked instead.

"Why shouldn't they? Anyway, it's me who has to live with the gentleman I marry. I shall dashed well have a hand in choosing him."

"But you might have anyone. When you return to London next month—"

"I don't want *anyone*. I want the man I want, not some well-bred suitor I'll discover during yet another tedious season. It's a matter of the heart, not the head. You'll understand that when you meet the right person."

Ivo once again lapsed into silence.

"It's not Miss Burton-Smythe, by the way," Kate said.

His gaze jerked to hers.

She gave him a knowing look as they ascended the front steps of the house. "James mentioned it before Christmas when he went after you. You weren't really calling on her, were you?"

"No," he said. "I haven't called on her."

Not formally. Not yet.

It wasn't for lack of wanting to. There had simply been no opportunity to do so.

As chance would have it, one didn't present itself until over a week later, the very day that Kate's guests arrived at Beasley Park.

Ivo remained just long enough to greet them in the drawing room along with the rest of his family.

Lieutenant Charles Heywood was as dark as the Beresford men were fair. He towered over Kate, and over Ivo, too, with an unmistakable military bearing. Ivo half expected the man to start barking at them to man the guns or swab the deck or some such thing.

Miss Heywood was markedly less imposing. A strikingly lovely girl with deep auburn hair, mismatched eyes, and a sweet softness to her features, she spoke in a low velvet murmur and scarcely made eye contact with any of them.

James looked at her rather too much.

Ivo felt a flicker of satisfaction. Could Miss Heywood be the girl to bring his toplofty brother low? Ivo wondered, but he didn't linger to indulge his curiosity. The moment Kate departed to show her guests to their rooms, Ivo slipped out unnoticed amid the chaos of family, servants, barking dogs, and overlapping conversations.

There wasn't time to saddle Snap. Instead, stopping only long enough to outfit himself in sturdy top-boots and a heavy greatcoat, he marched out the gate and into the snow.

The distance between Beasley Park and Letchford Hall was a negligible one. Only a mile at its nearest edge. A shortcut across three pastures, a leap over a frozen stile, and Ivo was within sight of the ancestral home of the Burton-Smythes.

It wasn't the way he'd envisioned meeting with Sir Frederick. Ivo was meant to have arrived in a carriage, unrumpled, at the house's front door, everything in proper order as befitting a distinguished man of business.

But needs must.

Bounding up the snow-covered brick steps, he rapped soundly at the massive oak front door. Razor-pointed icicles hung from the stone casing above, as lethal as a French guillotine waiting to behead the unwary. Ivo carefully avoided them. He hadn't come this far only to be injured by an undignified act of nature.

At length, a small, grim-looking old woman in a black stuff dress answered Ivo's knock. The housekeeper, he presumed. Her flinty eyes betrayed immediate recognition. A look of amazement followed. Her gaze shot past him, brows lifting as they registered the absence of a horse or carriage.

"Mr. Ivo Beresford to see Sir Frederick," Ivo said. "If you please."

The woman's mouth pursed so severely that, for an instant, it disappeared completely. She stiffly opened the door.

Admitting him into the house, she directed him to a small parlor off the entry hall. It was sparsely furnished, with heavy draperies, a mahogany-framed settee, and two carved Jacobean chairs.

"You may wait here, sir," she said after taking his hat and greatcoat, "while I inquire if Sir Frederick is at home."

Ivo smiled to himself. Of course, Sir Frederick was at home. Though, whether he'd see Ivo or not was an open question.

While he waited, Ivo straightened his riding coat, brushed the dirt from his breeches, and smoothed the wind-swept locks of his hair. He wasn't dressed for a business meeting. He was dressed for the out of doors. A country gentleman's uniform of broadcloth, Bedford cord, and leather. That it was cut well to his figure, made little difference.

Hopefully the notoriously proud and disagreeable Sir Frederick wouldn't take it as an insult.

But it wasn't Sir Frederick Ivo was thinking about as he paced the anteroom.

It was Meg.

Was she aware he was here? Did she want to see him? Twelfth Night had come and gone over a fortnight ago. Perhaps she'd given up on him calling. Perhaps she no longer wished to welcome him with tea and cake as she'd promised the last time they'd met.

He flexed his hands at his sides as he walked up and down the room. So occupied was he with his thoughts that the sound of the housekeeper's voice made him start.

"Sir Frederick will see you in his study, sir," the old curmudgeon said. "This way."

Composing his emotions behind a mask of aristocratic confidence, Ivo exited the parlor, following the housekeeper down a wide, flagstone-lined corridor.

The inside of Letchford Hall was as antiquated as its exterior. There was aged brickwork and exposed stone, along with faded landscape paintings, worn tapestries, and even an entire suit of armor standing guard at the foot of the stairs.

No wonder Meg's fancies drifted toward Arthurian

legends. Ivo might have believed he was stepping into one if the fragrance of silver polish, lemon oil, and beeswax had been slightly less obtrusive.

Sir Frederick's study was located near the end of the corridor, past the open doors of what looked to be a substantial library. The man himself was waiting inside, seated behind a dark, carved Jacobean desk of intimidating proportions.

Ivo came to a standstill as the housekeeper announced him.

It had been years since he'd seen Sir Frederick. Time hadn't been kind to the ginger-haired baronet. He was substantially heavier, with a fleshy face and puffy bags under his eyes that attested to his penchant for rich foods and drink. His furious red hair was now shot with gray, and his ruddy countenance damp as if the mere act of sitting upright behind his desk was aggravating his condition.

He didn't rise to greet Ivo as the housekeeper departed. He merely stared at him for a long while, too many emotions running through his eyes to properly catalog them. "You have the look of your father," he said at last.

Ivo smiled. "Indeed, sir," he replied amiably. "I trust you won't hold it against me."

Sir Frederick's mouth twitched. But it wasn't with humor. He was plainly holding onto his temper by a thread.

Ivo's spirits sank. Good lord. Sir Frederick must truly hate Ivo's father. And not only as a philosophical exercise, but as an acrid ever-present emotion. One that seemed to have been eating away at the man for a very long while.

Was Ivo's proposal to be doomed before it began?

"Sit down," Sir Frederick said tersely. "My daughter informs me you have a proposition to make about a railway coming to Maidenbridge."

"I do." Ivo availed himself of a chair. "Might I first inquire after your health? I understand you've been unwell."

"I'm well enough," Sir Frederick snapped. "About this railway—"

"The West Somerset Amalgamated Railway," Ivo supplied. "It's a company I've formed with Lord Pershore."

"Pershore? Any relation to the Marquess of Bruton?"

"His youngest son."

Sir Frederick leaned forward in his chair. "Is Bruton supporting this venture?"

"He is," Ivo said. "If Pershore and I can secure enough subscriptions, Lord Bruton has promised to present a bill in the next session of Parliament."

"You've been successful in petitioning Horsley, Stanhope, and Pinnock, I gather."

"I have. They understand that a platform halt in Maidenbridge will be good for business."

"And what does your father say about the idea?" Sir Frederick asked with deceptive unconcern. "Or, more to the point, your mother?"

"I haven't discussed the matter with them yet," Ivo replied. "I felt it was important to speak with you first. The name of Burton-Smythe is the most respected in the community, and your estate commands much admiration. Your adoption of the newest mechanisms for farming, for example, and your use of the latest organic fertilizers. You're an innovator in that respect."

Sir Frederick made a hoarse, dismissive noise. "It's not innovation, it's common sense. Agriculture is an experimental science. Only a fool leaves his lands untested, content to rely on the practices of the past."

"I quite agree," Ivo said. "Indeed, I suspect you appreciate the newest methods in science and engineering as much as I do."

Sir Frederick's eyes darkened with swift suspicion. "If your intention is to flatter me, boy—"

"By no means. My parents' good opinion on the railway is, of course, necessary, but it's you who holds the most sway with the villagers and landowners hereabouts."

"Damned right, I do. The farmers know me, just as they knew my grandfather and his grandfather before him."

"Which is why I'm here. Given your appreciation of where innovation is taking us, you must also appreciate the many benefits your estate would reap in having a platform halt in Maidenbridge." Ivo continued, giving Sir Frederick the same impassioned speech he'd given to Standish and Horsley.

"Do you have a prospectus?" Sir Frederick asked when he'd finished.

Ivo suppressed a relieved smile. "As a matter of fact, I do."

Nearly half an hour later, after discussing minute details of the route, the potential costs, and the proposed timetable for construction, the conversation was interrupted by a knock at the door.

Meg stuck her head in. "Pardon m-me for disturbing you," she said.

Ivo was immediately on his feet. His heart thumped heavily. "Miss Burton-Smythe," he said, bowing. "A pleasure."

"Mr. Beresford." She curtsied, only the faint blush in her freckled cheeks betraying that there was anything other than polite disinterest between them. She looked to Sir Frederick. "Shall I bring in the tea tray, father? Or will you c-come to the drawing room?"

Sir Frederick's gaze flicked between them. There was a hint of calculation in it. "No tea for me. I've too much work to attend to. You may entertain Mr. Beresford in my stead."

Meg couldn't hide her astonishment.

Ivo, on the other hand, appreciated his good fortune too much to question it. "I would be honored to take tea with you, ma'am." He looked to her father. "Unless you have any other questions, sir?"

"None at present," Sir Frederick said. "I shall contact you once I've heard from your partners. In the meanwhile, you've given me much to think on."

It wasn't a full-throated endorsement of the venture, but for the moment, it was enough.

"In that case," Ivo said, smiling at Meg, "pray, lead the way."

# Chapter Nineteen

Meg poured a cup of tea for Ivo, amazed by the steadiness of her hand. He'd never seen her in a domestic environment. Indeed, outside of their dinner at the vicarage, he'd never encountered her inside of a house at all.

When Mrs. Church had come to Meg's bedchamber earlier to inform her that Ivo had arrived to speak with Sir Frederick, Meg had been frozen to the spot.

"The brazenness," Mrs. Church had remarked unkindly as she departed Meg's room. "And no horse or carriage! I believe he walked all the way from Beasley Park."

Recovering from her episode of shock, Meg had shot up from the window seat where she'd been embroidering a handkerchief, and made straight for her wardrobe. Her first instinct had been to change out of her simple woolen day dress and into something soft and pretty. She'd just removed a pale blue cashmere gown when she forcibly stopped herself.

Ivo wasn't courting her. It wouldn't do to keep thinking of him as a suitor. To continue featuring him in her daydreams. He'd insisted on restricting their acquaintance to friendship, despite having kissed her and having repeatedly held her hand.

He didn't want a romance. Not one with her. She only diminished herself by desperately clinging to the hope of one.

With that in mind, she'd returned her cashmere day dress to the wardrobe and, after taking a brief moment to repair her hair, descended the stairs to the kitchen to see to arrangements for tea for Ivo and her father.

"No milk or sugar for me," Ivo said. "Nor lemon, either. But you may slice me a wedge of that cake if you please."

He was seated on the damask-upholstered sofa beside her, the loaded tea tray arranged on the table in front of them. It hadn't been Meg's intention. On entering the drawing room together, she'd anticipated him taking a chair. Instead, he'd sat down next to her, near enough that the full skirts of her gown brushed his leg.

Her pulse had been fluttering ever since. "You p-prefer your tea black?"

"Today I do. I must keep my energy up for the journey back to Beasley."

She passed him his cup. "Mrs. Ch-Church said you walked here."

A glimmer of rueful humor shone in his eyes. "I did. It was the only way to make my escape."

Meg cut a piece of Mrs. Stapleton's seedcake for him. As she handed him the plate, their bare fingers brushed. It sent another wild tremor through her veins. Her voice, when she spoke, was a trifle breathless. "You m-make it sound as though you're a prisoner at Beasley Park."

Ivo was quiet for the space of a heartbeat, his attention fixed on where their fingers had touched. When his gaze returned to hers, there was an intensity in it that hadn't been there before. "I own that it often feels that way. Particularly now I have somewhere else I'd rather be."

Her cheeks warmed. She poured out her own cup of tea, adding both milk and sugar in generous amounts. "Your parents don't know you've c-come here, I gather."

"Not yet." Still gazing at her intently, Ivo took a long drink of his tea, not seeming to notice how hot it was. "I'll tell them about it soon. I wanted to speak with your father first."

She hesitated to ask. "And did he—"

"He's receptive to the idea. Or, at least, he seemed so. Then again..." A frown crossed Ivo's brow. "I suppose he could merely have been being polite."

"That isn't his habit. If he seemed receptive to the idea, it's because he finds merit in it. Had he felt differently, he wouldn't have refrained from voicing his opinions in the frankest manner possible." She paused to sip her tea. "Has he agreed to support the venture?"

"Not yet. He says he must write to my partner, Lord Pershore, and to my partner's father, the Marquess of Bruton."

"Did he not trust you enough to take you at your word?"

"Who knows?" Ivo smiled again with that same irrepressible humor. "I'll say this, he isn't as monstrous as I anticipated. Not when it comes to affairs of business."

"No," Meg acknowledged. "He wouldn't be."

"But in other matters?"

"He's improving," she said. "Or I am, rather. I'm not as frightened of him, and he respects me the more for it. He'd never say so, but...that's what I believe."

"I'm sure you're right." Setting aside his teacup, Ivo tucked into his slice of cake. He didn't use the fork she'd given him, or even the napkin, merely picked the wedge up with his fingers and took a ravenous bite. "My parents appreciate boldness, too, even if it unsettles the balance of things for a time. Which this is certain to do when I tell them about it."

"Won't they support the railway coming to Maidenbridge?"

"It's not the railway. It's the connection to your father that will give them pause."

*And to you,* he might have added.

Meg could practically hear the unspoken words echoing in the air around them.

His parents would object to her. And Ivo loved his parents. He would never go against them. Perhaps in small ways, such as meeting her for rides or calling on her father, but he'd never connect himself to the Burton-Smythes in any permanent capacity.

This was surely the reason he'd insisted they remain friends and only friends. Not because he didn't care for her, but because he knew that anything else between them was impossible. She consoled herself with the thought, though it was poor comfort.

"I considered talking to my mother about it in advance," he went on as he made short work of his cake. "To prepare the way, so to speak. But there's been no opportunity. Christmas had everything in chaos. And now we've guests to contend with. I don't expect things will calm down until they leave."

Meg raised her porcelain teacup for another sip. "Guests?"

"A friend of my sister's from London. A gentleman by the name of Lieutenant Charles Heywood. He's the grandson of the Earl of Gordon." Ivo dusted the cake crumbs from his hands. "He's brought his younger sister, Miss Heywood, with him. A charming girl. She's nearly as reticent in company as you were when first we met."

Her lips stilled on the rim of her cup. She forced herself to continue drinking. The hot liquid scalded her tongue. It burned almost as much as the knowledge that Ivo's family was presently entertaining a fashionable young lady.

"My sister has all sorts of activities scheduled for them.

Rides, walks, cutthroat games of charades. She's even planning a dance tomorrow evening."

Meg's chest constricted. She carefully lowered her cup back to its saucer. Somehow, she mustered a politely inquisitive smile. "A d-dance?"

He returned his empty cake plate to the tea tray. "Nothing formal. But there will be waltzing, I'm told."

Waltzing.

The knot in Meg's breast tightened on an inexplicable wave of sorrow. She wasn't prone to self-pity, but...

She had never waltzed with a gentleman before.

Though she'd been taught the steps and could perform them creditably enough, she'd only ever danced with Miss Adams. To be sure, at the rate it was taking her father to come to a decision about her having a season, Meg despaired she'd ever properly dance with any man.

But she'd dearly love to dance with Ivo. Even if it was only just once. And even if it would only be as his friend.

She imagined him holding her in his arms as they moved across the floor. She was wearing her new apricot figured silk. It had just come back from the dressmaker yesterday—a simple but elegant gown made with a fan-pleated bodice. Not a ball gown, admittedly, but suitable enough for a dance in the country. Quite beautiful, really. If only...

Ivo studied her face. "You should come," he said abruptly.

Meg sharply returned to the present, having lost the thread of the conversation. "I'm sorry. To where?"

"To Beasley Park. It would do you good."

She stared at him blankly. She feared she hadn't heard him correctly. "Are you inviting me to c-come to your sister's party?"

"It's not a party, as such. We're just clearing the drawing room. But there will be dancing. I would have you be there for it, to partner me at least. We're well short of ladies, and a fellow can't spend the whole evening dancing with his mother and sister."

"What about M-Miss Heywood?"

"Ahh. Miss Heywood." Ivo's eyes gleamed behind his spectacles. "I suspect—indeed, I very much hope—that she may do for my older brother."

Meg blinked. His brother?

At one time or another, every girl in Maidenbridge, and surely in all the West Country, had set their cap for the gorgeous Viscount St. Clare. He'd been coolly indifferent to all of them, blind to their enticements and too clever for their traps. It was widely accepted that he would eventually marry a lady of extraordinary wealth, rank, and beauty.

"Miss Heywood m-must be very beautiful to tempt Lord St. Clare," Meg remarked.

"Not as beautiful as you are," Ivo said. "But she's singular. Her eyes don't match, for one."

"Indeed?" Meg inquired faintly. How else was she to respond when he'd just told her he thought her beautiful?

"I daresay you'd like her," Ivo went on, seemingly oblivious to the impact of his words. "She appears a genteel kind of girl, with no airs about her. And you already know my sister. Kate's as jolly as they come, providing you don't engage her in competition. My brother Jack is quite merry as well. He'll gladly dance with you, too, if I relinquish your hand—which I won't."

A smile pulled at Meg's mouth. This time it was genuine. "You can't only dance with me."

He smiled back at her. "I easily could. I'll wager you're a splendid dancer."

"I'm untested outside of the schoolroom."

"You've never been to a ball? Or an assembly?"

She placed her cup and saucer back onto the tea tray. "I'm not formally out."

"That shouldn't matter in the country."

"Everything matters when it's a lady's reputation in the balance. My father is quite strict. He doesn't desire that I make a f-fool of him in public."

Ivo's smile vanished at the suggestion. "You could never."

"I would," she said. "Merely by having freckles and red hair. And by stammering. I'm no conversationalist, Ivo."

He gestured to the space between them. "What is this if not a conversation?"

"It's not the same. You're..."

"Odd. As we've established."

She huffed a laugh. "I was going to say that you're my friend."

"That too." He gazed at her warmly. "By God, it's good to see you. If you only knew how I've longed to see your face. How many times I've tried and failed to ride to that blasted river in order to meet you there." His smile softened. "I've missed you, Meg."

Meg's heart swelled in spite of herself. "Oh, Ivo...I've missed you, too," she confessed. "I wish..."

He gently took her hand. His own hand was large, and strong, and faintly callused. The hand of a gentleman who could be as powerful as he was tender.

Her pulse thrummed in her ears. For an instant, she couldn't breathe.

"What do you wish?" he prompted, a husky quality in his voice.

She curled her fingers around his. "I wish we could see each other in a m-more public way. I don't like to feel as though I'm a secret."

He leaned closer to her. "Then come to Beasley tomorrow night."

"How?" she wondered.

"How indeed?" The pad of his thumb moved over the

back of her hand in a slow caress. "The dancing should commence between half past eight and nine. I can send a gig for you."

"No." She shook her head. "You can't. If my father or the servants were to see—"

"So what if they do?"

"My father would be furious. And you can't make an enemy of him. Not at the very moment you need his help the most. I won't let you do it."

His gray eyes gazed into hers with a soul-stirring warmth. "What a dear soul you are. To think of me instead of your own pleasure." Lifting her hand, he bestowed a kiss on the curve of her knuckles. "But you have to come, Meg."

The touch of his lips inspired a reckless impulse within her. It was foolish to even consider it, and yet...

She didn't see why she shouldn't.

Beasley Park and Letchford Hall were neighboring estates, after all. What did it matter if it was dark? Or if it was snowing? She wasn't made of spun sugar. She was a country girl born and bred.

"I *will* come," she promised. "Leave it to me."

# Chapter Twenty

Ivo returned to Beasley Park the same way he'd come, over pasture fences and across the snowy fields. He scarcely registered the cold and the damp. He was walking on air.

Meg's naked hand had felt delicious in his. Small and silken, though not lacking in strength. She'd pressed his fingers so sweetly. It had set his blood simmering to a dangerous degree.

It was *still* simmering.

Indeed, from the minute their hands had first brushed as she'd passed him his cake plate, his brain had ceased to function at full capacity. Her skin had been as soft as he'd imagined. And the turn of her countenance. So lovely. So dear.

He'd been so distracted by the look and the feel of her, by her rose-scented perfume and the gentle cadence of her voice, he'd shoveled his cake into his mouth like a fieldworker, without a thought for his fork or his linen napkin. Then, after being so presumptuous as to hold her bare hand, he'd had the temerity to invite her to Beasley Park tomorrow evening.

And why shouldn't he have?

Ivo walked on, jaw set with resolve. To be sure, perhaps this was the exact way to go about things. To force Meg on his family so they'd have no choice but to see how wonderful she was. No choice but to admit that she was nothing at all like her hated father. Only then would his parents be convinced to give up this ancient grudge. With luck, his brother would be persuaded, too.

Ivo marched through the snow, warming to the idea. That warmth didn't last long. As he approached the ice-covered stile, he spied an all-too-familiar figure waiting for him.

James leaned against the wooden rungs, clad in a heavy overcoat, hat, and gloves. His face might have been chiseled from a block of marble.

Ivo's stomach didn't sink this time. It clenched with fraternal wrath. "Speak of the devil," he said. "Been following me again?" He climbed over the stile. "Don't answer that. It's obvious you have."

"Someone must stop you from exacerbating your crime." James regarded him with lethal intent. "Please tell me that you didn't just call at Letchford Hall."

Ivo walked past him, hands thrust into his pockets, doing his best imitation of a man without a care in the world. "I did."

James kept pace with him. Controlled fury vibrated in his deep voice. "You bloody idiot."

Ivo chuckled. "Is that the best you can come up with?"

"You shortsighted fool."

That one hurt. Ivo was obliged to conceal a wince. "Nonsense. I'm the least short-sighted among us."

James shot a sardonic glance at Ivo's spectacles.

Ivo whipped them off and thrust them in his pocket. "I'm not talking about my vision, you literal-minded arse."

"Short-sighted in vision, and in every respect, it seems,"

James said coldly. "If you've paid a formal call on Miss Burton-Smythe—"

"Now *that* I haven't done," Ivo said. Wind bit at his face as he walked.

"Then what—"

"I was paying a call on her father."

James's jaw dropped.

Ivo felt a distinct flare of satisfaction. It was worth the tedium of his brother's lecture to see him temporarily put out of countenance. It so rarely happened.

"We talked for some time," Ivo said, pressing his advantage as he continued through the snow. "Sir Frederick's a most reasonable gentleman, I found, when it comes to matters of—"

James grabbed Ivo by the arm, bringing him to an unwilling halt. His grip was as strong as iron. "By God, Ivo, if you've made the man an offer for his daughter—"

Ivo easily wrenched free from his brother's grasp. "Don't be absurd."

"What else am I to make of this slinking around? To go to Letchford Hall, to call on Sir Frederick, and then to walk—to walk!—back to Beasley in these conditions? These aren't the actions of a man in his right mind."

Ivo gave his greatcoat a sharp tug to straighten it. "You're perfectly right," he said. "This slinking around, as you call it, has become tedious."

James studied him for a long moment. "I suppose he refused you."

"Suppose what you will."

"I could have predicted as much. Sir Frederick would no more give his permission for you to marry his daughter than Father would give for Kate to marry Roddy Burton-Smythe."

Ivo ignored the fact that his brother had just compared him to a notorious wastrel. "It scarcely matters now," he said.

James was blatantly skeptical. "Then you mean to end it?"

"I do." Ivo continued down the path. "There's to be no more slinking. If I'm to court a girl in future, my family will be well involved in the affair, you can be certain."

James walked at his side. His eyes betrayed a guarded relief. "If that's the truth...I'm pleased to hear it."

I'll bet you are, Ivo thought unkindly. But he didn't say it. He pasted on a smile. "We're in harmony, then," he said. "For I'm pleased, too. Very well pleased indeed."

<hr />

THE NEXT EVENING, AFTER HER FATHER HAD RETIRED for the night, Meg withdrew to her room to change. With her maid's assistance, she arranged her hair in a thick coil of plaits, dressed in her new apricot gown, and put on her heaviest cloak.

"Mrs. Church will dismiss me if she discovers I've helped you escape from the house," Lucy fretted as she passed Meg a pair of ivory silk slippers with grosgrain ribbon ties.

Meg tucked the delicate slippers into her reticule. "You're not helping me escape, Lucy. You're only doing your job. The rest is down to me."

"But you look dreadful, miss!"

Meg flinched. However, the maid wasn't looking at Meg's face or figure. She was staring at Meg's heavy leather boots. "Never mind them," Meg said. "They're only for the walk. I'll put my dancing shoes on when I arrive."

Lucy wrung her hands. "Your skirts will be soaked through."

"Not if I'm careful. And even if they are," Meg added earnestly, "it will have been worth it!"

She set off a half hour later as the clock in the downstairs hall was striking a quarter to nine. An anxious buzz, like the aggravated swarm of bees, vibrated in her chest. It was fear, pure and simple. The fear of being seen. Of being caught.

Fortunately, Mrs. Church was still upstairs attending to Meg's father. And Mrs. Stapleton was asleep in her chair by the fire. Her loud snoring permeated the kitchen as Meg tiptoed past to exit through the back door.

The snow had stopped and the night air, though cold as the dickens, wasn't as icy as it had been yesterday. A full moon hung in the sky above, its soft glow illuminating the Somersetshire countryside.

Inhaling a deep breath to fortify herself, Meg set forth.

She was a good walker, even in a new gown, with several layers of petticoats, and a bustle tied round her waist. The latter was comprised of a pad of wool, used to give her skirts a more pronounced dome shape. Not the best undergarment for a mile-long walk in the moonlight.

But Meg was determined.

She held her skirts high for as long as she could, avoiding the deeper patches of snow. By the time the torchlights of Beasley Park came into view, her fingers and toes were numb and she was breathing hard, but she was otherwise in tolerably good order.

The bees in her chest, temporarily quieted by her vigorous walking, buzzed to life again as she beheld the grand Palladian manor house, with its stately columns and snow-frosted windows. It was a beautiful structure, made of honey-colored limestone, as though in silent acknowledgment of the family who had built it so many decades before.

It was here where Meg's father had met and fallen in love with Margaret Honeywell.

Though it hadn't been in love, he'd said. But surely it must have been something to have burned so violently in Meg's father's heart for so long.

Meg walked to the back door, where a lamp hung overhead, and two housemaids were gossiping as they returned from the privy. Taking one look at Meg, they stopped in the snow.

Meg swallowed hard. Her father would never forgive her for coming here. Certainly not in this hurly-burly fashion, turning up at the kitchen door like a waif begging for table scraps.

But it was too late to second guess herself now.

She drew back the hood of her cloak.

The maids gasped. They immediately fell into curtsies. "Miss Burton-Smythe!"

"Good evening." Meg was mortified to hear her teeth chattering. "I'm expected by Lord and Lady Allendale this evening, but I m-must first change out of these boots. May I leave them in front of the kitchen fire?"

One of the maids looked behind Meg, searching for a horse, a carriage, or even an accompanying servant. Finding neither, she exchanged a scandalized look with her compatriot. "Yes, miss." Another curtsy. "This way, miss."

Straightening her spine, Meg followed the girls into the kitchen. It was not unlike the kitchen at Letchford Hall, though the staff was larger in number and the cook appeared much younger than Mrs. Stapleton's antiquated years.

A woman who could only be the housekeeper sailed forward. She had a brisk manner and an unmistakable air of authority. "Can I help you, ma'am?"

"It's Miss Burton-Smythe, Mrs. Lewis," the first maid said in a weighted undertone. "She's come for the dancing, but must leave her boots."

Mrs. Lewis betrayed no surprise. She cast a fleeting look at Meg's feet. "Indeed. Allow me to assist you." She addressed the maid. "You may tell Mr. Selby that Miss Burton-Smythe has arrived."

The first maid departed in a flash of skirts.

Meg divested herself of her cloak and boots, handing them off to the housekeeper. She felt the stares of every servant in the kitchen. A discomfiting sensation. She pretended as though she didn't notice as she changed into her dancing slippers, resisting the urge to explain.

"Would you care to stand in front of the fire a moment, miss?" Mrs. Lewis inquired. "Your hem is damp."

"Yes, thank you." Meg did as the housekeeper directed. The heat from the flames felt glorious, but she hadn't much time to enjoy the warmth of it. Only a scant moment later, an elderly butler appeared to escort her to the drawing room.

His face was as purposefully blank as the housekeeper's. "Miss Burton-Smythe," he said, bowing. "Master Ivo is expecting you."

Meg released the breath she'd been holding. Judging from the reaction of the servants, it had seemed as though Ivo had kept Meg's arrival a secret. But no. Of course his family knew she was coming. Ivo would never put her in the position of being an uninvited guest.

Or so she believed.

But when she arrived outside of the drawing room—when the butler announced her name—Meg knew just how wrong she had been.

"Miss Burton-Smythe, sir," he intoned.

And everything stopped. The music. The dancing. The conversation. Everyone in the drawing room came to a halt as one to stare at Meg with varying expressions of shock and horror.

And she knew.

Ivo hadn't told anyone she was coming.

# Chapter Twenty-One

Ivo had been waiting by the drawing room doors for the past two dances, rather conspicuously pacing the floor. He'd told Meg the dancing would commence between half eight and nine. But as the clock struck the hour, she still hadn't arrived.

His mother, Lady Allendale, was seated on a velvet stool in front of the satinwood pianoforte, wearing a blue moiré evening dress trimmed in a rich fall of lace. At two and fifty, she could still command the attention of everyone in the room, and no one more than Ivo's father.

John Beresford, Earl of Allendale stood over his wife, turning the pages of her music while she skillfully played a waltz. He was singularly, irrevocably devoted to her. And not in some rarified manner, as though she were perfection on a pedestal, but in an earthy, purely elemental fashion. The two of them were the closest thing Ivo had ever seen to soulmates.

Only a few years older than Ivo's mother, his father's golden hair was finely wrought with silver. He was still in perfect health, however. Lean, fit, and—at times—implacable.

A formidable patriarch, but a loving one. Just as he'd been in Ivo's youth.

Across the room, Jack hovered by the fireplace, warming himself. Meanwhile, Kate danced with Lieutenant Heywood, her arch expression softened by a smile. And James—

Ah, James.

Smitten to his ice-cold core.

Or so Ivo suspected.

The tall, frost-hearted heir apparent was waltzing with a blushing Miss Heywood, holding her with the stiff propriety of a dancing master, exactly an arm's length apart, as they turned across the floor. Outwardly, it was nothing very revealing. Except that James was gazing down at Miss Heywood with a brooding frown, a look in his glacial gray eyes that was impossible to read.

But Ivo could read it.

James was flummoxed.

Ivo experienced a flicker of unholy satisfaction. It served James right, the overbearing tyrant. Judging by Miss Heywood (whose attention was presently fixed at the approximate level of James's topmost waistcoat button) she wouldn't be easily won. Blushes notwithstanding, the girl had a core of steel.

She didn't eat animal flesh, for one—a compassionate gesture on behalf of her four-legged friends. And then, this morning, when Ivo, Jack, and Kate had accompanied the Heywoods for an impromptu ride and a bit of target practice by the gamekeeper's cottage, Miss Heywood had admitted to being a member of a new society formed to protect animal welfare.

She wasn't just singular, with mismatched eyes and a shy demeanor, she was, it transpired, a bit of a bluestocking.

Ivo could have crowed with laughter at his brother's expense.

But he didn't feel like laughing at the moment.

He continued pacing, his restlessness transforming into a palpable frustration.

Meg had said she would be here. She'd promised. He'd assumed she planned to arrange a ride with one of the servants, in a gig, perhaps. But it increasingly appeared her plan hadn't come to fruition.

It wasn't until a quarter past nine that Selby materialized in the doorway, a pained expression on his usually impassive face. "Miss Burton-Smythe, sir."

A thrill surged through Ivo as Meg appeared in the butler's wake. She wore a dress of pale, apricot figured silk, with elegant fan-pleats along the bodice, and full skirts that floated around her hips in a graceful swell of shimmering fabric. A gleaming tortoiseshell comb glinted amid the plaited coils of her Titian hair. And in her eyes—

Panic.

Ivo went to her at once, heart hammering against his ribs.

He vaguely registered Jack muttering something under his breath. The music came to an abrupt close. Kate and Heywood stopped dancing. So did James and Miss Heywood. The legs of the pianoforte stool scraped across the floor as Ivo's mother stood from her instrument.

Ivo ignored it all, focused only on Meg. He gave her a foolish smile. "You're here."

"I shouldn't be," she said, so softly he barely heard her.

"Of course you should. You look beautiful, Meg."

"Ivo—"

"Courage," he said. Gently taking her hand, he drew her into the room and, with no little pride, presented her to his family. "Mother, father. Seeing as how we were short of ladies this evening, I took the liberty of inviting Miss Burton-Smythe to join us. Meg, you remember my parents, Lord and Lady Allendale? And doubtless you recall my sister, Kate, and my brothers Jack and James?"

His introductions were met with resounding silence.

Ivo's temper rose. Is this how they meant to receive her? So stiff and cold? It was unpardonable. Couldn't they see how sweet she was? How worthy? How very different from her hated father?

He held his mother's gaze from across the room. Surely she, of all people, would offer a warm reception to the young lady he'd invited to Beasley.

Lady Allendale looked back at him steadily. A glimmer of reluctant understanding flickered in her sapphire blue eyes. She alone seemed to comprehend the feelings he'd kept secret from everyone else. Feelings he hadn't yet shared with Meg. Feelings he'd only recently begun to recognize for himself.

There was no more skirting about the matter. Meg had his heart absolutely.

It was unplanned. Unintentional. Dashed bloody inconvenient, truth be told. But it was the reality of things. And Ivo wouldn't be sorry for it.

"Miss Burton-Smythe," his mother said. "This is indeed a surprise."

Meg curtsied, her face blazing with warmth. "M-my lord, m-my lady. I was honored t-to receive your invitation."

Ivo inwardly winced at the fierce reemergence of her stammer. She was frightened and anxious. That much was apparent. There was little he could do to reassure her, other than remain at her side, still holding her hand, silently offering his support. She may feel alone in a drawing room full of Beresfords and strangers, but she wasn't. He was here, and so long as he had anything to say about it, Meg would be treated with the respect she deserved.

"Miss Burton-Smythe," Lord Allendale said, with a bow. "How fares your father?"

Ivo leveled a hard glance at his pitiless sire. Had it really been necessary to mention Sir Frederick so early in the evening? Or at all?

Lord Allendale returned Ivo's glance with the same icy promise as James was presently conveying. There was going to be a conversation later, that look informed Ivo. A conversation Ivo wasn't going to enjoy.

"His gout is t-troubling him, m-my lord," Meg replied, her stutter intensifying. "He's b-been abed all day."

Dropping Heywood's arm, Kate stepped forward. "Miss Burton-Smythe. It's been an age."

"Lady K-Katherine." Meg inclined her head.

"Kate, please. And may I call you Meg? Miss Burton-Smythe is so dreadfully formal."

Meg's shoulders relaxed a fraction. "Oh yes," she said. "If you p-please."

In that moment, Ivo could have hugged his impetuous little sister.

He drew Meg closer. "Allow me to introduce Lieutenant Charles Heywood, grandson of the Earl of Gordon. And this is Lieutenant Heywood's sister, Miss Hannah Heywood. They're staying with us until tomorrow."

Heywood and his sister greeted Meg, neither of them seeming to understand why the temperature of the room had dropped by several degrees since her arrival.

Ivo had no intention of explaining it. The best course was to keep moving forward. The others would warm to Meg soon enough. Until then, dancing was what he'd promised her and dancing was what he intended to provide.

"Now that our numbers have evened up," he said to his mother once the introductions were dispensed with, "James can take over your duties at the pianoforte while the rest of us dance. You won't mind, will you, James? We can't spare any of the ladies."

James glared at Ivo as though he'd like to remove his liver and feed it to one of the family's spaniels.

"An excellent idea," Lady Allendale said. She took Lord Allendale's hand, giving it a meaningful squeeze. "Shall we, my love?"

Lord Allendale glared at Ivo for a long moment before allowing Lady Allendale to draw him away.

Ivo didn't waver. He was in the right. "Play something jolly, won't you?" he said to James.

James's hand flexed at his side. For a moment, Ivo anticipated that his brother's control would break. But no. Despite the ample provocation, James didn't take the bait.

He strode to the pianoforte and sat down. Unlike the others, James didn't require music. He had a prodigious memory and could play most pieces entirely by ear.

It wasn't a waltz, but Ivo wouldn't quibble.

"Shall we?" he asked Meg.

Meg gazed up at him. Her blushes were still in evidence, but there was something else. A strange solemnity to her expression that gave Ivo pause. He wished he knew what she was thinking. "If you like," she said.

He led her out into the center of the drawing room as the other couples lined up across from each other. There was a decided tension in the air. It was impossible to ignore. Ivo could only hope that, once the dancing started, the exercise would dissipate it.

It was a jolly dance. One that necessitated the eight of them joining and separating again, both with their partners and with the other dancers, in a lively pattern.

His mother's smile was brittle, his father's face absent expression, and Jack betrayed an offended dignity in his posture. Even Miss Heywood seemed to be rattled by the arrival of Ivo's unexpected guest. She repeatedly looked to her brother for reassurance.

Only Kate was behaving with relative normalcy, too busy fretting over Heywood to be too much put out by Meg's arrival. At least, Ivo thought so. However, when his sister linked hands with him in turn, she met his smile with a reproving scowl.

"Are you satisfied?" she asked under her breath.

"Immensely," he replied. "I've often found that the best way of enacting change is to force it upon the resisting parties."

"You may have ruined my plans," she informed him.

Ivo doubted it. Unless he was mistaken, Heywood was as thunderstruck by Kate as James was by Heywood's sister. "Really?" Ivo inquired, still smiling. "My own are going swimmingly."

THERE WERE NO MORE WALTZES. FOR THE NEXT FIVE dances, whoever it was taking a turn at the pianoforte—first Lord St. Clare, then Lady Allendale, then Lady Kate—only played music that was bright, merry, and decidedly unromantic.

Meg couldn't regret it. This was no place for romance. Not tonight. Not now she was here.

Her presence had cast a pall over the room. Not even Ivo's perpetual good humor had succeeded in thawing it.

He seemed so sure that they would accept her.

And they did to an extent.

They none of them were rude or insulting. They were civil. Exceedingly, embarrassingly, civil. *"How is your father?"* Lord Allendale had asked the moment she'd arrived.

The Earl was one of the iciest-looking gentlemen Meg had ever encountered. Good gracious! This was the man who had shot her father! Who had, perhaps, engaged him in a bout of fisticuffs over Ivo's mother!

A gentleman must surely have a passionate nature to resort to violence. A duel was one thing. That required a certain level-headedness. But to fight another man? To grapple with him? To beat him with one's fists? That wasn't the action of a cold-blooded fellow.

Quite the reverse.

At the end of the next dance, while Meg was still catching her breath, Lord Allendale approached. "Miss Burton-Smythe." He offered his hand. "If you would do me the honor."

Meg had no choice but to accept him. She slowly took his hand, dreading what he might say to her once their dance began.

Ivo was obliged to relinquish her. He made no attempt to disguise his irritation. "I'd hoped for the next dance."

"You've had five," Lord Allendale replied coolly. "I believe you're due for a change of partner."

Ivo's jaw tightened.

Meg glanced back at him only once as Lord Allendale led her into the lineup for the longways set. It was another vigorous country dance, broken by moments of more sedate single and double turns.

"I wasn't aware you were acquainted with my son," Lord Allendale said as the music brought them together for the first turn. His gray eyes were identical to Ivo's, though lacking in Ivo's warmth and animation.

"We m-met at Mr. Colfax's," Meg replied, hating herself for lying. "There was a...a d-dinner."

"I see. And was your father in attendance?"

"No, m-my lord. My father hasn't left home since his health deteriorated."

"Pity," Lord Allendale said before they separated again.

Meg's dance with Lord St. Clare was even more awkward. If Lord Allendale was a block of ice, then the handsome viscount was the entire arctic shelf.

"You are not out, I believe," he said, holding Meg's hand lightly as they promenaded down the line.

Meg looked straight ahead. "No, m-my lord."

"You will be having a season in London soon, I presume?"

"Not in London," Meg said. "In...In B-Bath."

They separated then, each returning to the top of the line where they resumed their places across from each other. Lord St. Clare made no other attempts at conversation. The remainder of their set took place in silence. Bleak, disdainful silence.

Meg would have sooner fallen through the floor than continue dancing with the man. Even Lieutenant Heywood was a better companion. He at least made an effort at polite conversation when it was his turn.

"My sister contemplates a season in Bath," he said. "It is, I understand, less overwhelming there for young ladies of a gentle nature. Perhaps you'll be so good as to call on her during your visit? She has few acquaintances in the city."

Meg smiled at him gratefully as the two of them turned around each other once, and then again, to the lively rhythm Lady Kate pounded out on the pianoforte. "It would be m-my pleasure, sir."

"I will be accompanying her, of course, but a brother is a poor substitute for another young lady."

Meg spared a passing thought for Roddy, who had all but abandoned her. "Indeed. But you are a considerate brother, and one of those m-must always be appreciated."

Lieutenant Heywood returned her smile very slightly. It was the most emotion she got out of the somber ex-naval officer. He was a stoic sort, and what genuine interest he held for their evening amusement lay in Lady Kate's direction. He looked at her often, though generally when Lady Kate didn't realize it. Their romance, it seemed, was not yet on firm footing.

It wasn't until after Meg danced with Ivo's younger brother, Jack, that she was once again permitted to dance with Ivo. Lady Allendale was at the pianoforte this time, playing another march.

"Is this enough merriment for you?" Ivo asked. They clasped hands, turning together for a full circle.

"Yes. Very merry." She kept a smile affixed to her face as they returned to their places. It seemed to be frozen there. Her cheeks were beginning to ache.

"I know it was a trifle awkward at first, but..." A brief shadow of doubt darkened Ivo's brow, only to be dismissed. "Well, the point is, you're here now and the worst is over. It had to happen one way or another."

Meg didn't reply.

She understood what he was doing now, though she hadn't recognized it before. He was forcing the change he so believed in. Forcing *her* on his family, despite the position it put her in. He believed in progress that much, to the exclusion of everything else. It had blinded him to her feelings. To the very real mortification she must feel at being someplace where no one wanted her. Where no one valued her.

Signor Ruggiero had told her that Ivo had a weakness for the misfits of society. He offered his friendship and protection. Helped them to become their better selves. It wasn't affection. It wasn't *romance*. It was pity.

Ivo had promised Meg that that wasn't what he was doing with her. But she knew better now. He was managing her right along with his family. Improving her life, though he must break her into a new shape in order to do it.

It was unkind. Unfeeling. And not the action of a gentleman who truly cared for her.

Did he think he was her patron? Her guardian angel? He was meant to be her friend. Indeed, in Meg's heart of hearts, she'd believed he was meant to be more.

"What time is your coachman collecting you?" he asked when next they joined hands for a turn.

"I didn't come in a coach," she said numbly.

"Your servant, then."

"I didn't bring a servant."

Ivo jerked his head to look at her. "I don't perfectly understand—"

"I walked," she said. "Just as you walked to Letchford Hall."

They separated again.

He stared after her as she resumed her place in the line. When they met for another circular turn, he pressed her hands hard. "It's snowing, Meg."

"The snow has stopped."

"It's still freezing."

"The exercise did me good. I hardly felt the chill." Another lie. It was the only way to get through this wretched evening. An evening with no waltzes. No warmth. Nothing but hard, miserable truths she must face at last.

"I'm sending you home in a carriage," he said.

"You are *not*." She briefly locked eyes with him, her temper flaring with an alarming heat. "I will return to the Hall just as I left it—without causing remark."

Which is exactly what she was going to do.

Never mind her heart. She had her dignity. Sometimes that was all a lady *did* have when everything else was gone. Meg was resolved to hold onto it like a threadbare cloak in a blizzard. The minute the next dance was over, as soon as she could creditably make her excuses, she was walking out the door of Beasley Park and she was never coming back.

# Chapter Twenty-Two

Ivo regretted nothing.

Why shouldn't he have invited Meg to join his family for an evening of dancing and revelry? She was all of eighteen, a perfectly grown-up age, and she needed a bit of enjoyment in her life. Besides, their party had been short of a lady. And Meg wanted to dance with him, didn't she?

Ivo had believed so. He'd certainly wanted to dance with her. And they *had* danced, though there had been precious little enjoyment in it for either of them. Indeed, upon Meg's arrival in the drawing room, all the merriment had swiftly drained out of the evening.

It was his family's fault, drat them.

None of them had said anything. Not outright. They wouldn't have dared. But the Beresford frostiness had been on full display. Meg had undoubtedly felt it. It was why she'd been so dreadfully withdrawn since they'd departed the house.

He cast her a speculative glance as he trudged alongside her through the starlit, snow-covered pasture that led toward Letchford Hall. He wished he could make out her face in the moonlight. "You're angry with me."

She forged on without a word. She'd been silent since he'd gone with her to fetch her cloak and boots from the kitchen. Silent and resolute.

There had been no dissuading her from returning home by foot, the vexing creature. Who would have guessed that gentle Meg could be so stubborn as to shun the offer of a warm carriage with a hot brick in favor of freezing to death in the snow?

His own extremities were fast becoming numb. It was approaching eleven, and his boots, gloves, and greatcoat provided only moderate protection against the encroaching chill.

Ivo hardly felt it.

The only cold he experienced was the one at his heart. The persistent, niggling fear that he'd done something inexcusable. Something so thoughtless—so unfeeling—that Meg would never be able to forgive him.

"*Are* you?" he pressed.

Meg bent her head, the folds of her hooded cloak falling forward to further shield her expression from view. "Not angry, no."

"What, then?"

"I'm d-disappointed."

"In me," he concluded. It wasn't a question.

Meg answered it nonetheless. "In m-myself. I should have known b-better than to come here." Her teeth chattered.

Ivo stifled an oath. By God, she was freezing! "I *knew* I should have insisted you return in a carriage."

Meg's affronted gaze at last met his. Twin spots of color burned in her pale cheeks. "You've done quite enough insisting for the evening. You already brought me here based on a lie. You *will* let me leave how I choose."

Ivo's brows shot up. "A lie? What lie? We did the exact

thing I promised you we'd do. We danced together at Beasley Park. It wasn't the waltz, I grant you, but—"

"You didn't even inform the servants I was c-coming."

He was insulted by the suggestion. "Of course, I did. I spoke with Selby particularly."

"What about the maids? The housekeeper? They n-none of them understood what I was doing there."

"How was I to know you'd call at the kitchen? I thought you were arriving in a carriage, at the front door, for God's sake. Selby was waiting there to receive you."

"So it's my fault?"

"Of course not. I only meant that he was looking out for you. And he found you, didn't he?"

"In other words, the end justifies the m-means?"

"That's not what I—"

"No. I daresay you didn't. No doubt you were too c-caught up thinking about progress. Human b-beings aren't railway cars, you know. You can't force them in a direction against their will."

He gave her a look of pure bewilderment. "What is *that* supposed to mean?"

"And they're not railway tracks," she went on in the same heated rush. "That you c-can piece together in whatever form you want and then run straight over."

"I never—"

"You told me what I was from the moment you met me. You said I wasn't shy, I was inexperienced. That I wasn't happy being alone, I merely had no choice in the matter. You think you know best about everyone and everything. But you don't know me at all. If you did, you'd never have subjected me to such m-mortification."

"Meg—"

She marched on at an accelerated pace. In her haste, she forgot to hold firm to her skirts. Her hem dragged in the snow.

He easily caught up with her. "Slow down, would you? You'll ruin your dress."

"More would be ruined than m-my dress if my father discovers I'm gone. I m-must get home before the servants realize—"

"Please. I know you're angry with me, but—"

She whirled around to face him. "What were you thinking, Ivo? To surprise me that way? Didn't it occur to you that you were making everything worse?"

His stomach sank to his top boots. He made a valiant attempt at optimism. "I thought the evening came off rather well, all things considered."

"Oh yes. Your father only h-hates me. And your b-brother hates me m-more. A great success."

"They don't hate you. It's me they're upset with." Indeed, Ivo fully expected they'd be waiting for him upon his return, a severe lecture at the ready. He wasn't much looking forward to hearing it.

She resumed walking, gloved hands clenched at her sides. "The way they looked at me."

He kept pace at her side. "It was nothing personal. They're just stuck in the past, that's all. Now they've met you, it's just a matter of time before they come round."

"They n-never will, can't you see that?"

"I strongly disagree." By foisting Meg on them, Ivo had forced them to face the truth about her. It had been the only way. They'd never have welcomed her otherwise. Their opinions about the Burton-Smythes were too firmly entrenched.

Painful as the evening might have been, it had been necessary. Now, they could finally all move forward. He said as much to Meg as they walked, trying his best to explain his reasoning. Though surely it should be obvious?

She shook her head, not seeming to hear him. "We

shouldn't have done it. Spent so much time together all those days before Christmas. We should have realized that friendship was impossible."

He caught her arm, compelling her to stop. They were at the top of the rise, only yards away from the stile. It was the last barrier before they arrived at Letchford Hall.

"Please don't say that," he told her.

She looked up at him in the moonlight. Her face was taut, her pale blue eyes luminous with the threat of tears. "Why n-not if it's true?"

"It's not true. Meeting you that day at Sefton Bridge was the best thing that ever happened to me." His voice deepened with gruff sincerity. "I treasure your friendship, Meg."

She flinched.

"I do," he insisted. "And I'm sorry if I hurt you." He said it again for good measure. "I'm *sorry*. It was dashed selfish of me. I wanted so badly to dance with you, I didn't think of anything else. Only of how merry it would be to have you at Beasley with me. I so wanted to see you there, my own dear, sweet friend."

Meg's mouth quivered. For an instant it looked as though she was going to cry.

Ivo felt a jolt of alarm. Good lord, what had he said now?

She walked on again before he could ask her, arms folded in front of her.

He silently cursed himself. Bloody hell. He seemed to have made it worse. He stalked after her. "You'd think we'd committed a crime."

"We have," she said. "If d-disobedience is a crime."

He thrust his hands into his pockets. "Disobedience?" he repeated with a scornful huff. "We're no longer children. You're eighteen and I'm three and twenty. I think we can decide who our friends are."

Meg didn't reply. But she didn't refute him either.

They *were* friends. This wasn't some superficial infatuation, fallen into because she was soft and pretty. Granted, she was both of those things. But that wasn't the reason she'd come to fix herself so firmly in Ivo's heart.

He liked her intensely. Her kindness. Her spirit. The way she laughed and teased him. He adored the glints of courage she possessed that were only recently beginning to glimmer through. Above all, he wanted her to shine.

He wanted *her*.

There was no point in denying it to himself. But he had no intention of frightening her off. He was resolved to treat her with respect.

He offered his hand to assist her over the stile. "Can you manage in that dress?"

"Yes, thank you. I d-don't require assistance." Ignoring his offer of help, she climbed the steps unaided, skirts clutched in her hands. She passed over the top, descending safely to the opposite side.

Ivo was treated to a brief glimpse of her slim, silk-stocking-clad legs.

He was tempted to follow her. To walk with her the rest of the way to the Hall. There was nothing stopping him. Not his parents or his older brother or even Sir Frederick. Nevertheless...

Tonight, he remained firmly on his side of the barrier.

"Please let's don't end the evening on a quarrel," he said. "You must know I'd never do anything to hurt you."

Meg lingered long enough to look at him. "I know you m-meant well."

"I did." Ivo was beginning to realize just how naïve he'd been. "I'm only sorry you didn't have a better time. I'd hoped you would enjoy yourself a little."

"I know that. I'm—" Her voice faltered. She quickly recovered herself. "I'm obliged to you for thinking of me."

He gave her a lopsided smile. "I always think of you."

Her mouth tilted faintly in return. There was something infinitely sad in the small gesture. Something Ivo couldn't quite put his finger on.

But now wasn't the time to interrogate her.

The full moon shimmered in the midnight sky. It was nearly eleven. She really should be getting home and so must he. He'd call on her at Letchford Hall in a few days' time, when the dust had settled and they were both of them thinking clearly again. A formal call this time, with no pretexts about it.

Until then, he must be satisfied that she hadn't completely broken things off with him. "Goodnight, Meg," he said.

"Goodbye, Ivo," she replied.

He remained on his side of the stile for a long while, watching her march off across the pasture in the direction of the torchlights that marked the drive of Letchford Hall. She soon disappeared from view, lost in the icy darkness.

Ivo turned back toward Beasley Park. It wasn't until he was home again that he realized she hadn't said goodnight to him.

She'd said goodbye.

# Chapter Twenty-Three

M eg passed through the cobbled yard unnoticed. It was dark and empty, with no servants lingering outside to smoke or to use the privy. The Letchford Hall kitchens, by contrast, were aglow with lamplight. It shone from the windows, offering an ominous warning, as Meg approached.

She knew before entering what she would find there.

Had the evening gone better, Meg might have been less reluctant to face it. Scolding, scandal, and inevitable punishment was a small price to pay for a few hours of pleasure in Ivo's arms.

But she'd had no pleasure tonight, only pain. She'd said goodbye to Ivo, for heaven's sake. She nevertheless must face what awaited her within, no matter how terrible it might be.

Slipping into the house, she found Mrs. Church and Mrs. Stapleton seated at the kitchen table, nursing cups of tea, and very obviously awaiting Meg's return.

Meg set her shoulders. If she must be caught out, she'd rather bear the shame with dignity than allow the threat of ruination to reduce her to tears. Unfortunately, there was only so much countenance a lady could preserve when her teeth were chattering like mad.

Mrs. Stapleton immediately rose from the table and rushed to Meg's aid. "Frozen through!" she exclaimed. "And wet skirts besides. You'll surely catch your death."

"If she hasn't done so already." Mrs. Church came to assist the cook in divesting Meg of her wet outer garments. "I do hope he was worth it, miss. To have risked your honor and very likely your life in order to take the moonlight with a good-looking lad."

"I can guess who it was." Mrs. Stapleton clucked as she stripped off Meg's gloves. "When your father hears of it, we'll be lucky if it doesn't send him to an early grave."

"*Hush*," Meg said sharply. Shrugging off the two servants, she went to the fireplace. Flames blazed the stone hearth, casting shadows over the slate floor. Sitting down, she began to remove her sodden boots. "Neither of you know what you're t-talking about."

"Oh, but I do." Mrs. Church followed Meg to the fire. "Do you imagine I didn't see you from your father's window walking across the fields toward Beasley Park? Do you imagine I didn't realize at once what you were up to?"

Meg stilled in the act of unlacing a boot. "Did you t-tell him?"

"Sir Frederick was resting after taking his tonic. I wouldn't disturb his sleep. But you may be sure he'll hear about it in the morning. It's my duty to apprise him of what you've been about. He'll know how to act."

"A shame." Mrs. Stapleton draped Meg's wet cloak over the back of a chair. "No handsome lad is worth tarnishing your good name."

Meg finished removing her boots. She'd been so upset, and

had walked so quickly across the pasture, she'd scarcely noticed her fingers and toes turning into blocks of ice. But she noticed it now. She leaned closer to the fire, holding her hands up to the heat. The flames crackled and popped, sparks flaring as a piece of wood crumbled beneath the blaze.

The numbness in her limbs dissipated, but the numbness in her heart remained.

"Not only hers." Mrs. Church carried away Meg's boots. "The master's name, too."

"Foolishness," Mrs. Stapleton said. She bustled about the kitchen, pouring Meg an earthenware mug of tea and thrusting it into her hands. "Walking about after dark when there's snow on the ground? And you in an evening dress with only that cloak to protect you?"

Meg cradled the mug with both hands. "It wasn't that long of a walk."

Mrs. Stapleton exchanged a knowing look with Mrs. Church.

"I expect you think it worth a bit of frostbite," the old cook said. "Hoping he might propose, are you?"

"I daresay he made you promises," Mrs. Church said. "Did he tell you he'd marry you? Many a well-heeled scoundrel has employed just such a tactic to dishonor a girl."

A surge of sadness took Meg unaware. She knew what the housekeeper and cook were thinking. It was what everyone would soon be thinking. But it wasn't true. Ivo Beresford didn't look at her that way. He never had. After tonight, Meg knew it beyond all doubt. If Ivo ever thought of her at all, it was only with something akin to pity.

"Mr. Beresford is a gentleman," she said. "And our nearest neighbor. That's all there was to his invitation. Nothing more."

"Hmm." Mrs. Stapleton didn't sound convinced. She poured herself a nip of brandy before joining Meg in front of the fire. "I saw the young man when he came to meet with the master. A handsome gentleman, to be sure."

"Handsome is as handsome does," Mrs. Church muttered.

"Even so," Mrs. Stapleton went on, "you must have had a jolly time at Beasley Park."

"Yes, quite jolly." Meg sipped her tea.

She might have realized the two servants would expect a thorough report. They thrived on village gossip, and a Burton-Smythe attending a dance at Beasley Park was tittle-tattle of the juiciest sort.

If only Mrs. Church and Mrs. Stapleton realized how scandalous it had truly been!

Meg wanted to weep just thinking about it. The pain was still too fresh.

And she couldn't even fully blame Ivo for inflicting it.

He'd clearly thought he was acting in everyone's best interests—presenting his stubborn family with a fait accompli. It had been a generous impulse. One aimed at repairing the breach. In the end, all it had done was make Meg feel small and self-conscious and completely out of her depth.

She knew now that she had no place in his world.

"Was the family all in residence?" Mrs. Stapleton asked. "Miss Honeywell and Lord St. Clare?"

"Not Miss Honeywell any longer," Meg said. "As for Lord St. Clare—that title belongs to her eldest son n-now, not to her husband, the earl."

Mrs. Stapleton chuckled. "That's my age you're hearing. She'll always be Miss Honeywell to me. I remember her of old. And that dashing husband of hers—still a rogue, I take it?"

"Still devoted to her," Meg said. Despite his air of glacial reserve, that much had been plain. Lord and Lady Allendale had formed a united front from the moment Meg had entered the drawing room. United against *her*.

"What of their children?" Mrs. Church asked, unable to contain her curiosity. "Their other sons and their daughter?"

"They were all excessively civil." Meg took another drink of her tea. "They had guests staying as well. A Lieutenant Heywood and his younger sister."

Mrs. Stapleton nodded. "That'd be the gent who's courting Lady Katherine. A handsome devil, if he's as the housemaids describe him."

"I suppose," Meg said vaguely. It had been difficult to notice the raven-haired Lieutenant Heywood when Ivo was there.

Mrs. Stapleton seemed to sense the turn of Meg's thoughts. "You'll only have had eyes for Mr. Beresford," she said. "He's a handsome lad himself. And affable, too. Though, you'll know that better than me. I've not seen him much since his return to Somersetshire."

"You met at the vicarage dinner, I gather," Mrs. Church said with a disdainful sniff. "That upstart Colfax has a good deal to answer for."

Meg thought of how she'd really met Ivo, so many weeks ago on the banks of the river by Sefton Bridge. One moment she'd been near tears, struggling to stand, and the next he'd appeared on his great white horse to come to her rescue.

*"Are you hurt?"* he'd asked.

Meg couldn't recall how she'd answered. Some stammering, blushing, reply no doubt.

It hadn't mattered. Ivo had naturally taken charge of the situation. He'd caught her errant mare and helped Meg back into her sidesaddle. He'd even inspected her injury—a process which necessitated him raising the skirt of her habit and touching her stocking-clad ankle.

It was a memory that still made Meg's pulse quicken.

But it meant nothing to him.

*She* meant nothing to him.

And she never would.

Meg had realized that tonight with complete clarity.

A knot of inexpressible grief formed in her stomach. But she had no right to be grieving the loss of Ivo Beresford. He'd never been hers to begin with. It had been a fantasy, nothing more. A girlish, romantic dream.

It was past time Meg woke up.

# Chapter Twenty-Four

"I warned him to keep clear of her," James said. "I told him he was putting us all at risk. My reputation—"

"You're not my father," Ivo shot back. "For God's sake, you're only two years older than me!"

"Your brother was right to warn you off," their father's stern voice cut through their bickering. "To encourage a connection with that family is a great piece of folly."

The three of them stood in varying positions in the candlelit Beasley Park library. James was by the terrestrial globe, still in his evening clothes, though absent his coat and cravat. Ivo's father was in a similar state, arms folded as he leaned back against one of the bookshelves, rows of imposing leatherbound tomes stretching up behind him to the second-floor above. Ivo himself remained firmly fixed in front of the cavernous marble fireplace, still attempting to thaw out after his icy walk to Letchford Hall and back.

As expected, he'd returned to find his father and James waiting for him, still simmering with displeasure at what Ivo had done. No sooner had Ivo entered the main hall than James had appeared to unceremoniously haul him to the library.

There, Ivo had spent the last ten minutes being dressed down, primarily by his older brother.

"I'm not encouraging anything," Ivo said. "I merely invited a neighbor for a bit of merriment on a cold winter's evening. We needed another lady for dancing and—"

"Whom do you think you're addressing, Ivo?" Lord Allendale asked in a tone of perilous calm. "Do you imagine I'm not up to every trick?"

Ivo fell silent. Of course, his father understood. His mother likely did, too. Perhaps they all did. No doubt Ivo's invitation to Meg had been utterly transparent. He hadn't made it innocently—or ignorantly. He'd known exactly what he was doing in forcing her on them. At the time, it had seemed the only way for them to get past this.

But Ivo hadn't been completely calculating.

When he'd sat beside Meg in the drawing room at Letchford Hall, when he'd held her bare hand in his, the invitation he'd extended had come from his heart, not his head. Whatever Meg was feeling tonight, he hoped she knew him well enough to recognize that.

Lord Allendale regarded Ivo steadily. Unlike James, no glint of repressed fury smoldered in his eyes. His emotions were, as ever, firmly under control. "Your brothers and sister are of an age to marry. I'll not have the old gossip started up again."

Gossip. Is *that* what he was worried about?

"Meg doesn't care about any of that," Ivo said. "She's never mentioned—"

"Miss Burton-Smythe's father won't show such forbearance," Lord Allendale interrupted. "He has no love for the Beresfords."

Ivo's already frayed emotions rebelled in the face of his father's implacable resolve. He felt for a moment as though he was once again a boy of seven, trying to persuade his father to let him have a horse instead of a pony.

"He cares for Mother," Ivo said sullenly, though he knew full well that even that fact was in dispute. He'd disputed it himself not a month ago, along the banks of the river. It didn't prevent him from making the same feeble argument that Meg had made that day. "He named his daughter after her, didn't he? It follows that he must have some fondness for Mother's children."

"*My* children," Lord Allendale said. "Your mother's and *mine*. Fred hasn't changed so much in the intervening years that he'd refrain from destroying the lot of you. He wouldn't view it as hurting your mother. He'd view it as hurting *me*."

James drew closer, adding his voice to their father's. "If you won't think of me, think of Kate. She's barely out of her first season and still seeking a titled lord for a husband. She can't afford to have someone questioning her legitimacy."

"Kate's given up on a title," Ivo said. "She's interested in Heywood now."

"She's toying with Heywood," James said. "She'll soon grow tired of him. When she does, she won't thank you for tarnishing her good name. If you'd given a thought to her instead of indulging your childish urges, you wouldn't be standing here now."

"Childish? Is that how you label caring for someone?"

James's attention sharpened. "You *do* care for her, then?"

"Yes," Ivo said, provoked. "Deeply."

His brother shook his head, as though Ivo had just admitted to an offense punishable by law. "Perfect," he said. "Splendid."

Lord Allendale looked to his eldest son. "That's enough."

"But father—"

"You may leave us. I desire to speak with your brother alone."

James gave a humorless, laugh. "That changes everything, does it? He *cares* for her, so the rest of us can go to the devil?"

"James." Their father's tone held an unmistakable command.

"Very well," James said. He turned to leave, delivering one last parting shot as he went. "Good luck talking sense into him."

Ivo remained silent until his brother had gone, shutting the door behind him.

Lord Allendale contemplated Ivo with a thoughtful frown. "She's pretty," he said at last.

Ivo exhaled a frustrated breath. "It's not about *that*."

"Isn't it?"

"No." Running a hand over the back of his neck, Ivo paced the hearthrug. "If you must know, I met her by chance. And then...after that...it all got tangled up in some business I'm engaged in with Pershore." He paused, explaining. "I've been meaning to discuss it with you. Pershore and I, and several of our friends, have formed a railway company, with a view toward building an extension here in Somersetshire. Lord Bruton has offered his backing. Since I returned last month, I've been attempting to rally support for it. Subscriptions and so forth."

Lord Allendale betrayed no surprise.

Ivo stopped for an instant, his pacing arrested by a sudden, sinking realization. "You already knew?"

"You've met with Horsley, Standish, and Pinnock. It's hardly a secret." Lord Allendale studied Ivo's face. "I gather that this is the reason you met with Fred, and not some secret desire to wed his daughter?"

"Yes. That is...I did meet with him to talk about the railway. He was quite interested in the idea, if you must know."

"He would be."

"I found him rather reasonable on the subject. Not a pleasant man, by any means, but not at all monstrous."

"Is he not?"

"But that isn't why—" Ivo broke off again. He resumed pacing. "I haven't been using Meg to get to Sir Frederick. The truth is, I *like* her. I have from the first moment we met."

"Which was?"

"At the end of November. And I don't only like her because she's pretty," he added, "but because she's wonderful. She's sweet and kind, and she makes me laugh. We understand each other and enjoy each other's company. She's my friend. Indeed, we were friends first."

"Ah," his father said.

Ivo flashed him a narrow glance. "Why must everyone act as though friendship is a lesser affection? It's the purest form there is."

"There's an affection that's purer."

"Love, you mean."

"If you manage to find it."

Ivo stopped to face his father. His heart thudded heavily. "And if I have?"

Lord Allendale's eyes softened with something like compassion. "You're young, Ivo. Only three and twenty."

A flare of indignation brought a scowl to Ivo's brow. He wasn't some immature boy. He was a man grown, with a man's ability to know his own mind. "How old were you when you fell in love with mother?"

His father's mouth curved in a sudden smile. "You know the answer to that. It won't help you win this argument."

"I don't want to argue. But I don't see how you were better able to know your own mind at eighteen than I know mine at three and twenty."

This time, Lord Allendale's eyes smiled too. "Eighteen? Is that when you imagine I fell in love with your mother?"

"You were friends first, as well, weren't you?"

"It was rather different," Lord Allendale said. "I've loved your mother for as long as I've known her."

Ivo frowned. "Yet, you left her for a time. You didn't marry until you were eight and twenty."

The smile in Lord Allendale's expression diminished. It was replaced by a familiar look of brooding solemnity. The look Ivo's father often wore when discussing those parts of his past that were less pleasant in nature. "I did," he acknowledged. "That separation wasn't of my choosing."

"Don't say great-grandfather forbade you. I won't believe it. He adored mother."

"It wasn't your great-grandfather's doing," Lord Allendale said. "It was Fred's."

Ivo stared. "*What?*"

His father lapsed into silence for several seconds, as though contemplating how much he was willing to reveal. "I worked here at Beasley Park as a lad," he said at last. "I'd have stayed a servant forever if it meant remaining close to your mother. She was the whole of my world. And then, one day, Fred accused me of stealing the Honeywell jewels. He even went so far as to arrange to discover them in my rooms. It was a hanging offense."

Ivo didn't know what to say. He'd heard something of this, of his father's humble beginnings, the years spent in Somersetshire before Ivo's great-grandfather had rescued him from a life of poverty. Ivo had even heard whispers about the accusations of theft. But the threat of hanging...

This was something new.

"I was locked up in a loosebox in the stables, awaiting the magistrate. Your mother crept out in the night and freed me. She gave me all her pin money and lent me her horse to escape. The horse I returned, but the money I spent on passage to the continent. Had I remained in England, Fred would have seen me executed."

A chill set into Ivo's blood. It had nothing to do with his walk in the snow and everything to do with the significance of his father's words. "I had no idea."

"That isn't the worst of it." Straightening from the bookcase, Lord Allendale came to join Ivo in front of the fire. "In my absence, Fred became your mother's guardian here at Beasley."

"I know that much. Old Bessie told me."

"Did she. And did she tell you how Fred attempted to press his hand?"

Ivo was unwilling to ask. He dreaded the answer.

"I'd just returned to England after having been legitimized by your grandfather. I had a new name, unconnected with the accusations of the past, and was in the midst of courting your mother. One night, after a ball which we had all attended, Fred joined her and her aged chaperone for the carriage drive home. While her chaperone slept, he attempted to force himself on your mother."

The blood drained from Ivo's face. He sank down into one of the wingchairs in front of the fire.

"I intercepted them, naturally."

Ivo looked up at his father. "You shot him?"

Lord Allendale's brows lifted. "You've heard of that, too, have you?"

"Is it true?"

"It is. But it didn't happen then. That was earlier, in London, during a duel fought over a hand of cards. After the events with your mother, I delt with Fred in a different manner."

"I've heard stories," Ivo said. "People say you and Sir Frederick engaged in fisticuffs. Was this when—"

"Regrettably yes. It wasn't the first time we did so, though it certainly was the bloodiest. Far worse was the fact that your mother was present. She saw the entire affair, to my shame. It isn't something she's forgotten. Nor has Fred, I promise you. By the time I'd finished with him, he resembled a side of beef strung up in a butcher's window."

"Good God."

"It was a long time coming," Lord Allendale said. "Fred has hated me since I was a lad. He could never accept that your mother chose me over him. Not because he loved her, or because he desired her wealth and property, but because of his bloody Burton-Smythe pride. He couldn't wrap his head around the fact that she'd prefer a man he deemed so much less worthy than himself."

"You were more worthy. You were the heir to an earldom."

"A fact which Fred takes great pleasure in disputing. To him, I'll always be illegitimate. It's easier for him to think me a trickster than to acknowledge his own inadequacy. Your association with Miss Burton-Smythe will just serve to provoke him."

"Is it only the prospect of renewed gossip that troubles you? Or…are you afraid he'll try something else with mother?" Ivo was sickened by the prospect.

"No. Fred can't hurt me or your mother anymore. But harming our children isn't beyond him. He's an unhappy man. He makes everyone about him unhappy. I suspect he'd enjoy having you in his power."

Ivo recalled the odd look of calculation in Sir Frederick's eyes that day at Letchford Hall. The way he'd encouraged Ivo and Meg to take tea without him. Had he been scheming even then? Willing to facilitate a match between Ivo and Meg solely as a means of hurting Ivo's parents?

"As for his daughter," his father continued. "She—"

"She isn't like him," Ivo cut in with a sudden fierceness. "If you didn't recognize that—"

"I recognized it," his father said. "She seems a nice enough girl. But if you pursue this tendre you have for her, you reopen old wounds. Far worse, you invite Fred back into our lives."

Before Ivo could respond, the door to the library swung open.

His mother entered, a candle in her hand. She was in a chintz dressing gown, her heavy mink hair arranged in its long evening plait. "I thought I'd find you here," she said to Ivo's father. "Delivering a lecture to our son, I expect, thinking to shield me from some connection with Fred?"

Ivo stood abruptly. "Mother. I never knew. If I had—"

"I see I was right." Lady Allendale set down her candle on the mantelshelf. She gave her husband a reproving look. "I wonder, my darling, have you relayed the whole of it?"

"More than I cared to," Lord Allendale said grimly.

Ivo went to his mother. He gently touched her cheek. The very thought of any man putting his hands on her sent pure rage through his vitals. "By God, I could trounce Sir Frederick myself. That the villain dared hurt you—"

"Hurt *me*?" She took Ivo's hand, giving it a reassuring squeeze. "Nonsense."

"Father said that once, long ago, Sir Frederick attempted—"

"Fred forced a kiss on me, yes. It was exceedingly vile. But pray don't imagine me his victim." His mother smiled. "Do you think I hovered on the fringes of this battle between Fred and your father wringing my hands and weeping? Have you ever known me to be so poor-spirited? I was at your father's side, a horse pistol in my hand. Why—"

"Maggie," Lord Allendale said under his breath.

"He's of an age," Lady Allendale replied, "Tales of our wild youth won't scandalize him. Doubtless, he's already heard the rumors."

"Whatever Sir Frederick did, it must have hurt you," Ivo

said. "Why else would you still hate him?"

"I don't hate Fred," she said. "Hate is a useless emotion. I've no energy for it, and certainly no room for it in my heart. Still...I've seen what Fred's capable of. His conniving took your father from me for ten years. It's that which I can't forget—or forgive."

"I can forgive none of it." Lord Allendale set a protective hand on the small of his wife's back, even as he held Ivo's gaze. "You may require the man's support for a railway. I won't stand in the way of that. It's business. As for his daughter, I advise you to think very hard about what it would mean to foster a connection with her."

Ivo's mother pressed his hand again, as though her gentleness would be a salve on the sting of his father's warning. "It's one thing if your heart is engaged, my dearest. However, if this is just some passing fancy—"

"It isn't," Ivo said resolutely. "*She* isn't."

His parents exchanged a look. They appeared to come to a mutual decision.

"Very well," his father said. "Do what you will. You're of age. You don't require our permission."

Ivo stilled. "What about James?"

"You don't require his, either," his mother said. "But take care, sweetheart."

"Yes, do," his father agreed. "I strongly advise you not to rush into anything. You *are* young, though I know you hate to be reminded of it. Given time, you may find someone more suitable. Someone you can love without the burden of all this history."

Ivo didn't reply. There was no more point in arguing. Not tonight. Unless he was mistaken, his parents well understood him.

What need had he to wait for some worthy young lady to whom he might pledge his heart? He'd already found her.

# Chapter Twenty-Five

Meg huddled deeper into the bed of old Farmer Penny's cart, her slight figure hidden amid the bags of feed and cans of milk, as the rickety conveyance rattled down the snow-covered road toward the village.

Dawn was just peeping over the West Country hills, sending its rays streaking across the snow. Farmer Penny regularly made his rounds at this hour. It had been easy to stow away in his cart while he briefly stopped in the Letchford Hall kitchens to take a cup of tea with Mrs. Stapleton. None of them had noticed as Meg slipped out a side door of the house, swathed in a dark bonnet and drab cloak, with her carpet-bag clutched firmly in her hands.

It had been the only way.

It was either this or remain to face her father's wrath when he awakened. Then, any chance Meg had of a season would be gone. He'd already been reluctant to provide one, When he learned about her unchaperoned moonlight visit to Beasley Park—about how she'd danced with all of the Beresford men, and returned home with Ivo as her escort—he would forbid a season altogether. Indeed, she'd be lucky if he didn't ship her away to some dreadful school somewhere.

Meg wasn't interested in suffering another of her father's lectures. And she had no desire to take her punishment, however well deserved it might be. Her concern—her *sole* concern—was for her future.

Last night, her heart aching too much to allow for sleep, she'd lain awake in her bed and formulated a plan.

She'd resolved to go to Bath herself, even if she must take the common stage. It wasn't a matter of money. She had enough set by from her quarterly allowance to see her through. It was a question of taking her fate into her own hands.

During her eighteen and a half years on this earth, Meg had had countless hours to ponder her identity. Her conclusion? She had none. Certainly none bestowed on her by birth. She was the child of an unhappy marriage. Neither beautiful, nor graceful, nor blessed with an excess of wit. Even her name wasn't her own. It belonged to Lady Allendale.

But Meg wasn't going to think about the Beresfords today. They were part of the past now. As for Meg's father...

Once in Bath, Meg would apply to Miss Adams for sponsorship. Sir Frederick would be presented with a fait accompli, just as Ivo's parents had been last night. Meg prayed that this time the result would be more to her liking.

A chill wind whistled through the barren branches of the trees, making her bones ache and her teeth clack. She heartily wished there had been another means of getting to the village, but she hadn't dared risk implicating any of the servants in her scheme. The last thing she wanted was for a groom to lose his place on account of driving her into the village or for one of the stable lads to be let go because he'd witnessed her riding out on her mare.

She all but held her breath until the milk cart arrived in

Maidenbridge. When it drew up in front of the bustling coaching inn, Meg nimbly hopped off the back of the cart and slipped inside the building. Not twenty minutes later, ticket in hand, she boarded the mail coach for Bath.

As acts of rebellion went, it was right up there with her older brother having gone off to France. But Meg didn't consider it a rebellion. Not in the least. Her actions were practical. Sensible. And the only course, really, if she was ever to have an identity of her own.

---

THE SEVENTY-MILE JOURNEY TO BATH HAD TO BE made in stages. At each stop, Meg's nerves jangled anew. Young ladies of quality weren't permitted to travel unescorted. It was therefore understood that any female riding alone on a public conveyance must be the very opposite of a lady. An uncomfortable state of affairs. It left one open to all sorts of insults and encroachments.

Meg had armed herself with a very large hatpin for precisely that reason. It would be the work of the moment to extract it from her bonnet and convert it into a weapon.

Fortunately, she had no cause to do so. Most of the travelers she encountered on the road were working men and women. Honest folk, who had no interest in robbing her or debauching her. The worst Meg could say of them was that, at every stop, they drank excessively to warm themselves. When crammed next to her in the coach, shoulder-to-shoulder, they stank so strongly of beer it made her nauseous.

By the time she arrived in Bath, night had fallen and it was raining heavily. The mail coach deposited her at the busy coaching inn in Friday Street.

It would have been easy to be overwhelmed by the

experience. To crumple under the weight of her sudden independence. All was strange and new. But it was exhilarating, too. A true adventure, though Meg's exhaustion had dimmed the brightness of it.

She took deep breaths to manage her stammer, addressing the coachman, the innkeeper, and anyone else that was necessary. Come what may, it was she who was in charge of her future now. Going forward, the decisions were all hers to make.

Rather than book a room for the night, she engaged a one-horse gig to drive her the remaining few miles to Miss Adams residence in Pulteney Street.

"You sure this is the right address, miss?" the driver asked as he pulled up in front of one of the elegant townhouses. It was dark as pitch, with no light shining in any of the windows and no torches illuminating the path to either the front or the back door.

Meg swallowed hard. She hadn't considered that her first view of Bath would be at night. "I believe so. But...would you mind waiting for m-me? There's a small chance I m-might require a ride back to the inn."

The driver inclined his head.

Meg climbed down from the front seat without any assistance—no easy feat considering the breadth of her skirts. Collecting her carpet bag, she picked her way along the darkened path to the painted front door. Taking a deep breath, she knocked.

No one answered.

Meg's stomach sank. Perhaps Miss Adams and her future mama-in-law were away? The house was dark enough for it. And Meg had no idea what sort of schedule the ladies kept.

The full weight of the risk she'd taken in leaving home so abruptly began to sink in. Fear followed with it.

She was just raising her hand to knock again when a

creaking tread sounded from inside. Moments later the door was opened by a portly housekeeper in a plain cap and wrapper. She held a small lantern in her hand.

"Who is it?" she asked.

"Miss M-Margaret Burton-Smythe," Meg replied. "I have come to see Miss Adams."

"No one told me she was expecting guests. Not at this time of night."

"It's something of a surprise. I haven't—that is, I didn't—"

"What's going on, Florie?" a lady's voice called from the top of the stairs. "How am I to sleep with all this racket?"

"This girl says as how she's here for Miss Adams, Mrs. Philips," the housekeeper called back.

"She what? For Miss Adams, did you say?" Mrs. Philips descended the stairs in the halo of a taper candle. Iron gray hair peeped from beneath her frothy lace sleeping cap.

"Aye, ma'am," the housekeeper replied. "A Miss Burton-Smythe."

"I'm sorry I've t-taken you unaware," Meg said. "I hadn't time to send word in advance."

"It's going on midnight," Mrs. Philips said. "Shut the door, Florie."

The housekeeper moved to close it in Meg's face.

"Not before letting her in, you stupid woman!" Mrs. Philips exclaimed. "And you—" She addressed Meg with growing impatience. "Don't just stand there. Come inside before you let all the heat out."

Meg glanced back at the driver. He gave her a brief salute before clucking to his horse and departing. Meg hurried into the house. "I'm sorry," she said again as she entered. "I didn't intend to c-cause so much fuss."

Mrs. Philips looked her up and down. "Miss Burton-Smythe, is it? The baronet's daughter? Huh. Best repair to the parlor. Florie? Fetch the tea tray. And tell Miss Adams she has a guest."

A footman in hastily donned livery materialized to take Meg's bonnet, cloak, and gloves and to relieve her of her carpetbag.

Smoothing her plain wool dress, Meg joined Mrs. Philips in the parlor. The footman arrived a short moment later to stoke the fire.

Mrs. Philips lowered her aged frame into a high-backed velvet chair. She gestured for Meg to take a seat on the settee across from her. "You have no maid with you, nor a manservant, unless my eyes have mistaken me."

"No, ma'am." Meg sat down, folding her hands in her lap. Her gaze intermittently darted to the doorway, anxious for her former governess to appear.

"Have you run away?" Mrs. Philips asked. "It appears you have."

"No," Meg said. "I...That is...I did leave a n-note."

Mrs. Philips was unmollified. "Which means I shall soon have an angry baronet pounding at my door. And me in my dotage!"

Meg didn't know how to reassure Mrs. Philips on that score. She couldn't very well tell the lady that Sir Frederick cared nothing about his only daughter. Certainly not enough to chase after Meg with undue speed.

Guilt nevertheless rose up to plague Meg's conscience.

Had her father realized she was gone yet? Had he found the short letter she'd left on her dressing table?

And if he had, how had he reacted to it? Was he furious? Was he shouting at the servants from his bed? Threatening to sack them all without a reference? Or was he rousing himself to come to Bath? Was he even now bundled inside his carriage in dogged pursuit?

Meg swallowed the lump that formed in her throat at the

thought of her father's wrath. "I'm sorry, ma'am. I didn't m-mean to—"

"Meg?" Miss Adams entered the room swiftly. Even in her robe and slippers, she possessed the same air of practical efficiency that she'd had during her time at Letchford Hall— her shoulders set, her chin firm, and her dark hair worn in the same uncompromising knot at her nape. "Oh, my poor dear girl. What must have happened to bring you here in all this state?"

Meg was on her feet in an instant. Miss Adams was the closest thing she'd ever had to a mother. Seeing her familiar stern but kindly face worked on Meg in a powerful way. All at once, the full, overwhelming weight of her situation descended upon her.

She flew into Miss Adams's arms and promptly burst into tears.

<hr />

"GONE?" IVO STARED AT THE GRIZZLED LITTLE housekeeper. "What do you mean she's gone?"

Mrs. Church stood in the doorway of Letchford Hall, mouth pursed tight. It was she who had answered Ivo's knock. She'd offered him no welcome. On the contrary. She was all but barring his way. "Miss Burton-Smythe has gone away to Bath for her season," she informed him.

*The devil she had!*

"Since when?" Ivo demanded.

"She departed some five days ago, sir," Mrs. Church said.

Ivo's mouth went slack. It took him several seconds to formulate a reply. "Five days ago? But that..."

It had been but five days ago that she'd danced with him at Beasley Park.

Ivo hadn't called on her in the meanwhile, despite his desperate yearning to see her and to reassure himself she was well. He'd been attempting to exercise caution for once. To allow tempers to cool and better judgment to prevail. Not for his own sake, but for Meg's. Lord only knew how her father must have reacted to her defection. The sight of a Beresford so soon afterward would only inflame the situation. As a consequence, Ivo had forced himself to keep his distance.

More fool him.

Apparently, as he'd been biding his time at Beasley, Meg had been making arrangements to leave.

"Quite so, sir," Mrs. Church said acidly. "She departed the morning after your ill-advised little party. If that's all?" She moved to shut the door.

Ivo stopped it with his boot. "What about Sir Frederick? Has he accompanied her?"

"Obviously."

It wasn't obvious to Ivo at all. "I wouldn't have thought he could accommodate a lengthy journey, given his ill health."

An even sourer look came over the old housekeeper's face. "Then he shall suffer for it, shan't he? Another evil we can lay at his daughter's door. Had he not been compelled to chase after her—" The old woman stopped herself. Her lips thinned. "But I will say no more."

"You've said quite enough." Ivo removed his boot. The door promptly closed in his face.

Meg had run away. The realization struck Ivo like a thunderbolt. He was at once consumed with worry for her.

He was equally plagued by guilt.

Meg had accused him of rolling over her like a runaway train. Of ignoring her feelings—*everyone's* feelings—in favor of embracing what he knew to be a better future. At the time, Ivo had believed that achieving that future had been worth the temporary pain his actions had caused.

But he had been wrong.

He'd been so focused on progress, he hadn't stopped to consider the irreparable damage he could be doing to Meg's dignity. To her reputation.

To her heart.

She was a young lady he cared about, not a production timetable. A young lady who had been raised by his parents' oldest enemy. There was history to consider. Ivo had thought that it didn't matter. That he could ignore it. He'd been too idealistic to recognize that, while the past may not be sufficient to obstruct the future, it was certainly informed by it.

Striding back to his stallion, he began to understand how deeply his impetuousness had hurt Meg. Far worse, his actions had driven her to put herself in harm's way. Why, she could even now be injured or lost!

But there was no time for indulging his fears—or conscience.

Mounting Snap, he galloped back to Beasley Park. Once there, he bounded up the stairs to his room where he ferreted out a trunk and two of the battered leather cases that had accompanied him on his journey through Europe. He was midway through packing the entire contents of his wardrobe when Partridge scurried into the bedchamber, aghast.

"Master Ivo! If you required your things, you had only to summon me."

"I've no need of your valeting, Brutus." Ivo tossed two of his evening coats into the trunk in a haphazard heap.

Partridge groaned at seeing the fine fabric treated so carelessly. "But sir—"

"I'm going away for a time. I'll see to my luggage myself."

The valet gave him a long-suffering look. "Master Ivo, you must know it's impossible. Why, even in the most remote outpost of the Alps, you were ever in need of my services. The care and pressing of your clothes—the polishing of your boots—"

"I'll see to that myself, too." Ivo threw in a pile of shirts. "It can't be that difficult."

"The job of a valet is one of the utmost complexity. One must know how to preserve fabrics. To remove stains and attend to the mending. Not to mention the other errands I perform for you. Sending messages. Posting letters. Making inquiries into—"

"If you want to help," Ivo said, cutting him off. "Summon Andrew to bring the gig around. I require a ride to the coaching inn."

"The coaching inn!" Partridge did a fair impression of a man about to fall into a swoon.

"That's right." An idea occurred to Ivo. "By way of Mr. Pinnock's residence," he added.

Pinnock was no use to Ivo at present, but there was someone in his household who would be. Someone who could perform all of the necessary services Partridge had mentioned. And who, unlike Partridge or any of the other servants at Beasley, owed his unreserved loyalty to Ivo.

"Mr. Pinnock is joining you on your journey, sir?" Partridge asked with no little relief. "May I assume you're off on railway business, then? Not business of a personal nature?"

Ivo fixed the traitorous fellow with a cool glare. "Eager to inform my parents? Or is it my brother who awaits your report?"

Partridge hung his head. "Master Ivo—"

"Inform them, by all means." Ivo hoisted his trunk onto his shoulder. "You may tell them I have an appointment in Bath."

# Chapter Twenty-Six

Meg had been in Bath but two days when her father arrived in Pulteney Street. He was greeted by Mrs. Philips and Miss Adams in the parlor while Meg remained in her room upstairs, seated on the edge of the bed, so sick to her stomach at the prospect of facing him that she thought she might cast up her accounts.

It was Miss Adams who had told her to wait.

"I shall handle your father," she'd said. "He may vent his ire on me. By the time you join him, he will be in better spirits."

"I didn't think he would come," Meg had said hollowly. "I never expected—"

"Did you not? I thought you a sensible girl."

"I hope I am. It was my good sense that told me he'd refrain. His health is suffering after all. And...I m-mean nothing to him."

Miss Adams had only patted Meg's arm in conciliation as she'd departed. "Your good sense needs mending, my dear. We shall address that while you're here, you may be assured of it."

A half hour later, Meg was summoned to join them in the

drawing room. She found her father there, seated on the settee. He was rather pale beneath his freckles. The journey had plainly worsened his pain.

Meg felt a distinct twinge of guilt. "Father."

Sir Frederick rose with the aid of his cane. Whatever Miss Adams and Mrs. Philips had said to him had done little to assuage his anger. His eyes blazed as he looked at Meg. But there was something else in his expression too. It lurked there, a shadow so faint, she might not have recognized it if she hadn't been regarding him so fixedly.

It was relief.

"I would have a moment of privacy with my daughter," he ground out.

Miss Adams and Mrs. Philips stood. "Ring the bell if you require me," Miss Adams said to Meg. She curtsied to Meg's father. "Sir Frederick."

"Sir Frederick." Mrs. Philips inclined her head to him before withdrawing from the room with Miss Adams.

Meg sat down in the empty chair across from her father. Her spine was very straight, her hands folded in her lap. She maintained her composure through sheer strength of will. "Do sit, father," she said. "You shouldn't b-be on your feet."

Sir Frederick remained standing a moment, fingers clenched, white-knuckled, on the carved ebony knob of his cane, before he grudgingly lowered himself to the settee. "Have you anything to say for yourself?"

"No, sir."

"No excuses? No pleas for forgiveness?"

"N-No."

He stamped his cane onto the floor with a resounding thwack. "Impudent girl!"

She held his gaze. "If I am, you've driven m-me to it."

"*I? I* drove you to Beasley Park? Into the arms of a Beresford?"

"The Beresfords have nothing to do with m-my being here," she said.

He leaned forward in his seat. "Do you think me soft in the head, girl? I suppose it was a coincidence that you fled to Bath at the first opportunity after attending their infernal party." His expression darkened. "If that Beresford boy has offered you the slightest insult—"

"He hasn't," she said at once.

"Then what?" A dawning look of understanding came over him. "Don't say you're infatuated with the lad."

Meg's cheeks burned, but she gave no answer. Her feelings for Ivo were too raw. The last thing she wanted to do was discuss them with her father.

"And he doesn't return your regard?" Her father uttered a derisive snort. "I might have predicted it."

The words sent a crack through Meg's rigid composure. "Because I'm so lacking in grace or charm?" she retorted. "Yes, I know very well what you think of me, sir."

"You know nothing. If that boy has shunned you, it isn't because of *you*. It's because he's his father's son. The whole world smiles upon him. And in exchange, does he respect his betters? Does he behave as he should to a young lady of good family? To my daughter, by God!"

"Ivo Beresford did nothing to me. He was respectful and kind. He was—" She broke off, her voice fracturing on a spasm of emotion. "He *is* m-my friend."

"No *friend* would have permitted you to traipse across the darkened countryside unescorted in the snow, merely to attend his family's party." Her father's face reddened with anger at the very idea of it. "Oh yes, my girl. Church and Stapleton have told me all."

"If you must know," Meg said, "he offered to send a carriage to collect me at Letchford Hall. It was *my* idea to sneak away as I did. It had nothing to do with him and *everything* to do with you."

Her father's brows flew up to his hairline. "My fault, is it?"

"Your hatred for his family is a p-poison. You've poisoned m-me with it all my life. From birth, you inflicted it on me. Even m-my name is not my own."

Her father failed to conceal a flinch. "That tiresome charge again," he grumbled. "Margaret is a common enough name."

"I know why you gave it to me. You admitted it yourself." She gazed at him, her mouth tugging downward. Years of suppressed hurt threatened to break through. "How was I ever to thrive without an identity of m-my own?"

Her father looked back at her. Conflicted emotion warred with the depths of his gaze.

Meg saw it then, more clearly than she ever had before. He wasn't indifferent to her. He wasn't without remorse.

Her temper gradually began to ease.

"That man...," he said slowly, fingers tightening on his cane. "The noble Lord Allendale. He ruined my youth. Stole the lady I was meant to wed. Diminished me in the eyes of my father. Because of him, I was denied everything I wanted."

"The world doesn't end just because a m-man doesn't get what he wants," Meg said. "We *none* of us get what we want. Not all the time. We don't make other people's lives a misery over it."

"Your life, you mean."

Meg didn't answer. Not directly. "If you hadn't always been looking backward, you m-might have seen the harm you were doing in the present day. Not just to me, but to Roddy."

"Roddy hasn't been harmed."

"He was unhappy. Why else do you suppose he went so far away?"

"Because he wants to be master of Letchford Hall. He

wants the baronetcy. He'll return soon enough when I cock up my toes."

"You're always talking about us wishing you dead."

"Aren't you?"

"Had you given us cause to love you—"

"Love?" he said. "Don't speak to me of love. I've given my children something better. Something of substance. A position in local society. The best tutelage. The finest clothes. Roddy has had the larger part of my fortune already. And you! You exhibited skill at music, so I purchased that pianoforte for you, for no small sum. And what about your mare? I chose her at the sales myself, exercising the utmost care. There's nothing you've required that I haven't provided."

Meg was poised to tell him that all he'd done for her—and even for Roddy—had been done without affection. But a sudden realization arrested her speech. It struck her, all at once, that, to her father, duty *was* affection.

Perhaps, just perhaps, it was even love.

*His* kind of love, anyway.

It didn't excuse his many criticisms over the years. And it didn't excuse his bluster or his unreasonable fits of temper. But when coupled with his having followed her to Bath, it was nevertheless enough to convince Meg that she did have some measure of value in her father's eyes. Recognizing the fact was a salve to her spirit.

"I thought I had always been a disappointment to you," she said. "That's why you wouldn't give me a season."

"Rubbish. I never refused you a season. I'd have brought you to London in two or three years, and spared no expense in the bargain. Had you been content to wait until you were older and a trifle more mature—"

"I couldn't wait any longer. I m-must have a season this year. It's the only way I'll find a suitable gentleman to marry."

"Not Ivo Beresford, then?" He frowned at her. "Am I to assume you've given up on him?"

Meg couldn't deny it. She had come to Bath to forget Ivo. To find herself someone new to love. Someone better.

But there was no one better than Ivo Beresford.

She felt, much to her sorrow, as though she would never get over him. As though the anguish in her heart and her soul would go on aching for decades to come, giving her too much pain to allow for anything else. Any*one* else.

"It was he who encouraged me to look to the future," she said. "I don't want to live in the past, fixating on old heartbreaks. I want a chance for my own happiness. Miss Adams says that, n-now I'm here—"

"Yes, yes. She expressed the same sentiments to me. Infernal, managing female. Where is this elusive Mr. Philips, I wonder? Does he not realize he has women who need taking in hand? Were this my household—"

"Mr. Philips is in London on business. He'll return for their wedding in April. I should like to stay until then. To have m-my season and to see Miss Adams married."

Sir Frederick leaned back on the settee. A weariness came over him. He heaved a sigh. "Very well," he said at last. "Let it be as you wish."

Meg stared. "Do you mean that? Oh, Father—!"

He waved her thanks away, uncomfortable with her show of emotion. "None of that. It's as much for my own health as to indulge your whims. Spragg mentioned that the waters would do me good. I shall take a house in Camden Place. You'll join me there presently. Church has sent along some of your clothes. In the meanwhile, Miss Adams has recommended a dressmaker, along with various entertainments at the Assembly Rooms—"

Meg went to him in a rush before he could finish. She dropped down beside him in a flurry of skirts and, throwing her arms round his neck, pressed a kiss to his bristly cheek. "I shall make you proud of me."

His brawny hand came to rest on her back. "I'm already proud," he said gruffly. "You have the Burton-Smythe spleen. Just see it doesn't lead you into any more trouble."

# Chapter Twenty-Seven

"Still no sign of her." Ivo tossed aside his hat as he entered his hotel room in George Street.

Ruggiero came forward to collect his wet things. "You've been to the Pump Room?"

"And to Bennett Street, Russell Street, and the Circus. If only this bloody rain would stop, people might be out in greater numbers and then I could find her. As it is..." Ivo sighed, running a frustrated hand over his hair. "I daresay everyone is keeping to their lodgings, attending private parties and the like, rather than venturing out of doors."

Ruggiero retrieved Ivo's hat, coat, and gloves. During their week in Bath, he'd assumed the role of valet with a surprising display of enthusiasm. It wasn't because he had a burning desire to learn the trade. It was because he had a personal loyalty to Ivo, something the estimable Partridge had lacked.

The signore hadn't at all minded temporarily leaving his post at the Pinnocks, not if it meant helping Ivo in his time of need. Mr. Pinnock hadn't minded either. The idea that he could be, in some small way, involved in the great romance of a

Beresford and a Burton-Smythe had appealed to his matchmaking vanity. He'd all but packed Ruggiero's bag himself.

Ruggiero and Ivo had set out together within the hour.

Ivo was grateful. Nevertheless, during the past seven days, the signore's little lapses had begun to strain Ivo's patience. The fellow didn't know much about pressing delicate linens, nor about the correct proportion of blackening agents to polish fine leather boots. As a consequence, Ivo wasn't looking his best.

But that couldn't wholly be laid at Ruggiero's door. On arriving at the fashionable watering hole last week, Ivo had anticipated finding Meg easily. It hadn't been the case. He'd haunted the Assembly Rooms, the Pump Room, and the fashionable shops to no avail. Wherever Meg was hiding, she'd yet to emerge. Or possibly she *was* here, at all the places he'd visited, but he was cursed to be forever just missing her. Always two steps ahead or behind, always searching, but never getting any nearer.

His sense of desperation was growing by the hour.

If only he'd had the forethought to get the name of Miss Adams's future mother-in-law, then he might have managed to track down the lady's town house. But even if Meg had been there to begin with, it must be many days since Sir Frederick had caught up with her.

Perhaps they'd gone away again? Back to Letchford Hall or some other place, far removed from the reach of any of the Beresfords? Ivo wouldn't put it past Sir Frederick. After Meg's dinner at the vicarage, her father had forbidden her his carriage. What might he have done when he'd learned of her dancing at Beasley Park?

If this were the dark ages, Ivo would surely discover Meg locked in a remote tower somewhere or confined to one of those beastly gibbet cages employed in hanging troublesome people off the castle walls. Sir Frederick may not have those methods at his disposal, but there were plenty of other ways he could keep Meg under lock and key.

How in blazes was Ivo to find her?

He didn't know. He couldn't think. Couldn't function. His heart was breaking by degrees.

Sitting down on the edge of his hotel bed, he rested his head in his hands.

"I've been to the Saracen's Head in Friday Street," Ruggiero said.

Ivo shot the signore a dark glance through his fingers. "Have you, just. And what did I tell you about drinking during our stay?"

"I wasn't drinking. Not wine. I had a tankard of ale while I talked with the barman. He said as how a baronet arrived in Bath last week. A *gouty* baronet."

Ivo slowly lifted his head. "You're jesting."

"I'm not, sir. The man didn't know the gentleman's name, only that he was cross and kept his manservant on the trot."

Ivo suppressed a rogue flicker of hope. This was Bath. A gouty gentleman was no rarity. Not even one who was a baronet. The city was full to the brim with titled ladies and gentlemen nursing their infirmities. Nevertheless...

"Where is this gouty baronet staying?" Ivo asked. "Did the barman know the street or—"

"No address, Master Ivo. But he did say as how the baronet's manservant mentioned his master was attending the ball at the Assembly Rooms Monday evening."

Ivo knew about the ball. He'd heard mention of it at the tearoom only this morning. Two dowagers had been discussing it over currant buns. Ivo had thought he might attend on the off chance he'd learn something of Meg's whereabouts. But he hadn't dared hope to see Meg there herself.

He stood abruptly. "Ruggiero, I could kiss you."

The signore beamed through his beard. "Shall I obtain tickets?"

"I'll get them myself." Ivo collected his damp hat and coat, possessed of renewed energy. "I'll speak with that barman, too. You can press my evening clothes while I'm gone. And do try not to burn my cravat this time."

MEG HAD SPENT MOST OF THE LAST WEEK ENGAGED with the French dressmaker Miss Adams had recommended. The talented Madame Sandrine had come to the house Meg's father had leased in Camden Place. There, she'd outfitted Meg in day dresses, evening gowns, and ballgowns. Beautiful garments made in silks, velvets, and delicate crepes and gauze. Most of the dresses wouldn't be ready for another week, but Madame Sandrine had managed to run up a few pieces for Meg in advance, including a gown of rosy pink moiré silk for Meg to wear to her first ball at the Assembly Rooms, set to take place Monday evening.

When not closeted with her dressmaker, Meg spent the days leading up to the ball in tending to her father's needs—partnering him at cards or accompanying him to dinners at the houses of his acquaintances in town. The few hours she had to herself were used for visiting Miss Adams in Pulteney Street.

Meg's former governess was exceedingly kind and patient with her. But Meg couldn't fail to recognize that their relationship had changed since their time together at Letchford Hall.

No longer employed by Meg's father, Miss Adams had a higher loyalty now. Her attentions were focused on her impending marriage. On the needs of her future husband and mother-in-law. Meg could claim but a distant third place in Miss Adams's heart. Perhaps not even that.

"I enjoy our little talks excessively," Miss Adams said, walking Meg out after just such a visit on Monday afternoon. "But I won't monopolize you today, my dear. You must return home and ready yourself for the ball. You'll want to look your best. You'll have no end of partners, I suspect."

Meg wasn't so sure. "I've only met a handful of gentlemen in Bath so far," she said, "and there are none of them I desire to dance with overmuch."

"There must be someone, surely. Did I not see you at the Pump Room three mornings ago, surrounded by a crowd of good-looking young fellows?"

It hadn't been a crowd. Only a few gentlemen, really. Recent acquaintances cultivated by Meg's father. They'd been civil, to be sure, but most of their conversation had been directed toward Sir Frederick. As for good-looking...

They none of them had been anything compared to Ivo Beresford.

Meg's heart twinged to think of him. She'd been trying so hard to put him out of her mind. But it wasn't easy to stop thinking about a person one loved. About one's dear, best, and truest friend. For he *had* been her friend. She'd taken offense at the appellation before, believing it to be a lesser designation than the one she desired. She shouldn't have done. Friendship was nothing to sneer at. Not the kind she'd shared with Ivo.

"I understand that one of them is heir to a large estate in Northumberland," Miss Adams said. "Lord Beaumont, isn't it?"

"He hardly spoke to me," Meg said. "It was my father's opinion he was interested in. Something about farming methods. Indeed, the gentleman only addressed me to mention a possible outing tomorrow with a party of ladies."

Miss Adams linked her arm through Meg's. "Now that's promising. An outing to where, pray?"

"An estate called Prior Park. It belonged to Henry VIII at one time, I believe."

Miss Adams smiled. "And should therefore prove an interesting diversion for you. You were always enamored of history."

"Yes, well, it's a college now, or a school of some kind. We can't see the whole of it. Fortunately, visitors are still permitted to view the grounds and the observatory." Meg collected her umbrella from the footman who awaited them at the door. The sun was shining today, but one could never be sure in Bath. "It should be a pretty prospect if the weather holds."

"Then you must enjoy the excursion, just as you must enjoy the ball this evening."

"I will," Meg said with half-hearted confidence.

Miss Adams gave her arm a squeeze. "Promise me. No more moping. You desired to come to Bath and now you're here. You must make the most of it. Go out and see people. Make friends. Find yourself a suitor worthy of your affections. No more hiding in Pulteney Street with me."

Meg's shoulders drooped. Miss Adams was right as always. "Shall I not visit you again?"

"Don't be silly. I delight in your company. But I'll not have it take the place of amusements appropriate to your age. Go to the ball tonight and to Prior Park tomorrow. You may call on me again on Friday with a thorough report." Releasing Meg, Miss Adams kissed her cheek in farewell as the footman handed Meg into her carriage. "Take care how you go!"

Meg returned to Camden Place in time for a light supper.

After dining with her father, they both changed for the ball. Despite Miss Adams's encouragement, Meg had her doubts about attending. Her father had yet to accompany her to a public event. She expected they'd remain no more than a quarter of an hour before the discomfort from his gout would compel him to call for their carriage. It seemed to her there was little point in attending at all.

"We needn't have come," she said as the two of them made their way through the Upper Assembly Rooms.

A small crowd had gathered in the entrance hall, comprised of well-dressed ladies and gentlemen of varying degrees of rank and wealth. Most were of an older variety—people who had come to Bath to take the cure. The younger people among them were fewer and farther between, and not all of them of the first rank.

Music drifted out from the ballroom. The opening quadrille was nearly at an end. It was still early yet. Not much past nine o'clock.

"Nonsense," her father replied. "Lord Beaumont says this ball will be attended by the best of Bath society. Anyone of consequence must show his face."

"Oh?" Meg half-listened to her father as they advanced through the fashionable throng.

Her father hadn't known Lord Beaumont above a week, but the pompous Northumberland baron had already made an impression. He was a prosing gentleman who seemed to be an expert on everything. Rather than irritate Sir Frederick, the man's seemingly vast knowledge and endless well of flattery had served to divert him from fixating on his pain.

"I expect he'll be here," her father said. "He's asked us to join his party."

"Has he, indeed," Meg murmured. Rather presumptuous of him. Her father was the senior gentleman among them and the one of higher rank. He didn't require Lord Beaumont to lend him countenance.

But Meg had no opportunity to express her misgivings. She and her father had gone no more than a few steps farther into the ballroom when the man himself approached to pay his addresses.

"Sir Frederick." Lord Beaumont swept them a bow. "I'm gratified you could come." His lordship was a slender man, well above thirty, with a thick brown mustache, a close-trimmed beard, and a long, aristocratic blade of a nose.

"Beaumont," Meg's father said. "You've met my daughter."

Lord Beaumont inclined his head. "Miss Burton-Smythe."

"My lord," she said, returning his brief salute.

He cast a perusing look over her pink ball gown. What he saw seemed to satisfy his sense of importance. "If I may be so bold as to reserve your first dance?"

"What dance would that be?" Meg's father raised his voice to be heard above the music and the stomping of the dancers. "A galop? A polka?"

"There is indeed a galop and a polka on the program," Lord Beaumont said. "However, it's a waltz that's slated for next."

A waltz.

The very dance Meg had dreamed of dancing with Ivo. But that dream was no more. She supposed she must be satisfied to waltz with anyone. Even someone as officious and uninspiring as Lord Beaumont.

"With your permission, Sir Frederick," Lord Beaumont said, ignoring the fact that Meg had yet to give her own.

"By all means," her father replied. "I shall seek out a seat for myself."

"Allow me to assist you." Lord Beaumont ushered him to

a vacant chair along the dance floor. "You may rest here quite comfortably until we're finished."

There was faint applause as the quadrille came to an end. A surge of people brushed past, some couples exiting the floor and others moving toward it, eager to take their places. The orchestra commenced the opening strains of the waltz.

Mr. Beaumont extended his hand to Meg. "Miss Burton-Smythe. If you will?"

Before she could answer, a tall, handsome golden-haired gentleman emerged from the crowd. He was clad in elegantly tailored black-and-white eveningwear, his silver spectacles glinting in the flickering light from the crystal chandelier above. Jaw set with resolve, he strode forward to join their party, as confidently as if he'd been offered an invitation.

Meg's eyes went round.

Good gracious. It was Ivo!

"Miss Burton-Smythe. Sir Frederick." He sketched a bow.

Meg stared at him, her heart threatening to leap straight out of her chest. It was all she could do to keep her countenance. To stop her mouth from spreading into a foolish grin like any besotted simpleton.

He was here! He had come to Bath!

It was no coincidence. It couldn't be.

"Mr. Beresford," Meg's father said ominously. "At long last." He regarded Ivo from beneath sunken brows. "I wondered when you might arrive."

Meg turned her shocked gaze on her father. "You were *expecting* him?"

"I'm no fool," her father said. And then to Ivo: "What took you so long, lad?"

"Forgive my tardiness," Ivo said. "I've been in Bath all of a week and—"

"A week!" Meg echoed, stunned.

Ivo's mouth hitched in a fleeting, lopsided smile. "Indeed.

I'd have called sooner, but I seem to have misplaced your direction."

"We're in Camden Place," Meg blurted out.

"Camden Place. Of course." Another glimpse of a smile. Had Ivo not been so calm and collected, she might have thought him as foolishly smitten as she was. "How stupid of me."

Lord Beaumont's hand fell back to his side unaccepted. He addressed Ivo with barely disguised irritation. "I beg your pardon, sir. I haven't had the pleasure."

Meg hastened to introduce them. "Lord Beaumont, m-may I present Mr. Ivo Beresford, son of the Earl of Allendale. He is our neighbor in Somersetshire. Mr. Beresford, B-Baron Beaumont of Northumberland."

The gentlemen exchanged rigidly polite greetings. All the while, Ivo's gaze kept returning to Meg's and hers to his.

Music swelled all around them.

"The waltz, Miss Burton-Smythe," Lord Beaumont reminded.

"Ah yes, the waltz." Ivo's expression became gravely serious as he turned to her father. "May I beg permission to dance with your daughter, sir?"

Sir Frederick looked to Meg. "Well, my dear? What say you?"

Meg could hardly breathe for the butterflies swarming in her stomach. She somehow managed an infinitesimal nod.

Lord Beaumont drew himself up with offended dignity. Bowing to Sir Frederick, he stalked off to find himself another partner for the dance.

Meg's father's face bore a look of resignation. This wasn't what he wished for her. But he made no more objections. How could he? He knew what it was to be denied the person one wanted. The loss of Margaret Honeywell had blighted his life. Whatever he felt for the Beresfords now, it seemed that he'd ultimately decided to spare Meg that pain.

"Permission granted," he said to Ivo. "Providing you return her to me directly the waltz is over."

"I shall." Ivo offered Meg his hand. "Will you do me the honor, Miss Burton-Smythe?"

"Yes. I will." Smiling shyly, Meg slipped her hand into his.

# Chapter Twenty-Eight

vo led Meg out onto the ballroom floor. Her gown was a glorious confection of rose-pink silk, with short, tight sleeves that dropped down to reveal her creamy shoulders, and skirts trimmed in beaded lace and pink ribbon bows. A dress as sweet as it was alluring.

He'd never seen her in pink before.

"You look outrageously pretty this evening," he said as he circled her waist with his arm. "Have I mentioned that yet?"

The music for the waltz grew louder as all the musicians joined in accompaniment. Couples gathered around Meg and Ivo on the floor.

Meg didn't appear to notice them, not even when the skirts of another lady's gown brushed hers. She remained staring up at him, lips half parted, plainly still recovering from the shock she'd received at seeing him there.

She slowly set a gloved hand on his shoulder. "What are you d-doing here, Ivo?"

"Waltzing with you." He guided her into the first turn. "Isn't it obvious?"

"Yes. But...I don't m-mean now, I m-meant—"

"I know what you meant," he said gruffly. He gazed down at her as they danced. They had no real privacy to speak of. Not even the music could fully disguise their conversation. He nevertheless couldn't stop himself from asking the question that had been plaguing him since he'd left Beasley Park a week ago. "Why did you run, Meg?"

"I-I didn't."

"You did. Your father was obliged to pursue you, wasn't he? And now I find you here, looking breathtaking, and being courted by some dull dog with awful side-whiskers—"

An unwilling smile quivered at her lips. "Oh, Ivo—"

"Who is he to you, this Baron Beaumont person."

"He's n-no one to me," she said.

Ivo didn't trouble to disguise his relief. Jealousy was a new emotion for him. One he'd experienced at full force when he'd arrived in the ballroom to discover Meg preparing to dance with another man. "I'm gratified to hear it. I wouldn't like to have to challenge the fellow to a duel over your hand."

She bent her head. "Please d-don't tease me."

"I'm not teasing."

"You are." Her fingers gripped his shoulder as he swirled her around again. "Gentlemen d-don't duel any longer."

"If you say so."

"Why did you—"

"I came for you," he said. "I'd have been here sooner, but I thought—" A regretful frown creased his brow. "Forgive me, I thought I was acting for the best. Giving you time or some such gallant thing. But I should have gone to Letchford Hall the very next morning, shouldn't I have? It wasn't time you wanted. You wanted me."

She blushed furiously.

His fingers tightened at her waist. He drew her close, far closer than a gentleman should be holding a lady in the waltz.

"You do want me, don't you?" A flicker of uncertainty lent a huskiness to his question. "Because I want you, Meg."

Her bosom rose and fell on a sharply indrawn breath. "Ivo—"

"But if you say that you'd prefer I leave you alone—that you don't wish me to—"

"I do," she said. "Oh, but I do. I'm sorry I said those things. That I got so angry with you that n-night. I never—"

"It's me who should be apologizing. I used you abominably. You were right. I was impatient. I was trying to force the change. Instead, I hurt you and I made everyone else furious besides. It's a thorough muddle."

She went quiet a moment as they danced. "Do your parents know you're here?"

"They should," Ivo said. "They're not unintelligent."

"You haven't told them?"

He hadn't done. Not explicitly. But when he'd left the library the night of the dance at Beasley, when he'd parted from his parents to retire to bed, he'd had the sense that both of them had known exactly how it would be. They may not approve of his choice, but they wouldn't forbid it outright. Not if it was a matter of love.

Which it was.

"They're fully aware you have my heart," he said. "And once a Beresford man loses his heart, he's lost it forever. There's no going back."

"But if they don't approve of our friendship—"

"This is between you and me, Meg. Not my parents. Not my brother. Not even your father. Just you and me."

"We don't exist in isolation."

He smiled down at her. "In this moment, we do," he said. "I can't see anyone else but you."

She sighed, melting a little in his arms. "I-I feel the same. It's wretched."

He was surprised into a short laugh. "Only wretched? I think it's rather wonderful."

Her hand slid up his shoulder. "Yes. Wonderful, too. I said wretched because...I'm afraid there won't be a happy ending."

"Oh but there will be," Ivo promised. "Just you wait and see."

———❦———

PRIOR PARK WAS A GRAND NEO-PALLADIAN MANSION that had been built sometime in the early eighteenth century. Composed of pale stone, it resided on a hill overlooking all of Bath. The house itself, which was presently in use as a school, was only rivaled by its famous landscape gardens. It was these Meg had come to see, along with Lord Beaumont and several of his fashionable friends.

She'd hardly slept a wink the night before knowing that Ivo would be joining their party. What if it should rain? What if she was ill? What if he should change his mind about her?

All her worrying had been for naught.

Ivo had arrived at Camden Place just in time to accompany them on the journey to the Park. Once there, he'd wasted no time in drawing Meg away from the others.

Only then was Meg content. No, not content. She was happy. Gloriously, incandescently happy.

They were finally alone together in the bright uncomplicated light of day. Not meeting surreptitiously by the river. Not reduced to polite conversation in a crowded ballroom. There was just the two of them. Here in the open at last, Meg holding Ivo's arm as they walked down the slope on the north side of the property.

"I've been here before," Ivo said. He was dressed in a dashing blue coat, cord breeches, and polished top boots. The perfect image of a country gentleman, though he *was* wearing spectacles.

He'd been wearing them last night at the Assembly Rooms, too. Meg felt now as she did then, as if he'd come to her as his true self, with no artifice between them.

She flashed him a smiling glance. "Have you? Why didn't you say so?"

"Because it was long time ago," he replied. "I was young and with my friends. And I wasn't escorting the prettiest girl in Bath."

"Ivo—" she objected, cheeks warming at his flattery.

"In any case, there's something I want to show you. We can talk there. At least, I'll talk and you can listen. There are things I want to say that I couldn't say last night. We had so little privacy in the Upper Rooms."

Ivo had returned her to her father the moment the waltz had ended. They'd only danced one other time during the evening. Anything more would have been deemed improper. It was a galop. A lively dance for couples. But though it had been merry, leaving Meg laughing and giddy, it had afforded no opportunity for conversation.

"What do you wish to tell me?" Meg's pulse was already racing in anticipation.

"Wait," he said. "We're nearly there."

They'd already gone more than a quarter mile from the mansion. A short distance farther and Ivo at last caught sight of his intended destination.

"Ah. That's it, just there," he said. "Can you see it?"

Meg squinted into the distance.

Ahead of them, the cold February sunlight glinted on the surface of a lake. A stunning honey-colored bridge spanned the water. Built in the same style as the house, it was held up by rusticated stone piers and boasted a colonnade, in the style of a classical temple, surmounted by a stone entablature.

"The Palladian Bridge," Ivo said. "It's a copy of one in Wiltshire, built to resemble the Rialto in Venice. There aren't many of them left in the world."

Meg was enchanted. "Oh, but it's beautiful!"

"I rather think so. Not as treacherous as Sefton Bridge admittedly, and no rumors of deals with the devil to contend with, but I like to think that we left the peril of our early days behind us. Our future is on surer footing."

She smiled up at him. "Do you want to cross it together?"

"That's exactly what I want. Are you up for it?" He offered her his hand.

She accepted it, clasping it firmly. "I'm ready when you are."

Returning her smile, Ivo led her up the stone steps and over the water, passing through the colonnade. The water was still as glass beneath them. When they got to the center of the bridge, he stopped. His handsome face grew uncommonly serious.

Meg felt a flare of her old insecurity. It surely couldn't be anything good if he was looking at her that way, so grave and formal, so suddenly unlike himself. Her mouth went dry. "You had something you wanted to say to m-me?"

"Only this." Still holding her hand, Ivo gracefully dropped to one knee. "Will you marry me, Meg?"

Meg stared down at him. Her throat clogged with emotion.

"I love you," he said, pressing her fingers. "I *love* you. I can think of no greater honor—no finer state—than to go through life with you at my side. To marry you, my darling, and to belong to you as thoroughly as you would belong to me. Please, please say you will."

She nodded rapidly, tears spilling from her eyes. "Yes. I will. Yes, yes. With all my heart."

He was back on his feet in an instant and, in the next moment, she was in his arms.

She clung to his neck. "I love you, Ivo."

He kissed her cheek. "I swear I'll make you happy, Meg."

"You already have," she whispered in his ear.

His lips found hers. He kissed her again, deeply, sweetly, tenderly. A kiss Meg returned with building confidence. Her heart thumped hard. Or perhaps it was his heart, beating as heavily as her own. In that moment, it was hard to tell where one of them ended and the other began.

When Ivo at last lifted his head to look at her, his eyes were glistening, too. "Well, my dear," he said, a bit unsteadily. "It appears we're only halfway across. What do you say to our continuing to the other side?"

Meg beamed up at him. Her friend. Her love. The man she was going to marry. "Yes," she said. "Let's."

# Epilogue

Ivo remained in Bath for another month, walking, riding, and shopping with Meg and escorting her to concerts and dances at the Upper Rooms. Just because she was no longer on the marriage mart didn't mean she shouldn't enjoy the city to the utmost. Indeed, they both enjoyed it all the more because they were in love.

Most mornings, they accompanied Sir Frederick to the Pump Room so he could take the waters. His health was gradually improving, even if his temperament was not. Ivo often caught the grumpy baronet contemplating the pair of them with a frown. Though he'd given his approval for the match, Sir Frederick plainly recognized the many difficulties a connection between the Burton-Smythes and the Beresfords would bring.

Ivo's own parents arrived in the third week of March, in company with Kate, James, and Jack. Kate was newly betrothed to Lieutenant Heywood, who would be joining them there with his sister the following month.

Like Sir Frederick, Lord and Lady Allendale gave their approval to Ivo and Meg's engagement, though in a more open-hearted fashion. To their mind, Meg's pedigree was no longer at issue. After all, once Ivo and Meg wed, she would no longer be a Burton-Smythe. She would be a Beresford.

That didn't mean the obstacles were at an end. There was still the first meeting between Sir Frederick and Ivo's parents to contend with.

While Kate and Jack settled into the family's rented house near the Circus, Lord and Lady Allendale, and James along with them, contrived a meeting with Ivo, Meg, and Sir Frederick at the Pump Room.

It was by way of being neutral ground, and therefore a more desirable location to confront their childhood foe than in either of their drawing rooms.

Sir Frederick all but turned to stone when he saw them enter the Pump Room, his glass of cloudy Bath mineral water held, untasted, in his hand. He stood a bit straighter, still relying on his cane for support.

Ivo's parents, by contrast, appeared entirely unaffected. Lady Allendale's hand was tucked in her husband's arm, the two of them close as ever, providing mutual support and protection. Only their eyes betrayed the truth of their acrimonious history with Sir Frederick. Ivo had rarely seen his father's gaze so icy. And as for Ivo's mother... Her sapphire blue eyes fairly shot sparks.

"Fred," she said.

"Margaret." Sir Frederick offered her a rigid bow before turning on Ivo's father. The remnants of hatred, nurtured too long to dismiss, lingered in his face. "*Lord* Allendale."

"Sir Frederick," Ivo's father said coldly. "Isn't this an interesting pass?"

"That's one word for it," Sir Frederick grunted in reply.

Ivo's mother shot an arch glance at his glass. "Are you not going to drink your medicine?"

Coloring with embarrassment, Sir Frederick downed the

foul-tasting water. His features contorted in a grimace. "A bitter brew"—he gave the empty glass to a attendant— "but a necessary one."

"Quite," Lord Allendale said. "We must all swallow our share of bitterness for the children's sake."

"It's their happiness that's important now," Lady Allendale concurred. "Not our ancient grievances."

Ivo and Meg stood side by side, all but holding their breath. Their gloved hands were clasped in silent solidarity. They both knew how important this meeting was. They also knew that, regardless of its outcome, they still had each other. There was nothing that could change that now. Nothing that could prevent their marrying.

That didn't mean they were careless of the feelings of their parents. Ivo understood now just how much the past impacted the future. It couldn't simply be swept under the rug in the name of progress. But perchance, in time, a certain harmony might be found, sufficient for them all. Not a reconciliation precisely, but a means of healing and moving forward.

Meg squeezed Ivo's hand before releasing it. Her father looked very alone at the moment, as though he was standing against the world. Given his past conduct, perhaps he deserved to be alone. But these old grudges served no one. Like Ivo, Meg was looking to the future.

She went to her father and slipped her arm through his to offer her support. "Shall we t-take a turn about the room?"

"An excellent idea," Ivo's mother said. She smiled up at her husband. "Shall we, my love?"

"I am, as ever, at your service," Ivo's father said.

Ivo lagged behind as the four of them strolled off together—an unlikely quartet, but one that was soon to be bound inextricably by the bonds of Ivo and Meg's marriage.

"I never thought I'd see the day," James remarked, coming to join him.

"Nor I." Ivo walked on, his sights firmly fixed on Meg. She was but a few yards ahead of him, the gentle sway of her pale pink wool skirts unmistakable in the milling crowd.

James walked at Ivo's side, hands thrust into the pockets of his trousers. His austere black suit stood in stark contrast to the more colorful, and often dated, ensembles worn by the other gentlemen in the Pump Room. "They'd only endure it for your sake," he said. "Were it me, I'd never have asked them to."

"I didn't ask them." Ivo cast his brother a narrow glance. "Anyway, you mustn't disapprove entirely. If you did, you wouldn't be here."

James looked at Meg. "She is rather perfect for you, I admit."

Ivo's brows lifted. "I'm sorry. I seem to have suddenly lost my hearing."

His brother smiled slightly. "I can admit when I'm wrong."

"And can you apologize?"

"I shouldn't think it necessary. My concern was only for our parents, and for the preservation of the title. Sir Frederick knew our father as a boy. He set out to destroy him once. I don't give second chances."

"Maybe you should start," Ivo said. "Some people are capable of changing, you know. Anyway, he won't hurt us now. Not now that Meg and I are to be married."

"I trust not." James paused. "By the way, Pinnock is putting it about that he had a hand in orchestrating your betrothal."

Ivo gave a short laugh. "I'm not surprised."

Ivo had sent Ruggiero home last month. Companionable as he was, his valeting skills had left a great deal to be desired.

Doubtless, on returning to Maidenbridge, the signore had given his new employer a full report on the state of Ivo and Meg's romance.

"And I still haven't heard an apology," Ivo added.

"Very well," James said. "If it will shut you up. I'm sorry if I was—"

"An arse? You were. But I accept your apology." Ivo flashed his brother another look. "Though I'm not such a gudgeon as to believe you came all the way to Bath merely to show your support for my engagement."

"True," James said. "I'm eager to talk with you about this railway business of yours."

"Oh?"

"Father gave me the impression that it would take as many as seven years to complete building the extension through Somerset."

"A standard amount of time."

"And you've obtained enough subscriptions?"

"I have," Ivo said. The acknowledgment contained a wealth of satisfaction. Now that enough money had been pledged for the expansion, all that remained was for Parliament to approve the scheme. "But I wasn't talking about the railway. There's another reason for your being here that has nothing to do with my engagement, *or* with my business prospects."

James lapsed into silence.

"Miss Heywood is arriving next month, is she not?" Ivo asked.

His brother's stern face was immediately wiped clean of expression. "What has that to do with me?"

"Nothing, I imagine. She's not a duke's daughter, is she? Nor an heiress or a princess. She's merely a very interesting young lady. A beauty, to be sure. I wager she'll make a match in the first month."

"Ivo—"

"The first week," Ivo added remorselessly. "You'll have to act fast."

James glared at him. "Are you quite finished?"

"For the moment. But do recollect, I'm poised to marry the woman I love this summer. If you require my advice on courtship, you need only ask me for it. Or you could always ask Kate. She's about to marry as well. Indeed, it seems we've both beaten you to the finish line."

James's mouth quirked. "And here you're supposed to be the least competitive of all of us."

"That doesn't mean I don't like to win." Ivo grinned. "If you will excuse me?"

Still privately laughing at his overly serious older brother, he caught up with Meg. At the first available moment, when Sir Frederick and Ivo's parents were engaged in a seemingly safe conversation about their adjoining estates, Ivo drew her aside.

Meg's eyes shone with happiness and no little relief. "It's going better than I'd hoped," she confided to him in a whisper.

Ivo again took her hand. He sunk his voice. "Yes. I'd feared they'd be at each other's throats."

"No chance of that in the Pump Room."

"Less chance, anyway. We'd best not leave the three of them alone for long."

"No, indeed," she said. "We must return to them promptly."

They gazed into each other's eyes, both of them smiling a trifle foolishly. A month straight of daily outings had not been enough. Ivo wanted more of her time. More of her. He wondered if he'd ever get enough.

"I know," she said softly, replying to him as though he'd spoken his thoughts aloud. "I feel the same."

"Soon," he promised her. "Only a few months more until we marry. And then..."

"And then, we'll have the rest of our lives to spend together. To live happily-ever-after, just as you said we would."

Ivo raised her hand to his lips. He pressed a kiss to her knuckles, loving her as dearly as he knew she loved him. His words were an unbreakable vow. "And so we shall."

# Author's Note

At eighteen and twenty-three, Ivo and Meg are the youngest couple I've ever written. As such, they have a few moments of immaturity that I felt were realistic to their ages. It doesn't mean their romance is on less solid footing than that of the heroes and heroines in my previous books, but it does explain some of their behaviors leading up to their engagement.

If you've read *Return to Satterthwaite Court (Somerset Stories, Book 3)*, you may have already recognized that Charles and Kate's romance overlaps Ivo and Meg's. That's the main reason I wrote *Appointment in Bath* next, as opposed to going straight to the love story between James Beresford and Hannah Heywood. In terms of the timeline, it made more sense.

And of course, if you've read *Gentleman Jim (Somerset Stories, Book 2)*, you'll recognize Sir Frederick as the villain from that story. As a former villain, I couldn't make him completely redeemable. I suppose I still can't forgive him for his past crimes. It's why he's had to suffer so much. Shot and beaten in the first book. Injured, gouty, and ill in this one. It's no less than he deserves. However, for Meg's sake, he had to have some humanity. Enough, at least, that she was able to maintain some type of relationship with him. I hope you'll forgive me for giving him a semblance of a happy ending (though he does have to swallow some bitter medicine in the end!).

Bridges are a theme in this story, both literally and figurately. Sefton Bridge, the clapper bridge that crosses the River Barle, is based on the Tarr Steps, a famous medieval clapper bridge located in Exmoor National Park in Somerset. There's lots of folklore associated with the Tarr Steps, including the long-held belief that the bridge was built by the devil.

The bridge at Prior Park is also a real bridge—and an extraordinarily beautiful one. You can see it in the background of the book cover!

Finally, some of you may be wondering what happened with Ivo's railway venture. During the mid-1840s, after the completion of the Bristol and Exeter Railway, there were many proposals to extend railway access through west Somerset. Most of these proposals came to nothing. Unfortunately for Ivo, I based his railway venture on these failed proposals. In reality, it would be over a decade before a proposal for expanding the railway was successful. The West Somerset Railway Company was incorporated by Parliament in 1857. Construction for a line from Taunton to Watchet was started in 1859 and completed in 1862.

# An Excerpt from A Lady of Conscience

Read on for a Sneak Peek into the next book in Mimi Matthews' Somerset Stories series, featuring the frost-hearted James Beresford, Viscount St. Clare, and the shy, young bluestocking, Hannah Heywood, who is as devoted to animals as her mother, Phyllida Heywood.

Coming June 2024 and now available for pre-order from your favorite retailer.

PROLOGUE

*Beasley Park*
*Somersetshire, England*
*January 1844*

Hannah Heywood slipped out the kitchen door of Beasley Park, her hooded velvet cloak drawn up over her head against the winter chill. There was a full moon tonight. It shone, luminous as a pearl, in the midnight sky above, shimmering over the snow that covered the empty stable yard. She raised the small oil lantern she carried in her gloved hand, lighting the way to the stone stable block beyond.

After an evening of dancing and merriment, she'd been too restless to sleep. It didn't help that she hadn't successfully settled into her room. Her first night as a guest at the grand West Country home of the Earl and Countess of Allendale had been marked by much tossing and turning, and this night promised to be no better.

She was missing her pets, of course. Hannah supposed it was to be expected. This was the first time she'd left them—*or* her parents—for any length of time. Worries had begun to plague her from almost the first moment she and her older brother, Charles, had departed Heywood House. Thoughts about Evangeline, her three-legged spaniel, refusing to eat, or about Tippo, her aged pug, whining at the door of her empty bedchamber for hours on end, waiting in vain for his young mistress's return.

They were no overly sentimental imaginings. They were rational fears motivated by fact. Hannah knew her pets. She knew they would be pining.

But it was only for a day longer. She and Charles were traveling back to Heywood House in the morning, their brief stint as the guests of the vivacious Lady Kate Beresford, daughter of Lord and Lady Allendale, at an end.

Hannah was eager to return home. In the meanwhile, her restlessness was best assuaged by checking on the only animals of hers that were still readily within her control.

She let herself into the darkened stables. Her family's team of carriage horses—Dandy and Walter—had been housed inside since Hannah's arrival three days ago. Along with Evangeline and Tippo, they'd never been far from Hannah's thoughts during her stay. She made a point of personally looking in on them every day.

Each time she'd visited, it was always the same. They'd been comfortable, well-fed, and contented. It was no different on this occasion. Entering the stable, she found them dozing peacefully in their looseboxes, settled in for the night on thick beds of fresh straw. She was moving toward them, their names on her lips ("Walter! Dandy!"), when a sound arrested her step.

There was someone else in the darkness of the stable. A gentleman stood in front of one of the looseboxes at the end of the aisle, his tall, broad-shouldered frame just visible in the glow cast from her lamp.

Hannah's heart leapt into her throat. She recognized that icy blond profile. That height, those shoulders, and the adamantine firmness of that uncompromising chiseled jaw.

It was James Beresford, Viscount St. Clare.

Lord St. Clare was the eldest of Lady Kate's three older brothers. He was also, quite possibly, the handsomest gentleman Hannah had ever beheld. So disturbingly handsome that, from the minute they'd been introduced to each other, Hannah had found it rather difficult to look him in the eye.

It was childish, really. He'd been nothing but civil to her. Coldly, excruciatingly, civil.

But she'd felt his penetrating gray gaze on her at the dance this evening—both during the giddy, stomach-fluttering moments when they'd waltzed together, and during those moments when she'd been dancing with someone else.

No doubt he found her an oddity. Her mismatched blue and brown eyes were often an arresting sight to strangers, and her extreme shyness frequently put them off. Even the warmest people sometimes found it trying to converse with her. And Lord St. Clare was the very opposite of warm. He didn't laugh or jest like the rest of the Beresfords. Indeed, he rarely spoke at all except when absolutely necessary, and only then, with the strictest formality.

But there was nothing formal about him now.

He was in his shirtsleeves; absent the impeccably tailored evening coat and elegant black silk cravat he'd worn when he'd waltzed with her earlier that night. His golden-blond hair was mussed, his mouth curved in something like a scowl. He was out of countenance, possibly even angry—the tight hold he kept over his emotions temporarily relaxed because he'd believed himself to be alone.

She lowered her lamp, instinctively shrinking back into the shadows. There was little worse than intruding on a person's private moment, especially if that person was a frost-hearted viscount who prided himself on his unrelenting sense of control. He wouldn't thank her for having spied him without it. Quite the reverse.

But there was no hiding. Not now he'd seen her.

"Miss Heywood," he said coolly. He bowed to her in the darkness.

Hannah swallowed hard. Stiffening her spine, she made herself step forward, revealing her face to his view. "Lord St. Clare." She dropped a reflexive curtsy. "Good evening."

Unsettling as his presence was, it behooved her to stay on good terms with him. She doubted this would be her last visit to Beasley Park. Unless she was very much mistaken, her brother Charles was halfway to being in love with Lady Kate. Which meant that, eventually, the two of them would marry. It also meant that very soon Lady Kate's three brothers would be as good as family to Hannah.

One brother in particular.

Lord St. Clare came down the aisle to join her. "Dare I ask what you're doing out here at this time of night?"

I might ask you the same, Hannah nearly replied. But she wasn't one to banter. Neither was she an accomplished flirt.

Her shyness prevented all but the barest conversation with strangers. Unless, that is, she was talking about her animals.

"I'm looking in on my horses before retiring," she said.

His gaze was inscrutable. "Had you reason for concern?"

"Only that they're in a strange place, far from home."

"You need have had no apprehension on that score. Our head groom is excellent."

"I'm certain he is, sir."

"Yet still you're here." He dropped an enigmatic glance down the front of her velvet cloak, to where the cloth gaped to reveal the silk gown beneath. "And still in your evening dress."

A flare of self-consciousness heated her cheeks. She drew her cloak more firmly about herself. "I-I was too restless to retire to my room after the dance," she said, stammering a little. "I've had no opportunity to change."

He looked at her steadily, his fathomless gray gaze impossible to read. "Ah yes. The dance. I'd almost forgotten."

Hannah's blush deepened. Naturally it hadn't meant anything to him. He was a gentleman of breeding and bearing. A man of five and twenty, far older in both age and experience than her meager nineteen years. The waltz they'd shared this evening had been a thrillingly romantic event to her, but one he'd plainly forgotten the instant the music had ended.

"I'm not accustomed to parties," she said in an effort to explain. "We live a quiet life at Heywood House. Even a small dance in a private drawing room is a great cause for excitement."

He joined her at the side of the loose box. His arm brushed lightly against hers as he cast a brief look in at Dandy. "Whatever the cause for your excitement, you may be assured your horses are content."

Her pulse fizzed at his touch, the same way it had fizzed when he'd taken her hand to dance with her. He wasn't a comfortable gentleman to be around by any means. His very proximity did odd things to her circulation.

She followed his gaze into the loose box, ignoring the quivering in her stomach. Dandy was snuffling in his sleep, one back foot cocked at rest. Hannah's mouth curved in a fond smile. "Yes, I see that now."

"You weren't genuinely worried, I trust."

"I always worry about my animals." She paused, struggling to explain in words what she so easily articulated in the letters and anonymous opinion pieces she wrote in support of the burgeoning animal welfare movement. "They can't speak for themselves, you see. Not in a way that human beings can readily understand. It's up to me to give them a voice. To be their advocate, if necessary."

Her words were met with a prolonged silence.

Hannah's growing sense of discomfiture increased exponentially. She supposed that, given her shyness, she didn't strike him as much of an advocate. Naturally he underestimated her. He knew nothing about the strength of her convictions or about the lengths she was willing to go to for a noble cause.

"An admirable philosophy," he replied at length.

She couldn't tell if that was sarcasm in his tone. "It's not a philosophy. It's a moral duty."

"Is that why you don't eat animal flesh?"

He was the first one of the Beresfords to ask Hannah about it outright. The others had merely accepted her dietary restrictions as a matter of course. Hannah suspected that her brother had privately addressed the matter with Lady Kate when they'd arrived, thereby avoiding any awkwardness with the menu during their stay—or any awkward questions.

But Hannah didn't mind questions about her convictions. Not if they were asked in a spirit of sincerity.

"In large part, yes," she said. She'd given up eating meat

several years ago, in consultation with her long-distance correspondent, Miss Mitra, and other female members of the movement. "It isn't exceptionable. Many in the world refrain from eating animals. The Hindu, for example."

Lord St. Clare's icy expression didn't change. Hannah nevertheless thought she detected a faint hint of incredulity at the back of his eyes. As though he'd expected her to be ignorant of the world or wholly immature—or both.

"I read books," she informed him. "And I correspond with all manner of interesting and well-informed people."

"Do you indeed?"

"I do. I'm a capital correspondent."

The barest trace of a smile shadowed the firm line of his mouth. "I'm sure that you are."

She drew back from him with a frown. She didn't like to be teased. Not by him. Not about something so serious as her feelings toward animals. "You think me amusing, I daresay."

Lord St. Clare met her eyes in the lamplight. "What I think, Miss Heywood, is that your commitment to your beliefs shows a rather impressive largeness of mind."

She blinked. "Oh."

"I also think that if you remain out here for a moment longer in service to those beliefs, you're likely to catch your death."

"I'm perfectly warm in my cloak," she assured him. She hesitated before adding, "It's you I worry about."

His brows lifted slightly. "I?"

"Do you often venture out into the snow without your coat or your neckcloth?"

"No. Not often." His forehead creased. He lapsed into silence again for several seconds before admitting, "I've just come from the library, and a rather heated exchange with one of my brothers. The snow was the best remedy for my temper.

That and a visit with my stallion. A few moments in his company never fails to restore my equanimity."

Hannah nodded in immediate sympathy. She knew there had been tension in the house this evening, much of it owing to Lord St. Clare's younger brother, Ivo Beresford, having invited the daughter of an estranged neighbor to their family party.

"Horses have that talent," she said. "Troubles never seem so great when you're standing beside one of them. It's owing to their size, I believe. It dwarfs us, and our problems."

"Very well put."

"I contributed a brief article about the effect to a new journal on animal welfare that one of my correspondents is publishing in Bath. I mean to procure a copy for myself when next I visit."

He gave her another of his unfathomable looks. "You'll be traveling there in the spring?"

Hannah was surprised that he knew of her plans. She hadn't talked about her upcoming season in Bath during her visit, except when in company with Charles and Lady Kate. "It's to be my formal debut." She felt compelled to add, "London wouldn't have suited me. I prefer things to be simple."

"Don't we all." He offered her his arm. "If you will permit me to escort you back inside?"

She cast a last glance at Dandy and Walter before taking it. "Very well."

The muscles in Lord St. Clare's arm were powerful under the curve of her gloved hand, unhindered by the thick layer of his coat. He was an athletic gentleman. A man as strong in his body as he was in his self-restraint.

His composure had been wobbling tonight in the aftermath of his argument with his brother. A disconcerting sight. She wondered what it would look like if the viscount ever lost control completely. If he ever succumbed to the wild, reckless, passionate nature for which the Beresford family was rumored to be famous.

It wasn't likely to happen. And even if it did, Hannah wouldn't be around to see it. In the spring she would go to Bath, where she would meet and marry a sensitive, bookish gentleman, as unlike the cold-blooded viscount as night was to day. It was for the best. She required warmth in her life. She required joy. Despite the cracks she'd observed in his armor, Lord St. Clare didn't seem capable of either.

Back at the house, he held the kitchen door for her and waited as she preceded him inside.

She drew back the hood of her cloak, revealing the plaited coiffure of her dark auburn hair. "Thank you, my lord," she said breathlessly. "I shall bid you goodnight."

"Sleep well, Miss Heywood."

"And you, sir." With that, she hurried from the kitchens, her heart beating heavily at her throat. She was certain she felt the weight of his lordship's gaze at her back, following her until she'd disappeared from his sight.

# Acknowledgments

This book wouldn't have been possible without the help and support of my excellent team. Many thanks to Jocelyn Bailey for editing; to James Egan for cover design; and to Anne Victory and Crystalle for proofreading. I'm also endlessly grateful to my amazing assistant Rel Mollet and to my brilliant agent Kevan Lyon.

Thanks, love, and gratitude are also due my wonderful mom, who read this book more times than I can count. And to my devoted menagerie—Stella, Jet, Tavi, Bijou, and Asteria—who give any story of mine that features animals their full endorsement (which is to say, *all* my stories).

Last but certainly not least, I'd like to thank you, my readers, for sticking with me, and with this series. You mean the world to me!

# About the Author

*USA Today* bestselling author Mimi Matthews writes both historical nonfiction and award-winning proper Victorian romances. Her novels have received starred reviews in *Publishers Weekly, Library Journal, Booklist, Kirkus*, and *Shelf Awareness*, and her articles have been featured on the *Victorian Web, the Journal of Victorian Culture*, and in syndication at *BUST Magazine*. In her other life, Mimi is an attorney. She resides in California with her family, which includes a retired Andalusian dressage horse, a Sheltie, and two Siamese cats.

Connect Online
MimiMatthews.com
Facebook: @MimiMatthewsAuthor
Instagram: @MimiMatthewsEsq
Twitter: @MimiMatthewsEsq

# Want More?

Would you like to know when Mimi's next book is available? Sign up for her newsletter (https://www.mimimatthews.com/newsletter/) to keep up to date.

Join Mimi's exclusive Facebook group, Mimi Matthews' Victorian Reading Room (https://www.facebook.com/groups/mimimatthewsvictorianreadingroom), for exclusive access to Mimi as she shares her love of writing, historical romance, Victorian fashion, brooding heroes, independent heroines, and of course, her beloved pets!

Finally, the more reviews a book has, the more other readers will discover it. Every review helps, so if you have a moment to post your thoughts about this story, Mimi will be ever grateful.